Copyright
All rights reserved. No part
any manner without the prior written permission of the copyright
owner, except for the use of brief quotations in a book review. All
characters and situations are products of the author's imagination and
any resemblance to persons or situations living or dead, past or present, is purely coincidence.

Jordin,

You're awesome!

Meredith Tate

Howl at the Moon
Marked Book 2
by Meredith Spies
copyright 2023

HUGE THANK YOU TO:

Editing by Cate Ryan (www.cateedits.com[1])
Cover and Promotional Art by Samantha Santana (www.amaidesigns.com[2])

---

1. http://www.cateedits.com

2. http://www.amaidesigns.com

Potential Triggers:

Mentions of assault (on page but also described, and a past event), death, death by violence (described, past event), mentions of deadnaming (not shown on page but referred to), homophobia (off page), depression, internalized ableism regarding possibly life-altering injuries, child endangerment, kidnapping of adult and child, imprisonment of adult and child, car accident (no deaths).

Chapter One

There was a werewolf in my bedroom.

And he couldn't be quiet if his life depended on it, which, all things considered, is a bit ironic. "I'm trying to sleep, asshole," I muttered.

Ethan chuckled. "Sorry. Shorty at the station called. They need all hands; something big going on at the Jenner farm."

I rolled onto my back, only able to get one eye to cooperate at oh-god-thirty in the morning. "Probably just Anthony Jenner drunk off his ass again," I muttered. Still... "Am I gonna need to suit up? Any deaths?"

"Not sure yet. You know the drill, though." He leaned in and kissed me hard and fast as his phone buzzed again. "I'll call you later. Maybe we can meet for lunch if this isn't too messy."

I grunted and rolled back onto my face, his soft laugh drifting behind him as he let himself out of my room, then out of my house. Ethan's car rattled to life, and I winced inwardly, sure I'd be getting the look from my neighbor, Mr. Cullen, about that. Timothy Cullen had only just moved into the small Craftsman next door, and already he was a one-man HOA, sending little 'helpful notes' as he called them to all of us on Larkspur Court.

Apparently, there was a correct height for grass and none of us on the street had achieved it aside from Mr. Cullen.

He'd even sent a message to the neighborhood WatchOut group about the unnecessary levels of enthusiasm regarding a recent family of deer that had passed through the vacant lot at the end of the road.

I bet he was a lot of fun at parties.

Cullen also hated Ethan's car beyond what I thought was a reasonable measure—and considering how much I hated Ethan's old Ford Escort, that was definitely saying something. Cullen had taken to standing on his front porch like a creeping creeper whenever Ethan came over in the evenings, staring at us with a slow shake of his head every time I came out to meet Ethan before one of our few dates (it was weird, this dating gig—nothing like when we were teenagers but nothing like anyone I'd dated since—and I wasn't sure if it was because now we were adults or because of what we shared, but it was... weird).

Ethan shrugged it off. Cullen was harmless, he'd said. Bored. Needed a hobby. "Besides," he'd said, just a few days before, "he's not technically doing anything illegal. Being a bad neighbor isn't against the law. It's just annoying."

"I mean, if he killed me, that's both a bad neighbor and illegal," I'd muttered, stretching my legs across Ethan's lap, *America's Worst Bakeries* playing in the background.

"Yeah, and he'd get arrested for the murder, not the bad neighboring."

Needless to say, we'd have to agree to disagree about the criminality of Cullen's shitty behavior.

A soft scuffling noise outside my window dragged me from my grumpy musings. My first thought—Cullen's gone too far this time, peeking in to see if I'm here so he can bitch at me—was rapidly replaced by *fuck, someone's trying to break in!* as the sound of scraping replaced the scuffling, something hard pressing and dragging in the wood below my window. Someone trying to pry it open, maybe, or jimmy the old-fashioned window locks.

I hesitated for just a moment or two (okay, maybe five). It was early, I was tired, and really there wasn't anything in the house I couldn't replace...

The mental image of Ethan's expression, his rumbled *You let someone break in so you could get more sleep?* dragged me out of bed, though, and I shoved my feet into the old slippers I kept by the bed, shuffling toward the window and flinging back the drapes before my half-asleep brain realized I didn't have a weapon or even my phone.

Which was a moot point, seeing as there was no one outside. At least not that I could see. The faint tingle racing up my back told me I wasn't alone, those scared rabbit senses that had dogged me my entire life, that only finally began to make sense a year ago, waking up and sending up flares of alarm as they got to work.

"Fucking hell. I do not need another werewolf this morning."

Slippers traded for boots and a large, sharp chef's knife and my phone procured, I made my way to the front door and tried to peek out through the sidelight without being obvious about it.

The soft shuffle came again, just inches away, through the wood.

Fuck.

I slid away from the sidelight, trying to remember those calming exercises I'd looked up a few months ago at Ethan's urging. Breathing in, two three, out four five, hold six seven, scream in panic eight nine...

The shuffling stopped, then the sound of light steps tripping down my front porch sounded, then hurried ones across the gravel drive and toward Cullen's house. My native panic was replaced with a surge of annoyance. A quick fumble with the lock, and I threw the door open, striding out after Cullen. "Asshole," I whisper-shouted (I might be pissed, but I did have other neighbors, a few of whom actually liked me). "Get back here!"

The click of Cullen's front door shutting punctuated that little would-be encounter. Across the street, Dave Allen was getting into his car, his sleepy toddler clinging to his neck for the daily trip to grandma's for babysitting while Dave did whatever Dave did—I kind of tuned out around hour two of his life story. "Morning, Doctor Babin!" he called. "Casual Friday?"

Shit. I was glad I'd never been able to commit to sleeping nude like Ethan. Nothing was sadder than a man naked save for a pair of shoes, out there looking like a half-decorated Christmas tree with his bits and bobs flopping around from the ankles up. "Er, something like that. Hey, did you just see Tim Cullen out here?"

"Sorry, man. I was wrestling Thing One into her car seat." He nodded at the car where the vague lump of a car seat could be seen peeking over the back seat. "Thing Two's gone all spaghetti noodle on me, so I wasn't really looking. All good?"

"Ah, yeah. Just... wanted to borrow some sugar or something," I mumbled. "Have a good day!"

I didn't wait to hear his reply, marching my sleepwear-clad self back toward the house only to draw up short when I caught sight of the bright pink sticky note flapping on my front door.

Doctor Babin

Leash your dog! It is against community regulations to have a dog free-roaming!

ETHAN WAS DISTRACTED when he answered. "I'm driving, Landry," he said. "Can this wait till I get to the office later?"

"It's just real quick. Are you alone?"

There was a pause, then a vaguely amused drawl. "Are you asking for fun reasons or serious reasons? Because if you've suddenly decided to give phone sex a try, I gotta say your timing isn't great."

My face warmed, and I have no shame (okay, maybe a tiny bit, given the circumstances) in admitting that other parts of me perked up a bit at the thought. I wasn't good at the whole talking dirty thing, something Ethan found either endearing or amusing; I couldn't decide which. He still teased me about the first time I fumbled at it and asked him to *Do that thing, you know? The one that's all... like that?* complete with some weird hand motions that looked like a failed audition for *Cats.*

Nothing ruins sexy time faster than your partner laughing so hard they fall off the couch and get hiccups.

"No," I grumbled. "Not now, anyway. I just wanted to know..."

"Yes?" he drawled, the clicking of his turn signal like an annoying game show timer in the background.

It made me feel itchy, and as much as I'd like to blame my not-quite-human senses for that irritation, it was just me being, well, twitchy. "Was Cullen outside when you left this morning?"

"Oh god," he muttered. "Landry, it's just past the ass crack of dawn. It's too early for this good neighbor bad neighbor bullshit. I mean, love you, but for crying out loud—"

"Okay, one, we're circling back around to that love you thing. Don't think you're getting out of it," I interrupted in a rush, that heat from earlier pulling back and leaving me feeling cold and anxious. Another reminder that maybe he wasn't as all in this as I was. Possibly.

Shit.

"And two?" he muttered.

"Two what? Oh! And two, you didn't let me finish. Cullen left a note about me having a dog off the leash."

When he spoke again, his words grated over disbelief and maybe a shred of disappointment. "Are you asking if I shifted? In the open? In a non-pack area?"

"No," I drew out. "Maybe? Or maybe if Tyler or someone had been sniffing around."

"Sniffing around, Landry? Really? And dogs? Seriously?" His wounded tone was clear and sharp.

"Ethan!" I snapped. "Come on! This is not the time to get all prescriptive about language." His heavy sigh added a pang of guilt to my morning—it had been insidious, this creep of subtle accusation, that I wasn't taking this seriously enough, or worse, that I was somehow not taking him, specifically, seriously. I was so in my head about what had happened with the clinic, with Cleverly and Garrow and, shit, everything that I forgot I wasn't the only one involved.

And maybe he was right about that.

Sometimes.

A little.

But... Fuck!

"Ethan, please listen to me."

Ethan made a soft, frustrated sound, and the noise on his end of the line changed. "I just got to the office. I need to grab one of the work vehicles to head out to the scene before dealing with all this bullshit here, so I don't have long."

I wanted to be annoyed, but he sounded so tired, absolutely already done with the day. I swallowed the urge down and told him about the shuffling sounds outside my window, at the front door. The sharp pang of fear I'd felt... "It wasn't just nerves," I added when he did one of those deep sigh, my boyfriend is being weird things. Swallowing down the nerves that threatened to choke my words, I said in a rush, "This was... this was my wolf."

The sigh morphed into a snorted, choked laugh, and suddenly that heavy exhaustion he was wearing, the stress of dealing with the rat bastards at work, was gone, at least for a moment. "I'm sorry. It was your what?"

"My wolf," I muttered. "Are you laughing at me, Ethan Jeffrey Stone?"

"My middle name isn't Jeffrey," he snickered. "You should know that, Landry Wolf Babin."

"Shut up. I'm hanging up on you now."

"Wait!"

"What?" My face felt hot, and even though I knew he couldn't see me, I ducked my chin. Calling that strange part of myself my wolf had been Tyler's suggestion. He was a dick but could be surprisingly sympathetic about the whole suddenly-not-entirely-human thing. *Call it your wolf. Treat that part of you like it's a whole creature, you know? Take ownership of it.*

After months of struggling with trying to shift, trying to make that secret part of me just fucking obey, it had sounded like excellent advice.

Though, now that I was thinking about it and listening to Ethan wheezing softly as he tried not to laugh, maybe he was an even bigger dick than previously thought and he'd intended for me to make an ass of myself like this.

"I'm sorry," Ethan muttered, his words shaking with barely suppressed laughter. "It just... it sounded so 1970s Harlequin. *My Wolf: A Story of Love, Chewy Bone, and Shedding.*"

"I'm not talking to you anymore," I announced crisply. "Fuck off."

His hoots of laughter chased me as I fumbled to disconnect the call.

When he called back a few seconds later, I ignored him.

Because fuck him, that's why.

I kept on ignoring him as I started the coffeepot, took a quick shower, and got dressed for the office.

I kept ignoring him while I stared out my bedroom window, the narrow strip of yard between me and my neighbors still in shadow as the sun wasn't fully up yet. Still, even with the low light, I was able to see the ground had been disturbed.

My phone's ringtone switched to a shrill, unforgiving screech. "Ah, good, he's calling from his desk phone now."

I shut the ringer off.

Maybe I was being a brat. Or maybe he was. I just know that some days were harder than others, trying to get a handle on my new reality. Ethan had been trying to help me learn to shift, learn to use my previously latent abilities, but it had been one headache after another. When I suggested that maybe I was just meant to exist in the weird liminal space I'd been inhabiting, he'd growled—actually fucking growled—at me. "It takes time," he'd told me, "even for those of us who know from birth what we are."

"What I am," I'd muttered, staring at the disturbed lawn outside my bedroom window, "is tired."

It took just a few minutes to check the side yard. I may not be as astute with my senses as Ethan, Tyler, or any were who'd been were since birth, but I was better than an ordinary human. There'd definitely been something not human there, but it wasn't quite an animal either. The scared rabbit impulse I tended to get around weres was softer, more of a murmur than a scream.

Whatever it was had been a predator, but not a wolf.

Not a were.

The prints, though, were distinctly human-shaped. Or at least shoe-shaped. A quick mental image of some bipedal animal in human clothes danced to the fore of my thoughts and was at once funny and terrifying. Shaking it off, I followed the tracks from the muddled spot by my window, then around the back of the house, where they headed off toward the pond between our lane and the edge of the wilderness preserve.

The steps remained human-shaped, but the gait lengthened. They were running, I thought. Running away, or running to?

The rattle and squeak of a screen door opening dragged my attention away, toward Cullen's house. He stood on his back porch, fully dressed in his usual neatly pressed slacks and stark white shirt, clutching his monstrously large Maine coon to his chest.

I was pretty sure the cat could take Ethan, if given half the chance.

"Hey," I called, taking a few steps toward him. "I got your note. What the hell, man?"

He sniffed, shifting his hold on the cat. "You need to keep an eye on those dogs," he spat. "They could hurt someone. Children! My Esmerelda!"

The cat made a sound suspiciously like a snort.

HOWL AT THE MOON

Yeah, I didn't think any creature could hurt that beast.

"I don't even have dogs," I said, throwing my hands up in frustration. "As close as you watch me, creeper, you should know that!"

"I've seen those dogs sniffing around all the time," he seethed. "If they're not yours, you need to stop making your place an attractive nuisance for the damn things! If I see them again, I'm calling animal control!"

"Do it!"

Cullen stiffened, a flicker of surprise dancing across his features before his scowl settled back into place. "You'd like that, wouldn't you? Those beasties dragged off and euthanized! Just so you could shirk your responsibilities—"

"Dude," I groaned. "What the hell are you talking about? It's too early in the morning for this level of what the fuck. I have a job to get to. Just stay off my property, okay? No notes, no sneaky pics of my boyfriend's car you can post on the neighborhood loop and complain about the muffler, alright? Mind your own business."

Esmerelda bared her teeth and emitted a low growl I'd never in my life heard a cat make.

"You share this space," Cullen said, shouldering Esmerelda like a toddler. If a cat could ever look awkwardly embarrassed, she was doing it.

"Yeah, well," I called back, "so do you!"

Not my best comeback, but I'd only had the one cup of coffee so...

My phone rang again, and this time I shut off the ringer.

Getting ready for work was a fight. I wanted to call in, tell Reba I was just over today already, and spend the rest of the day holed up at home... waiting. But shit was already hitting the fan at work thanks to state-wide budget cuts, meaning my full-time job was cut to three-quarter time, and might be zero-time before all was said and done. Between that and Ethan's crappy experiences at the sheriff's office lately, it felt like this being a responsible adult gig was just too much.

Maybe I should've just gone into regular medicine, I thought, yanking a pair of my work slacks from the closet. See runny noses and rashes all day, assure people they're not dying no matter what WebMD says.

I hesitated at the door, the very faint scent of strange were lingering in the air outside as I stood, one foot in and one foot out. Whatever Ethan thought, I knew what I'd sensed.

I knew that I hadn't been alone that morning.

A strange were had been watching me.

Chapter Two

"Shit's hitting the fan," Reba muttered as soon as I stepped into the office that morning.

"It's Friday. Of course, it is." I sighed. "What's going on this time?"

"Check your email, but this came in the interoffice drop off this morning."

Interoffice mail from the state office was never good. Doubly so when you were already on thin ice after 'concerning incidents' and 'extended absences' on top of your entire department, state-wide, being the first in line for budget cuts.

Fuck.

I saluted Reba with my coffee and headed into my office, dropping my satchel off at the desk before opening the dreaded manila envelope. "Dear Doctor Form Fill Here," I muttered, feeling a breath of relief that it was apparently a form letter based on the generic wording, and while it did have my name in the address, it was a bland *we hope you are doing well in these difficult times* sort of letter that gave off heavy budget cut vibes.

Sure enough, paragraph two was the guillotine blade. Reba was waiting for me when I threw open the office door. "What the fuck is *as needed*? What the fuck?"

She opened her hands sympathetically. "The email said we were being cut down to one day per week with additional hours as needed." She sniffed, eyes a bit bright. "We do get a stipend for being on call but it's not enough to cover what's being lost."

I read—maybe a bit too loudly—the text of the third paragraph. "Until such a time as an assessment of the county finances can be made, we will be limiting the hours and services of the offices in the following counties." I glared at her. "There's sixteen counties on here!"

"And apparently, all of them have relatively low violent death rates." She sighed. "I think last year was an outlier for us."

I grunted. "This is... this is..."

"A fucking mess," Reba declared, sniffing wetly. "I already called Susan at Doctor Clark's office in Misston, and she said she'd pass the word to the other offices so all y'all pathologists out here can have your monthly bitch and moan meet up a week early."

The thought of not coming in to work every day, not seeing Reba—who'd become like an odd auntie to me since I started at the office—made my eyes sting. I shook my head. "What are we gonna do?"

"Well"—she heaved a mighty sigh—"you're going to see to that stack of reports on your desk and I'm going to start on these invoices. Then we're going to get a drink after work because lord knows we both need one."

"Drinking midweek, Reba?" I chided gently, though with no real censure. "I'm shocked."

"Honey, I've seen things that'll curl your hair. Now get. This is a normal work day until five when we go get a beer. Then we haul ass home and scream in the comfort of our own four walls."

REBA HAD CURSED ME when she said it'd be a normal day, and I should've realized that as soon as she'd said it. But I was so fixated on the message from the higher-ups and fielding texts from several of my coroner friends that I let myself slip into a false sense of normalcy as I signed off on forms and sent, *I know, right? What the fuck!* texts.

I had never been thankful for expedited file requests before, but a sudden glut of them coming in from the Dallas medical examiner's office was an unexpected relief. It meant I didn't have the time or headspace to dwell on what was happening and my sudden sense of being useless.

Again.

Instead, I filled out the request top sheets, dotted my i's, crossed my t's, and got in touch with the ME in Dallas to sort out a courier. Because of course they wanted the hard copies and not digital, and of course they seemed to be unaware of the fact I could only give them copies because no way was I letting hard copies out of my office. Not when my job was hanging by a thread. I kept my head down and worked until I heard Reba leaving for lunch. "Shit," I muttered. It was already one o'clock and my stomach seemed to finally catch up to the fact we'd gone past our usual break time. Shutting down everything, I switched my phone to cover and grabbed my bag, intending to grab something quick from the grocery's pre-made food counter.

Tyler Stone had other ideas. "Hey!"

He came loping up to me with a sort of long-legged grace inherent in people who think running is super fun and should replace all caffeine intake as a means of getting your blood pumping in the morning.

Weirdos.

"Were you sniffing around outside my house this morning?"

Tyler stopped a yard or so away and scowled. "Why the hell would I do that? I don't want to know what you and my brother get up to. Freak."

I shook my head, sighing. There'd been my last hope it was all a mis-understanding. "Ethan said it wouldn't have been you, but—"

"But you didn't believe him?" He smirked. "Gotta say, I thought y'all'd last longer till the bloom was off the rose."

My gut clenched at that. Had Ethan said something to his brother about being unhappy? Or thinking I was? Maybe getting back together as adults wasn't what Ethan had hoped it'd be, and... I was spiraling. Fuck. I forced myself to plaster a bored expression on my face and sigh. "What do you want, Tyler?"

"No, seriously, why did you think I was sniffing around your place?" He took another step toward me, leaning forward in a parody of sharing a confidence. "Are you sneaking some other were into your place now, dude? That's uncool. Does Ethan know?"

"Fuck off, Tyler." I stepped around him, mentally ticking off the minutes left in my lunch break and rearranging my plans. No salad, then, just a sandwich—I could eat that and walk at the same time instead of spending a few minutes decompressing at my desk, since it seemed like Tyler was intent on wasting my precious time.

"Sorry, I know it wasn't funny. But seriously, do you know other weres? Because—"

"Because no. I just know y'all," I hissed. "And there's people out here, dumbass!"

Tyler snorted, loping up beside me and shooting a wave to one of the guys walking toward us. "Hey, man. How ya doin'? See the full moon last night?" He added a small, comical wolf-howl. The man stumbled, startled, but waved and kept walking, shooting us backward, confused glance.

"Are you high, Tyler?" I demanded. "Drunk? What is going on with you?"

"I'm running on like three hours of sleep and a gallon of gas station coffee." He stepped in front of me, stopping me when I would have crossed the street to the grocery. "Listen, I need to find Oliver. Have you heard from him at all? He's not answering his messages, and Ethan's neck deep in some bullshit about a dead cow."

"I haven't seen or heard from Waltrip in days, at least." I sighed. "Tyler, look, I appreciate you're... whatevering here, but I have less than twenty minutes now to get some lunch, eat it, scream into the void, and get back to my desk. Can this wait? Or, I don't know, be done over text or something?" Or never. Never is good.

HOWL AT THE MOON

Tyler grinned, wide and manic. "Come on, let me buy you lunch," he insisted, slinging his arm around my shoulders and half-dragging me across the street.

"Dude!" I shrugged him off, striding ahead of him and not slowing down until I reached the sliding doors of the grocery. Tyler jogged up beside me and looped his arm through mine. "Why are you so damn touchy feeling all of a sudden?" I growled. "Let me go!"

"Hey! Look! Melons! C'mon, I bet they have those tiny watermelons. Those are great, aren't they? You're being followed. I mean, I can eat a lot, but a regular sized watermelon? Guy looks like he smells dog shit. It's just too much, even for me. Those tiny ones, though?"

"What?"

Tyler had led me to the giant melon display in the middle of the produce section, only stopping when the towering pyramids of honeydew, cantaloupe, and watermelons were between us and the door. The cloying smell of sweet fruit slowly starting to decay, undetectable to most noses, mingled with the faint odor of dirt, of sweat from my own body, and the sharp tang of were from Tyler's. It stuck in my throat and made me want to sneeze. Tyler reached up and pressed his finger under my nose and made a face. "He's acting casual. Grab a melon."

"The fuck?"

"Here. Get that tiny watermelon. I was just rambling a minute ago, but now I have a craving."

Tyler looped his arm over my shoulders again and started handing me produce to hold. That damn tiny melon, a plastic bag of carrots, an onion that was truly monstrous, a hard-shell full of rosemary, a packet of sugared lemon peel, all the while keeping his attention on the front of the store. He kept himself between me and whoever he was keeping in his sights. "I'm gonna describe this guy to you," he murmured, "and you tell me if you've seen him before."

I nodded, focusing on the display of turnips.

"Medium height, maybe a bit taller than you, but not by much. Sandy hair, going gray. Looks fussy as hell. Pressed, pleated—good lord, is this the eighties? —slacks, tucked in fucking Izod shirt. Pinched up face, like he's judging everyone."

"That's about half the people I see on a daily basis," I murmured, but his description of the clothes pinged hard. "Might be my neighbor, Tim Cullen. He's got a stick up his ass about... well, everything." Briefly, sotto voce, I told Tyler about my recent run-ins with Cullen and the note he'd left on my door about 'my dogs.'

Tyler's growl was practically subsonic. At the front of the store, something clattered and Tyler bared his teeth. "He heard that," he chuckled. "Your neighbor's not human, man. He's not were either, though."

"What?"

Tyler shook his head, staring, not even bothering to attempt acting subtle now. "I was coming to your office to tell you what I'd found about Justin so far."

"Justin?" I straightened, nearly dropping my armful of produce. "Where is he? Is he... is he alive?"

Tyler slid me a glance. The near-manic demeanor he'd been sporting since intercepting me outside my office was gone and his usual Resting Bitch Face was back in place. He gave me one sharp nod, then looked back at Cullen. "He's seen me," Tyler said, a slow smile curving his lips. "Good. Wait here." He strode toward Cullen, grabbing one of the turnips as he passed.

"Tyler!"

"Hey," Tyler called, lobbing the turnip at Cullen, missing him, but not by much. I swear even the canned music overhead went silent. "What's your problem, asshole?"

"I'm buying groceries," Cullen retorted. "Do I know you?"

"Why are you following Doctor Babin?"

HOWL AT THE MOON

"Sir!" one of the women wearing the red manager pinafore snapped, striding out from behind the customer service booth. "I'm going to need both of you to leave. I will call the police if you don't get off store property immediately!"

Tyler held up his hands in a no harm gesture. "I just want to know why he's been stalking my friend here."

Every eye in the store swiveled toward me. Or that's what it felt like. I wiggled my fingers in a tiny wave, careful not to drop my armful of produce.

Cullen sniffed. "You have delusions of importance," he announced, aiming the words at me. "There's one store in this town, and only a handful of routes to reach it. The fact I had to walk past your office doesn't mean I'm following you, you narcissistic asshole."

Tyler scooped up the turnip and fished some money out of his pocket, handing it to the customer service lady. "Here. For this," he shook the turnip. "I'm leaving, but I know what you are," he added in a low rumble. Cullen visibly paled before turning a deep pink that made me worry for his blood pressure. Tyler saluted me with the turnip. "Meet you back at the office."

Cullen sniffed again, his upper lip curling to bare some teeth. "This is ridiculous. I should press charges."

"For what?" I demanded.

The woman threw up her hands. "Get out. Both of you."

"But my melons," I blurted. "I... I don't even want these, actually. I have watermelon at home. And I don't like carrots."

She pinched the bridge of her nose between her thumb and forefinger, using her other hand to point at the doors. "Just put them down at register two. And go!"

An awkward shuffle and muttered apology later, I edged past Cullen with his empty handbasket—he'd apparently been lurking near the front of the store, by the magazine racks, so I don't know who he was trying to fool with his grocery shopping excuse—and made a beeline for the opposite side of the street, where Tyler waited with his damn turnip.

"Ever had these mashed?" he asked, shaking the fronds at me. "I kind of remember my mom making them mashed, but that might be one of those things you think you remember, but it's just your imagination, you know?"

"Tyler." I sighed. "What are you doing?"

"Come on. Walk with me." He shoved the turnip into his pocket and nudged me in the opposite direction of my office.

"I need to get back."

"We're just going around the back way. Come on. Walk and talk. Tell me about these footprints."

Fuck it. I started walking with Tyler and gave him a rundown of the past few days with Cullen's weirdness, the signs of something not human outside my house, but I left out the tiff I'd had—maybe was still having—with Ethan.

Tyler grunted softly to himself as we rounded the corner and headed for the alleyway between shops, which would spit us out in a narrow alley between the side of the deli and the larger row of offices where mine was tucked away. "Cullen, he's not human. At all. Can't you smell it on him? I thought you were all tuned in to the weirdness, dude."

"I think maybe it gets muddled when I'm around weres," I admitted. "Ethan's been trying to help me, um, develop things, you know? Get better at understanding what my senses are telling me, untangling them from fear triggers. And also the shifting."

"Yeah?" he asked, smiling a little as we strode down the gross-smelling alley, dodging puddles of dumpster goo. "How's that working out?"

My face warmed. "Eh."

"Not so much, huh?"

I shook my head. "This isn't exactly something Ethan has experience teaching, you know? And I doubt there's a were out there who does."

"We learn it when we're children. It's more instinct than anything." He slowed his steps, drawing us to a halt behind Bernie's Wigs-N-More with its dumpster full of old mannequin heads and wads of out-of-date wigs tossed to make room for new merchandise.

I wondered what the -N-More was, or if it was just more wigs.

"Ethan says I'm... I'm as much were as y'all," I muttered. "But I can't even do things a child can. And now I have my neighbor stalking me, and apparently he's were, too? This feels like some weird crossover of Ugly Duckling and Little Red Riding Hood, but without the whimsy."

Tyler snorted. "He's not were. But he's definitely stalking you. Or he was, at least today. And maybe this whole time. Those steps outside your room might have been his. I can't be sure though."

"He's not were, but he's not human," I said slowly. "What does that even mean? Is he a fucking cryptid or something?"

"God, no. Cryptids want nothing to do with us."

"What?"

He carried on as if hadn't just yelped at him. "He's... he's something that's pretending to be a regular human. Maybe he's like you, and it's throwing me off. But he doesn't smell like a were at all. You, though," he paused and made a show of taking a deep sniff of the air over my shoulder. "Definitely have that were scent to you."

"You're so fucking weird."

"I'm weird, but I'm right. And I'm also on Justin's trail. Whatever happened when he took the Lycaon, it's stuck. He's not like you. No offense. I just mean that he's..." Tyler shook his head, tipping his face up to the narrow strip of blue sky overhead as he sorted out his words. "He's changed. But doesn't understand anything about it. It's not something he's grown up with, or something that's even been part of him. Garrow using regular humans for some sort of control group went catastrophically bad. Some of whom we think are regular humans have were traits in their genetic makeup, maybe from some long-lost relative or maybe some other mechanism we don't understand. So much of our own history wasn't recorded, and what was is often muddled up with mythology and folklore. And two, those traits can—and did—get triggered by Lycaon. A handful of deaths over the past few years that were attributed to some hemorrhagic fever or even an overdose have been traced back to Bluebonnet, thanks to Elio and Diz's research."

"But Justin's alive," I murmured. "He's alive, right?"

Tyler lowered his chin to give me a curious look. "If he's not, will you be sad?"

I threw up my hands. "Of course I will, asshole! We weren't best friends or anything, but he's still a person, and I knew... know... him. He doesn't deserve to suffer."

"He's alive," Tyler said after a beat. "But he's not well. Whatever the Lycaon caused inside him, it's pushed him toward being a full-fledged were."

Maybe I was mistaken, but I thought I heard a hint of pride in Tyler's tone, like he was impressed by something out of Justin's control.

Never mind that twinge of envy I felt—Justin was going through literal hell, and here I was wishing I had the same reaction to the damn medication, so I wouldn't be in this weird half-state of being.

"Where was he last?"

"He'd been staying down around Houston for a while. There's a huge rogue community there, but I don't think that's where he was headed intentionally. Elio was able to track down a great-aunt of Justin's that has a condo there, and apparently it's been sitting empty while she's on one of those fancy multi-month cruises. Looks like that's where he ran when shit got hairy—heh, hairy—but she was due back a month ago, so he ran. Diz picked him up on security cameras in the city, living rough apparently, but there's been some rumors that a new were's hit the scene a bit south of the city."

"And it's Justin?" I whispered. "He's... he doesn't know the rules, you know? How were communities work? What if he pisses someone off? They're not going to know about the situation down there. Hell, they—"

"There's another lab." Tyler's voice was low and flat, already tired of the bullshit that hadn't really happened yet. Or maybe that never stopped.

My breath left me in a whoosh as anxiety skyrocketed. "Shit, Tyler..."

"I'm on it. I actually was in Dallas meeting with Elio at his little tech cave when he and Diz confirmed their suspicions. There's an old army base near the Oklahoma border, been out of use since the seventies, but even then, it was barely functional, just a leftover from the last big war. A private company bought it up in the nineties, but it's just been sitting there, at least from the outside. Diz did some picking when a few things popped up on her favorite dark web shopping site, and the owners are tied to Bluebonnet. They funded a huge chunk of the research there."

"And... this site. It's another lab."

He nodded slowly. "Bigger, less obvious. It's far enough off the public grid that folks don't notice. And it's a comparatively small op. But the problem—"

I scoffed. "There's another one?"

"Hold your horses because this gets bad, Lan. The clinic is putting out feelers in the rogue community. And Justin is suddenly heading north, toward this Podunk town, and allegedly closed base."

"They got to him?" I asked, reedy. "Tyler..."

I shook my head, unable to unsee the mental image of Justin—goofy, irritating, TMI-sharing, always-smiling Justin—turning into some sort of B-Movie monster and murdering innocent people.

"I'm on it. But I need to find Oliver, and I was hoping you or Ethan had heard from him."

"Why would I?"

"He was on the trail of Mal Benes, the guy from your cohort."

Shaking my head again, I muttered, "I have no idea. And why do y'all keep making it sound like Benes and I should know one another? I don't remember any other kids from the experiment other than little flashes of memory from waiting rooms."

"Oliver dropped off the grid a few days ago," Tyler said as if I hadn't complained. "He left a message with his office that he was on his way to a meeting with a potential source and that was it. I was hoping he'd come back to this area to follow up on a lead."

"You mean harass me and Ethan?"

Tyler shrugged. "Either way. But there's been no trace of him. Which either means he's gone to ground because he's in trouble, or," he paused, swallowed, affected cool nonchalance that was frayed around the edges, "he's dead."

Chapter Three

Tyler followed me back to the office, pointing out where he'd noticed Cullen lurking before I'd come out, tucked into a narrow nook that had once housed a payphone in front of the tax prep office across the street from where we stood. "I parked down by that deli you like—what the fuck is with traffic today? This place is usually a ghost town."

"Autumn in the south," I muttered. "Homecoming season."

"Ugh."

"Basically."

"I'm going to leave word for Ethan about this," Tyler murmured warningly. "Maybe you should let him know yourself, too."

"I don't need him babysitting me."

"No, but maybe he needs to know someone not human is on clan territory?" Tyler noted. "And maybe he'd like to know his boyfriend lives right next door to the guy?"

"Why didn't Ethan notice him, then? He's met Cullen."

Tyler shrugged. "Are you certain?"

"I mean, he's been there when Cullen's been bitching about his parking, or the noise or..."

"Or maybe he made sure to stay a distance away from Ethan? Not get close enough to get pinged."

I nodded slowly. "Maybe so." My mental slideshow of interactions with Cullen almost all involved him standing on his porch or driveway, holding that giant cat of his and refusing to come closer as he shouted at me, or leaving notes in mailboxes or online. Or in the case of this week, directly on my door.

He never approached us any closer than that.

Was he afraid of getting knocked the fuck out, or was it something else?

"Shit."

Tyler nodded. "Yep. Pretty much. Okay, if Oliver turns up, tell him I'm looking for him. I need to get, otherwise I'll miss Justin. He's been showing up at the same unhoused camp for the past few nights and I want to be there when he gets there."

I nodded, giving Tyler a wave as he trotted back toward his car, leaving me to trudge into the office on my own.

Reba was waiting for me, eyes wide and lips stretched into that too-big, panic-smile she sometimes got. "You've got a visitor."

She looked uneasy, her fingers twisting into knots at her waist as she darted glances at my office door. "Okay?"

She nodded. "Just... be careful," she whispered. "He's weird."

Stranger danger some hysterical part of my brain shrieked as I neared my office door.

Great. My early warning system had gone from klaxons to child-hood PSAs.

Breathe, focus on that feeling, Ethan had told me during most of our practices by the pond. That part of you is scared because you were never taught to understand these signals. Someone who was raised with it, it's not fear we feel but awareness. Someone is near, someone like me. It doesn't always mean harm.

The edges of my anxiety dulled a bit but were still pressing against me from the inside out as I opened the door and stepped into my office. A man in a sharp navy-blue suit and bright pink shirt sat across from my desk in one of the guest chairs. He popped to his feet as soon as I stepped through the door. "Doctor Babin," he said—not a question, just letting me know he knew. "My name is Travis Hiller."

And you're not human, are you, Mr. Hiller?

HOWL AT THE MOON

"I'm afraid this office is an appointment-only situation, Mr. Hiller," I began, but he cut me off with an airy wave and a smirk.

"I can be quick."

"Most folks wouldn't admit that out loud," I muttered. "Reba, you alright?"

She nodded. "Sure, just dandy! I'm going to go grab lunch!"

"Sure thing," I said, tipping my head toward the exit. She'd just gotten back from lunch but frankly, I didn't blame her for bolting while she could. "Take your time."

Reba broke land-speed records fleeing the office, leaving me in the brightly lit lobby with a werewolf.

"No," I murmured. "You're one, aren't you? A were."

He flashed me a grin. "How can you tell?"

I could feel my brain trying to work it out, shaking dust off senses that had been mothballed for decades. The urge to flee was still there, simmering, barely in check, but something else was pinging, too. *Wolf,* my thoughts whispered. *Wolf but dangerous, not like Ethan, not like Tyler...*

His smile didn't waver, but tightness rimmed his eyes. "Again, how can you tell?"

"What can I do for you. Mr. Hiller? I have patients to examine, whose families are waiting so they can take care of their final needs. I'm assuming you're not a salesman?"

He shook his head slowly, smile finally dimming. "You haven't checked your messages."

Again, not a question. "Did you come here just to make declarative statements?" I shifted my weight to the balls of my feet. He noticed, a quick flick of his eyes downward, a barely perceptible tensing of his entire body. One of us was going to run, the other was going to give chase.

"I'd been hoping to get in touch with you before you reached the office this morning but needs must. Do you have your phone with you?"

"I'm really getting a vacuum salesman vibe here," I snarked. "Instead of pouring dirt on my floor to show me how well it cleans, you're going to brick my phone to convince me to buy one of your company's?"

"We'll just use mine then." He pulled a brand-new smart phone, one of those ridiculously expensive kinds that could probably colonize Mars while performing open heart surgery. "Ah, can we sit?" he asked, motioning to Reba's desk.

"No, we're good here."

He rolled his eyes, not even bothering to hide it. "My client would like to hire you, Doctor Babin. He feels your particular background—"

Danger! Danger, Will Robinson! "Stop right there. I don't do contract work and even if I did, I have zero clue as to who would want to hire a forensic pathologist to do freelance jobs." I took a step back—there was no way to be subtle about it and at this point, I didn't care.

He'd be fast. He was tall, all legs really, and had a barely restrained sort of tension to his movements that made me think of something bursting from the underbrush, something feline and sharp that would be on me before I could turn around to flee.

Where would I run? The exam room? Hide in one of the empty morgue drawers?

No, I needed to focus. To pay attention to what these senses were saying, beyond the fear and flight response.

One, this man wasn't human. Two, he was a were like Ethan, Tyler, Waltrip. Three, he was working for someone who knew what I was, which meant I was super double plus unsafe.

Hiller cocked his head, not looking up from his phone. "If you'd checked your messages, we could already be done now." He flipped his

HOWL AT THE MOON

phone around to face me and I staggered back—no hesitant steps this time.

"Christ!"

Hiller frowned. "I'd hope this isn't how you react to every dead body you see."

What was on his phone was only a body in the loosest sense of the word. A vague suggestion of life might be more accurate. Red, with only a few solid pieces to indicate all that blood had once been *inside* someone, filled the screen. "You sent me that?" I snarled. "Fucking hell! What's wrong with you?" I pushed his hand back, forcing him to move or lose his phone. "Get the fuck out of this office!"

Hiller thumbed the screen, and another image popped up. This one more identifiable as a person but no less dead than the last. Without being able to see the body in person, I could only guess as to what happened but the way they were twisted, I would guess torture was involved. "What the hell is this?" I demanded. "I don't know what you think I *do*, but you—or your employer—can fuck off with this!"

"Doctor Babin," Hiller said, voice crisp and firm as I turned to go back into my office and put several locked doors between us. "Don't run from me."

My feet stumbled, like his words could compel me. "Get out of my office before I call the police."

"Your lover? Sheriff Stone?" He quirked a smile. "I think you'll find his presence useless in this situation. In fact, he would likely tell you to hear me out." Without looking, he thumbed to the next image. It was one I'd seen before, one Waltrip's assistant Elio had dug up earlier in the year. Mal Benes, one of the people who'd been in my experimental cohort as a child. His parents had taken him to Colorado around the age of six or seven.

In the picture, he was looking at someone off to one side, making an exaggerated face of surprise, eyes crinkling with humor. My stomach cramped—*he has a kid*. "Is he... Those pictures..."

"No." Hiller tucked his phone away finally and folded his hands at his waist. "But the shifter clan in Penny Mine—and I use the term *clan* loosely," he sniffed, "believe your Mr. Benes is responsible for these deaths."

I shook my head but paused. I had no idea about Mal Benes, beyond our shared roots in the Garrow experiments. Maybe he was a horrible person. Maybe he'd been able to reach that were part of himself and it had fucked with his head. Instead of fear and anxiety, he felt power, bloodlust...

Or maybe he was just a fucking psycho killer and thought slicing and dicing people in the backwoods of Colorado was a super fun happy time to be had by all.

"I don't understand what this has to do with me."

"My employer wishes for you to clear Mal Benes of wrongdoing. There is a, ah, *private* investigation underway and those in charge require forensic evidence to render the appropriate verdict and potential punishment. Shifters are not so thick on the ground these days that we can afford to lose this many."

My lips were numb when I asked how many.

"At last count, sixteen."

"Jesus Christ... That's not a private matter, Mr. Hiller. That's fucking federal levels of unstable behavior. You need to involve *actual* authorities." Beneath my surface, I could feel that need to run bubbling, but this time it was different. Not run away, I realized, but *toward*. *Defend, chase, protect...*

"That isn't possible. Not within our circles, Doctor Babin. Something you would know if you stopped insisting on hiding from what you are."

Reba's return, marked by the sound of her fussing with the key card and fumbling her paper bag of goodies, made us both turn toward the door. "Check your email, Doctor Babin," he said with a tilt of his head. "I'll be in touch."

HOWL AT THE MOON

Reba slid past him as he gave her a cordial nod and toothpaste ad smile, slipping into the corridor and striding to the elevator at the end of the hall.

"Who was that?" Reba hissed the second the lock engaged. "Lord, I didn't know whether to drop my drawers or call the cops! Or both! Are you okay, hon? You look like you're gonna be sick!"

I did some odd maneuver between a headshake and a nod, finally settling on a frantic sort of giggle. "Sorry, just a really pushy asshole."

Reba grunted in annoyance, setting her bag down on the desk and opening it up, letting out a waft of cinnamon and sugar and grease. "I went by the bakery and got some cinnamon rolls, and one of those poppyseed bran things you like. They were out of the hazelnut vanilla coffee though, so you're gonna have to make do with a flat white."

I nodded. "Sure. No worries."

She glanced up at me, halfway to seated in her chair. "Seriously, are you okay? He was giving off weird vibes. He didn't *do* anything wrong, you know? It just *felt* off. And I've read *The Gift of Fear,* so I know I gotta listen to my gut, especially being a lady in this day and age. But..." she paused, finally sitting and sweeping a concerned gaze over my face. "Landry, are you *sure*?"

I nodded, this time firmly and enthusiastically. "He was just pushy, is all. It's fine. I'm gonna go have this," I held up the muffin she got for me, "and down the coffee before I start on Mr. Lemon." *And try to call Waltrip again.* The fact not even Tyler could reach him was... well, *concerning* didn't seem like a strong enough word. Even when Waltrip wanted to be all mysterious and shit, he couldn't shut up. The fact he was off the radar was a huge flashing red warning light.

Something bad is coming, and it either took him off the grid or he's trying to get ahead of it on his own.

I must have made a face because Reba shot me another concerned look and I forced a smile, taking a bite of the muffin. "All good, I promise," I mumbled around a mouthful of orange cranberry poppy seed carby goodness.

"For god's sake, don't talk with your mouth full," she sighed, shaking her head. "Go, work!"

I nodded, waving the muffin again as I headed into the inner sanctum of my office. First I'd try Waltrip, then start on Mr. Lemon. One was definitely more urgent than the other.

THE REST OF THE DAY was an odd dream state. I couldn't shake what Hiller had shown me, couldn't unwind the way my thoughts wrapped around the knowledge someone outside of the little clusterfuck of last year knew about me, sought me out.

It didn't feel good.

By the time I wrapped up for the day and closed up the office, I'd almost—*almost*—forgotten about the fluff with Ethan that morning. It felt like days ago at that point, but it was less than twelve hours. I reluctantly checked my phone—the Unknown Number messages from Hiller were there, as well as several messages and missed calls from Ethan, and one message from Waltrip (at least that meant he probably wasn't dead). The last message from Ethan had been sent around nine that morning, before his day got hectic no doubt, and just said *I'm coming by tonight. We'll talk then.*

That didn't feel good, either. While my feelings *had* been hurt, my reaction had been, well, bratty. Less than mature. And I needed to suck it up and talk to Ethan like an adult and not just tuck my very metaphorical tail and sulk.

Though he really did owe me an apology for laughing at me.

Hmph.

Waltrip's message was more concerning though.

Don't talk to anyone. Bringing you something to keep safe.

That could be anything from a flash drive of info to, knowing Waltrip, something dangerous and illegal.

And there'd be no finding out until he decided to show up with whatever it was.

Shit.

ETHAN DIDN'T COME BY until after seven. I'd only been home about half an hour, long enough for the faint buzz from my beer with Reba to wear off and the pile of bills on the hall table to taunt me into another attempt at organizing them.

They weren't overdue yet, but it was going to be a skin-of-my-teeth situation getting them paid on time. I'd already cut out a lot of the *extras*—streaming services, the higher tier internet package, dropped to a lower cost phone plan, and even changed what I was getting at the grocery in an effort to cut costs when my hours got reduced. Now, with the news that I was pretty much unemployed, I was in a low-key panic about what to do next. A quick job search at the bar with Reba showed me what I already knew—pathology wasn't exactly a happening field. There were a few openings in Houston and Austin or even farther afield out of state, but that would mean moving and...

I sighed aloud. Ethan was here. My life was here, such as it was. I didn't want to move, even if I could afford it, but if something didn't change soon, I might not have a choice.

Hiller's offer tugged at my thoughts. He'd sent one more email before Reba and I split for the night. It listed a truly bananas sum for my "freelance services."

Enough to cover my bills, including my house note, for a few months. Hell, I could even get Netflix back if I felt daring.

Enough to buy me some time to find something new. Maybe do the unthinkable and change specialties, if I had to.

Reba's suggestion of starting a funeral home was... something. And I may have looked that up when she ran to the ladies' room after her second Lone Star—it was way more work than most people realized, and more money, especially seeing as it would require all sorts of different schooling and certifications and licensing.

Not all jobs with the dead are the same, kids.

Morosely, I took a handful of the second notices and aggressively worded first notices outside and sprawled on the Adirondack chair on my porch, watching the way the sun smeared the sky with orange and deep pink, ignoring the clattering coming from Cullen's porch as he tried to pretend he wasn't snooping on me. I closed my eyes and tried to will myself not to freak out, but that was useful as tits on a boar hog, as Aunt Cleverly would've said.

Damn it. Now let's add some angry-sad-anxiety to the mix, thinking of Cleverly and Garrow and Tyler's news about the new lab.

Ethan's car rumbling up my drive was a spike of relief, piercing through the dark fog that nibbled around my edges. I stood as he pulled up and Cullen drifted to the end of his porch, fussing with some of his hanging plant baskets and now just openly watching us.

"You alright?" Ethan called as he got out of his car. "You've got a whole"—he gestured at his face with a sort of circular motion—"thing going on."

Ethan was in a pair of old, battered jeans and a plain t-shirt, his boots (not his sturdy work ones, I noticed, but an ancient pair of Docs I remembered from high school) dusty and looking worse for wear as he walked toward me. He looked like something out of one of those country music videos where they warble about high school sweethearts and my man this and that.

I hated country music with a burning passion to rival the intensity of a thousand desert suns, so this was a very complicated moment for me.

"I'm fine. Just a very confusing boner right now."

One corner of his lips tilted into a smirk. "Didn't know if you'd mind me coming by to talk, but I figured, since I didn't hear back from you all day, you either had a real busy day today and maybe might want some company to decompress, or you were still mad at me for laughing this morning and I needed to talk to you in person so you couldn't avoid me."

I sighed. "Bit of both, to be honest." Moving to meet him at the top of the steps, I tentatively rose up on my toes to kiss him as he joined me. The dark circles under his eyes drew me up short (ha, no height jokes please). "Hey, are *you* okay?"

"Another long day," he admitted, and my gut twisted. Ethan had been having a shit time at work for weeks (that he'd admit to, so that meant it was really longer). Long, late days, meetings out the ears... And I hadn't asked him how he was doing for ages.

Shit.

"I'm selfish," I murmured, resting my head against his shoulder. "I'm so sorry I've been a brat and you've been—"

"Hey," Ethan interrupted. "Let's go inside, alright? Get out of the heat. Then we can talk."

I nodded hesitantly, wondering if this was Ethan's way of telling me to drop it, or if he felt I really didn't care. Cullen's door slammed, and I glanced over as we headed inside. His massive cat was staring back at me from what would be his living room window, her squinty little eyes almost hidden in the sea of floof. She bared her teeth in a silent hiss before I looked away. "They do say pets start to act like their owners," I muttered.

"Who says that?"

"They do."

Ethan snorted. "Alright then." He stepped aside so I could open the door, following me into the cool dark of the house. He locked up behind us, even setting the deadbolt and chain. "Just in case," he muttered at my look.

"Okay, safety man," I chuckled. "Let me get clean and changed. I feel gross."

He didn't offer to join me in the shower like he sometimes did, and I felt a pang of something unpleasant. Maybe I'd fucked up worse than I thought?

By the time I'd taken a fast shower to get the lingering funk of the day off me and thrown on some joggers and an old t-shirt, Ethan had gotten us out the pitcher of sweet tea I kept in the fridge and was cooking dinner as if it were his kitchen.

And really, given the amount of time he spent at my place, it might as well have been. We didn't stay at his much, and part of me wondered if that was due to the fact he lived right in the middle of were territory. Several local families made up a clan of weres, and he was the de facto head of the group since his father's death. Ethan had assured me several months ago, after having to deal with some squabble between the Dermott and Keeler families about a property issue, that his role as head was really not that big a deal and had become more symbolic over the years.

I couldn't help but wonder if he kept me away from that part of his life because of how I was. Because I wasn't like them and never would be, even if I could get the hang of shifting into a wolf form. I wasn't part of the community, or the culture.

I was and always would be an outsider.

Ethan looked up from chopping vegetables and offered me a small, tender smile. "You're thinking so loud it's giving me a headache."

I huffed, crossing the kitchen to steal a carrot from his chopping block and kissing him on the cheek. "Today was not a great day. And I'm sorry I got mad at you for laughing at me this morning. I mean, I think it was a dick move to laugh at me like that, but I'm sorry I got mad and didn't tell you why that hurt my feelings."

He set the knife down and carefully scooped up the celery he'd been slicing, transferring it to the skillet where he was making either a very ambitious stir fry or getting experimental with the contents of my crisper. "I shouldn't have laughed."

"I mean, if it was funny," I mumbled, and he shot me a sideways glance. "I just don't understand why."

"Babe, you referred to 'your wolf,' like it's a pet or something. Or that ridiculous fake proverb about having the two wolves inside you. It's not a separate thing. It's you. You are it. There's no barely restrained beast waiting to come out. It's not something beyond your control—"

"Except it kind of is," I pointed out. "If I could control it, you wouldn't have worn yourself out this past year trying to help me shift."

He took the carrot from me and set it aside before pulling me into an embrace. I sighed into it, letting him take my weight against his chest and hold me up with his arms, his larger size making me feel safe and wanted and like I wasn't going to fly into a dozen pieces. "Whenever I'm at work, I don't feel like this," I muttered.

"Hm?"

"Nothing."

"You're lying."

"I'm avoiding."

He tipped my chin up. "Feel like what?"

"Like I'm going to fall apart," I admitted. "At work, I'm good at what I do. I'm beyond competent—"

"And so modest, too," he teased, shifting me to a one-arm hold so he could stir the vegetables. "The problem is—at the risk of being an armchair shrink here—that you don't like not knowing how things are going to turn out. At work, even if you have a weird case, you know they're still dead. They're not going to be something unexpected. And if you do have a bit of a what the fuck to deal with, you know there're only so many answers."

I made a face. "That's not entirely true."

"How about this, then? At work, you're doing something you've trained to do for years. You know what you're doing, you know how to find answers when you don't. But this"—he tapped my chest with two fingers—"you don't know. Maybe you suspected something was different about you when we were kids, but you didn't know. And all this information has not only been dumped on you, but in the worst way possible."

"I don't know." I sighed. "Maybe? Or maybe I'm just really bad at this." I tapped my chest where he had. "And I need to accept that."

Ethan frowned, pulling away to shut off the burner and move the skillet before catching me back in his arms again. "What's going on, Landry?"

For a brief second, I thought of brushing off the question, or bringing it back around to my whinge over the whole poor me, can't wolf thing. But I caved to my better judgment and told him about the visit from Travis Hiller and about Waltrip's text message. Vague, yet unclear. Just the thing to make my day better.

Ethan made me show him the messages from Hiller, his expression tight and grim and growing more so with each picture. "Said they were in Penny Mine?"

I nodded. "Sounds like one of those ghost towns out west, doesn't it?"

"Mmm. Just a sec." He pulled out his phone and dialed someone. When they didn't answer, he tried again. Then again. "Oliver," he finally said when the voicemail picked up a fourth time. "It's Ethan. Call me." For good measure, he sent off a text too, before taking my phone to look at the images again. "Did he say how they knew about you, this employer of his?"

I shook my head. "I assumed it was because of Garrow and Bluebonnet, really. You've told me before the were community isn't as big as all that. I figured word carried once shit went bad last year. He said the shifter—"

"Shifter?" Ethan's head snapped up. "Not were? He specifically said shifter?"

HOWL AT THE MOON

I nodded slowly. "It's the same thing, isn't it?"

His wince was subtle, but it was there. "Not exactly. There're some weres that use the words interchangeably but to most of us? There's a big difference. A shifter wouldn't want to be called a were-anything, and a were wouldn't want to be lumped in with the shifters."

"What do you mean, were-anything?"

Ethan thumbed out of the images and handed me my phone back. "Don't erase that. Oliver needs to see those. And I mean that weres are weres. Shifters are..." He floundered. "Okay, so it's technically splitting hairs here, but shifters can be other animal types. Almost anything," he added, then held up a finger to silence me when I was about to burst out with a million questions. "Almost. They're not shapeshifters like in the movies, able to take on any form or something. They function like weres. Mostly." He made a face at that, offering me an apologetic shrug. "Most of it is cultural, from what I was taught as a kid. But I just know when you say shifter, that can mean anything from a wolf like me to a freaking chameleon or something."

"Huh."

He handed me my beer from where I'd left it on the counter. "This is the part when I admit I don't know much about how these other groups work. I've never had to. We only have one shifter community in Texas and they're mountain lions, way out west in the Davis range. There were rumors for a while that some black bear shifters had moved into the Red River area," he said, nodding in the direction of the river on the far side of the county, "but that was never proven. They might be there, or maybe it was some kids high on magic mushrooms having a real bad trip. Weres, as a rule—and I mean that literally—tend to avoid interfering in shifter groups."

Rolling my beer back and forth between my palms, I regarded him with a heavy dose of what the hell. "But shifters are weres. And vice versa. I mean, isn't the only difference you shift into a wolf, and they shift into something else?"

Ethan groaned, but it wasn't aimed at me so much as at whatever layers of were and shifter politics he was about to have to explain. "It's more complex than that. There are wolf shifters who aren't considered weres. While on the surface it's down to what we change into, it's deeper than that. There're centuries of culture, politics, socioeconomic development, of—" He broke off and shook his head. "The easiest thing is to say we're wolves, they're not. But it's like saying you're exactly the same as someone from a different culture just because you're both pathologists."

"Ah." At his skeptical look, I smiled softly. "I'm getting it. It'll just take time to organize into my mental filing cabinet, you know?"

He nodded, but it seemed a little hesitant. "If this Hiller person was specifically calling them shifters, this is outside of anything I can help with," he said finally. "I'm head of this clan, so there're all sorts of hoops I'd need to jump through to be able to interact with whoever is trying to get you to do this for them."

I reached out, laid my hand over his to quiet him for a moment. He looked at me, dark eyes wide under his heavy copper-colored brows as he searched my face worriedly. "Baby," I said, "they didn't ask for you. Or us. Just me."

The concerned look folded into one of annoyance and frustration. "And you don't see that as a problem?"

"Oh, I definitely do," I assured him, taking another sip of my beer. "But I don't know the first thing to do about it."

Ethan picked at the label on his bottle before catching my gaze, his shoulders slumping just a little as he sighed and said, "I think you do, though."

"What do you mean?"

"He gave you enough info to inform the authorities in Colorado, didn't he? Locations, his own name—"

"If that's actually his name!"

HOWL AT THE MOON

"Involved Mal Benes," he pressed on, talking over my protest. "Lan, he gave you enough to call someone else about this, remove yourself entirely. But you chose not to."

"I still could," I murmured. "He doesn't know..."

"This worries me for a lot of reasons, Landry. I don't like not knowing who this is, who knows you like this. And I don't like that they're trying to involve weres in shifter business."

"So, I'm one of y'all now?"

Hurt flickered over his features. He pushed his beer away and took mine, too, before capturing both my hands in his. "I told you that already. After Bluebonnet. Did you think I was kidding?"

"I think..." Thoughts of him coming to my place instead of us going to his, not inviting me to clan meet-ups, my own insecurities, all bubbled and seethed together, making my eyes throb. "I think I'm tired," I admitted after a moment. "Maybe we should just have dinner."

He stared at me a moment or so longer before nodding and pushing away to get plates down while I grabbed cutlery and glasses for the sweet tea.

Dinner was uncomfortable. We talked about the usual things, laughed at inside jokes, I praised his cooking and he got all bashful about it, but there was something sitting between us, wiry and sharp, just growing large and larger until I felt it pressed against my throat, and from the way Ethan was fidgeting, it was scraping at him too. I quietly gathered up our dishes and took them to the sink, getting the basin set up (my kingdom for a dishwasher) when Ethan broke.

"I'm not mad at you," he said softly. "I'm just... dealing with a lot at work. And it's weighing heavy on me, Lan. I don't want to drag you into it because I know you'll blame yourself and—"

"Wow, way to put words in my mouth," I grumbled, squirting way too much dish soap into the dirty side basin. "Good ol' Landry, overreacting."

"That's not what I said." Ethan sighed. "But tell me you wouldn't if you knew that I've been dealing with clan bullshit for the past three months, half of 'em thinking it's wrong to welcome in people like you and the rest thinking the first half is full of shit. It's like trying to herd cats. Angry cats," he added, scrubbing his hands over his face. "And, for the record, I'm not about to cut you out of my life, Landry. I'll leave the clan before I do that."

"Jesus Christ," I muttered, shutting off the water. "Ethan, that's insane. The clan is your life—"

"No," he snapped, getting to his feet. "You're my life. Wait, that sounds creepy. But you're a huge part of my life. I love you—have since high school, for fuck's sake. And the old guard wants us to stay small, hidden... they're dying out. Even if I didn't know you, Lan, I'd be fighting against the push to keep our clan cut off from the others."

The soft hiss and pop of dish soap dissolving and bubbles breaking was the only sound in the room for a long moment. "Ethan..."

"My dad used to say some of the old timers were howling at the moon," he chuckled dryly, hands shoved in his pockets like he couldn't figure out what to do with them. "I thought it meant they were really going out, you know? Like the old days when packs would still hunt as wolves. I found out later it means wanting something that's impossible to have. A wolf crying for the full moon..." he drifted off. "Well. That's that."

I padded barefoot across the kitchen, slipping my hands under his arms and resting my head on his chest, hearing his heart thump against my ear, his breath catch for just a moment. "I don't want to be the cause of a break," I whispered. "I wouldn't make you choose."

"You're not." He took his hands out of his pockets and pulled me in tighter. His lips brushed my head as he repeated the words, the pair of us swaying slightly as the soap fizzed away in the sink, pulling apart only when a light, rapid knock fell on my front door. Ethan groaned and

HOWL AT THE MOON

tipped his head back. "It's Cullen," he muttered. "I can smell that damn cat of his."

With a growl of my own, I headed to the front door and opened it on an unsmiling neighbor. "Cullen." I sighed. "I'd love to tell you to fuck off in a creative way, but I've had a very long day, and the best I can do is a good ol' 'get fucked,' so," I made a have at it gesture, "I'll leave you to it."

"Doctor Babin," he called, voice oddly calm, "you'd do well to mind what I'm telling you."

"Right, right, dire threats, HOA, yada, yada, yada. I need to go clean the kitchen, so if that's all?"

He stared at me, sour-faced, as I stepped back to shut the door. "Doctor Babin," he said sharply, like the words hurt his tongue. "I know you've been visited by Mr. Hiller. And I know about Colorado."

I paused, the door half-closed. "Most people know about Colorado, at least in passing. I mean, it's been a state for a while now."

His eye roll must have hurt. "We need to talk, Doctor Babin. No pretenses. I understand that you have no reason to hear me out—"

"That is the first thing you've said to me that doesn't make me want to pluck my eyebrows out just to feel something other than deep annoyance. Excuse me, it's getting late, and I want to get things done and head to bed."

"I work for the International Committee of Were-Shifter Relations."

My feet stopped moving and I swear I heard one of those needle drop sound effects. "The what now?"

He huffed softly and folded his arms across his narrow chest. "It's a cumbersome name, I'm aware. The IC, for short. We're working toward creating a network, so to speak, between were and shifter communities the world over. To make it safer for us while keeping our existence as quiet as possible, off the world stage."

"And a fuck-off huge committee is being subtle?"

"It's amazing what you can get away with so long as you smile and nod and keep your head down. We're not a flashy group, Doctor Babin. The world is becoming smaller by the day, and it is more and more difficult for the truth of our existence to remain hidden. And thanks to groups like Garrow's and the satellite branches of his research clinic, the threat isn't always from outside."

"The call is coming from inside the house," I muttered.

"Part of the same but separate." Cullen shrugged. "Like a cancer. The main tumor has been excised, but a few cells remained and are determined to grow." Across the street, the little girls who lived there sent up a wail as their dad tried to wrestle them inside for the night. "May we step inside?" Cullen asked, exasperation clear in his tone. "This is hardly something to share with the neighbors."

"Probably a big ol' HOA violation," I agreed. Behind me, inside the house, Ethan cleared his throat and made sure Cullen knew he was there but waiting, just in case. Cullen rolled his eyes and turned his attention back to me.

"Hiller... whatever he's asking you to do, it's dangerous, and he's lying about it. He offered you a job, didn't he?"

"I think you already know the answer," I replied slowly. "What the hell is going on here, Cullen?"

"What is it that Hiller is asking you to do, Doctor Babin? Is he trying to hire you as a physician for the compound?"

"What? What compound?" I shook my head, a thousand thoughts buzzing around against the inside of my skull, each one fighting for dominance.

"Because I have to say that is far more dangerous than you think, especially with their current, rather... unstable... situation."

"No, he asked me to help with the autopsies of several murdered shifters. Something about an internal investigation and—" I paused. "Oh, you got me spilling my guts, you sly dog." I sighed, not missing how he bristled at being referred to as a dog even colloquially.

HOWL AT THE MOON

"Well. The fact remains, Hiller is a liar. Whatever he is asking you to do is not for some benevolent and just internal investigation. The IC has been attempting for months now to work with the Penny Mine shifter clan and the Shoot Well weres. The weres are reticent but coming around—they've been in the area for over a hundred years and have strong ties with the indigenous groups and several treaties in place. The shifters..." He shook his head. "They're far less surefooted. The original shifters in the area were more... laissez-faire with their establishment. Far more Wild West," he added with a moue of distaste. "Their lack of a firm foundation has led to their current predicament. A history of grasping violence and now an unstable, unsuitable leader."

"So why ask me to come in and look at these bodies? What will that accomplish?"

He spread his hands, a sharp, nasty grin crossing his features. "You're not only an outside source, you're not were nor shifter. It could be argued that your findings will be more objective as you have no skin in the game, so to speak."

"Why not just turn this over to their court system or whatever?"

Ethan made a startled sound at that.

"There's no internal court system for shifters and weres—not yet, anyway," Cullen smiled. "Whatever he is asking you to do, it's either to entrap you or someone else."

"Of course. Of course, it is. Fuck my life."

Cullen sniffed. "Well. Now that we're on at least adjacent pages, will you listen to my proposal?"

"Oh, sure," I groaned. "Why the hell not? Go for it."

"Such enthusiasm. Take Hiller's offer."

"What?" I stood straight and glared down at him, his smirk only driving my anger higher. "After all that, you're telling me to take his offer?"

Cullen nodded. "Take his offer. And report back to me what you find. We've been trying for some time now to get a better look at the

Penny Mine situation, but the clan is not open to newcomers or visitors. This opportunity will make you perfectly placed to be our eyes on the ground." He wrinkled his nose, waved his hand, and added, "Or whatever that saying is. You'd be compensated, of course."

"Of course."

"I am not unaware of your current predicament with your job, Doctor Babin."

"How the hell do you know this?"

"Because I read the news. The budget cuts were announced today and are in the online version of most state papers." He sniffed, glancing past me to look at Ethan. "Sheriff Stone."

Ethan jerked his chin in acknowledgment. "This IC group, why haven't I heard of y'all? I'm the clan head for his area."

"Some of the more rural areas have not been approached yet, but in the case of Belmarais, I believe that is down to your father refusing our first agent about ten years ago."

Ethan made a startled sound, rocking back on his heels. "What the fuck?"

Cullen shrugged. "It was before your time, Sheriff, but if you're interested in working with us"—he produced an ecru colored card from his breast pocket and held it between two fingers, offering it to Ethan—"call us."

"I DON'T LIKE THIS," Ethan muttered. "But this might be something."

"Wait, not even an hour ago, you were telling me Hiller was up to no good, that this was like federal levels of bad. Now you're warming up to this?"

HOWL AT THE MOON

Ethan shrugged, turning to meander to the living room. "I didn't know about the IC," he admitted. "And... maybe this is something to consider."

I wanted to fight about it, but... not really. Maybe I felt like we should fight about it, like I was afraid to admit I was tempted. "It'd pay." I sighed. "Which, gotta admit, is weighing heavier than the possibility of walking into a cluster fuck. I can deal with cluster fuck if it means keeping a roof over my head."

Ethan scowled. "I wish you'd let me help."

"Ethan..."

"I know, I know. Still, just know the offer stands."

I nodded. We'd gone around about it once or twice, me refusing to ask him for help with my new economic straits, but unless there was no other option, I wanted to do it on my own.

And apparently agreeing to check out some dead people for a creepy asshole was a viable option.

Ethan ground his jaw for a moment then seemed to melt into a boneless slump of acquiescence. "Tell Hiller you'll take the job, but we're gonna talk to Cullen before we go."

"*We?*"

He grunted. "I need a shower."

"That mean you're staying the night?" I called after him as he headed toward the bathroom.

He didn't reply.

I got my phone out and hesitated after opening the most recent text from Hiller. *Damn it, in for a penny...*

Me: I'll do it. Is there a contract to sign or something?

Several minutes passed before Hiller replied.

Creepy McCreepface: No. Be there in three days.

Me: I need time to make arrangements!

Me: Four. Soonest.

Creepy McCreepface: Three.

Shit.

I fluttered around the house listlessly, turning off lights and wiping down the counter before making myself go to the bedroom. Ethan was still fussing in the bathroom, the shower was off but the sound of him brushing his teeth drifted through the partially open door along with the scent of his body wash that had made its way to my shower. I fully intended to stay up till he came out but was deep asleep within minutes, not waking till my alarm blared in the morning. I woke alone, the bed cold on his side and a post it stuck to my phone.

Don't go to Penny Mine. Wait for me.

"God damn it, Ethan." I sighed. "Fuck."

My phone rang before I could decide if I wanted to call him or not. Reba's name was flashing on the screen.

"Hey," I said by way of greeting. "Everything okay? It's early."

She laughed nervously, a bit out of breath. "I left my bag of wax melts here last night and thought I'd come by and grab them to take over to my sister's house before she goes to work since she's giving the candle making a go, and um..."

I sat up, heart kicking into gear at her tone of voice. "Reba, what's wrong? Are you okay?"

"How soon can you get here, Landry? There's something... someone... you need to see."

Chapter Four

Reba was waiting beside her desk when I rushed in, uncaffeinated and already picturing the worst.

Werewolves cornering her. Zombies suddenly becoming a thing.

The state sending someone to kick us out in person.

"Are you okay?" I asked, stopping on a dime at the sight of her too-wide smile that came nowhere near her eyes.

"Oh... um. Yes. You've got a visitor. Again."

"Again?" I froze. "Same guy?" I didn't feel anything off, no trace of Hiller in any sense of the word. A wash of relief pulsed through me before I realized that meant it had to be Waltrip. "Oh my god," I muttered. "Is it a big, burly redhead?"

"That guy from early this year?" she asked, expression crinkling in confusion. "No. Well, not anymore. He was here earlier and said he needed to drop something off for you, but when I tried to stop him, he just pushed past me and... Well, go see."

I shot her a sideways look, dreading whatever it was. "Damn it, it's not the state, is it?" I muttered. "Can't they just do this via email?"

"It's not the state," she tittered nervously. "Just, I didn't know what to do, so I let her stay in there. Your, uh, redheaded friend, he took off and left her there, said you'd take care of her."

"Take care of who? Christ, did Waltrip leave a cat or something in there?"

Reba's laugh was shrill and definitely anxious.

I shot off a text to Tyler, telling him Waltrip had been there (so he definitely wasn't dead), and cautiously approached my office door. A faintly sweet, cotton candy, artificial scent teased my senses. Some sort of cloying pink smelling plastic odor mingled with slightly sour milk and something like peanut butter.

And the faint sound of something electronic, a beeping game sort of noise.

The fuck?

Reba made a shooing motion at me. "Best get it over with because, lord, I have no idea what the follow up on this is going to be," she muttered.

I nodded and gave my door a gentle nudge.

And just stared.

Behind my desk, bundled in a purple fuzzy blanket—the kind you get cheap at Walmart—emblazoned with butterflies and flowers, a little girl sat with a Switch in her hands and her attention laser-focused. "Hey," she said. "Mr. Waltrip said you were okay."

TYLER FINALLY ANSWERED on my third attempt. "Fucking hell," he hissed. "What's your problem?"

"I need to get hold of Elio or Diz. Wait, they're still working for Waltrip, right? I need them to track him down."

Tyler sighed gustily. "I told you, he's been incommunicado for days now. Hell, if he turned up dead at this point, I wouldn't be shocked." His worried tone told me he'd definitely be hurt, though.

And maybe, maybe I would too. But I wasn't going to let Waltrip know that. The better-not-be-dead bastard.

There was a rustle of sound then a whoosh as if he were stepping through a sliding door or something. "Why?"

I glanced at the little girl behind my desk, sipping the grape soda Reba had run down to the corner store to grab for her. "I have questions."

HOWL AT THE MOON

Tyler snorted. "Good luck, man. Waltrip's off grid, according to Elio. I tried to get hold of him just an hour or so ago, and his phone's not only off, Elio can't ping it anywhere. Diz had him heading west, but that's it."

"Shit."

The little girl cleared her throat. When I glanced back at her, she was staring at me expectantly. "What?" I demanded.

"You cussed."

"Is that a kid?" Tyler whispered.

"She can't hear you."

"Landry, why do you have a kid? Oh my god, does Ethan know? Don't tell him yet. I'm only like three hours out. I stopped at the Buc-ee's for some beaver nuts, but I will get back I my car right now and be there in two hours if the state troopers aren't out."

"What?"

"I have to be there when you tell Ethan you've got a kid."

"Oh my god."

"Is that cussing?" the girl demanded.

"No," I hissed. "It's exasperation. Tyler, she's not my kid—"

"Dude, it's fine. We all experiment, you know? You hooked up with someone one night and weren't thinking, now a few years later there's a kid and—"

"And I'm hanging up now."

"Seriously! Wait until I'm back before telling Ethan!"

The kid was still staring at me when I turned around, shoving my phone into my pocket. "You're weird," she said flatly. "Can I have something to eat?"

"Here we go!" Reba trilled, hustling in as if summoned. She brandished a paper bag with the logo from the nearby bakery. "They were all out of sprinkled donuts, and I plumb forgot to ask if you wanted something sweet or savory, so I got a half dozen holes and a cheese croissant." She plopped the bag on the desk, hurried to the tall beige filing cabinet, and pulled out a bright pink paper plate I recognized as one of the ones she sometimes used for her own lunches. The girl's eyes widened at the sight of the donuts and croissant, her game forgotten as she snagged one of the sprinkle-covered holes and shoved it in her mouth with a happy sound.

"You track down her daddy?" Reba asked sotto voce. The girl made a face, shoving another hole in her mouth beside the half-chewed one. "Slow down, hon," she urged. "You're gonna bust your gut eating like that."

"My dad's in Colorado," the kid mumbled. "These are so good!" She reached for a third one and Reba gently pulled the bag back. "Mr. Waltrip said you an' Dad were friends when you were little."

A funny feeling behind my eyes, like someone clapping their hands really hard but soundless, burst at her words. Colorado. Waltrip. Knowing her dad. "Mal Benes." I sighed, closing my eyes.

"You know her dad?" Reba asked, skeptical. "Why didn't you mention you were going to have a kid in the office today, Landry? Or that you even knew anyone with kids? When I asked you last month about babysitting Jenna's niece, you said you were allergic to anyone under the age of twenty-five."

"One, I barely know Jenna. I couldn't pick her out of a line up if you paid me."

"Jenna! You know her!" Reba threw up her hands in exasperation. "The children's librarian with the brother who does security?"

"And two," I went on as if I hadn't heard her, "calling Mal Benes a childhood friend is overstating things. But yes, I did know him when we were much, much younger." So young I couldn't remember him if you paid me, but she didn't need to know that.

Mariska made a happy growly noise as she tore into the croissant. "Shit." I sighed. "I need to handle this."

Reba tapped her acrylics on her desk regarding me thoughtfully. "Well, if nothing else, it'll keep your mind off the whole... technically

HOWL AT THE MOON

unemployed thing. Call me if you need help, hear? Kids are no joke. Especially when you're not used to 'em." She narrowed her eyes at me, raising one finger to jab in my direction. "You're gonna tell me what all this is about ASAP though, you got me? Because if you think for one minute I'm gonna believe you're just surprise-babysitting the kid of an old childhood friend, you must think I'm dumb as a box of hair."

"Reba," I sighed. "Come on. Cut me some slack here. Why else would a kid be in my office if it wasn't some sort of emergency?"

She folded her arms and gave me a *look*. "You tell me."

"It's fine, I promise," I lied.

Reba stared at me for a moment longer, the quiet broken by the sound of the kid decimating pastry with happy little growls. "Fine," she huffed. "Fine. I need to get going but Landry... Promise me you'll call if this," she waved her finger at the kid and me both, "is too much to handle."

"I promise."

I waited for Reba to gather up her bag and the wax melts that had brought her there in the first place. Only when I was sure she was gone did I turn back to the little girl. "Come over here," I ordered, maybe sharper than I should have. The girl twitched, scowling, before sliding from my chair and marching past me, her blanket dragging on the floor and game device held under one arm as she clutched her makeshift cape with her hands.

Holy shit, holy shit, holy shit, what the hell do I do now?

Call Waltrip again. There. That's what I do. And if he doesn't answer, try Tyler again. And Ethan. And the National Guard and... shit, what the fuck is my life...

The girl sat at Reba's desk, resuming her game. Every once in a while, she'd rummage in a pocket and pull out a piece of sticky pink candy—the source of the smell I'd noticed earlier. "Are you gonna stare at me a lot, or what?" she demanded. "It's weird."

"Just sit tight," I muttered. "We'll get this sorted."

"It'd help if you knew my name," she pointed out. "It's Mariska. I'm named after a TV star Mom liked. It's Hungarian for Maria, which is something else for Mary, which comes from the name Miriam, and that means a lot of things." She paused and gave me a skeptical look over the rims of her purple-framed glasses. "Mr. Waltrip said you were a safe person and could help me."

My laugh was wild and high. "Mr. Waltrip might be functioning under some false information. I mean," I added at her sudden, nervous expression, "I'm safe. I won't hurt you. But I don't know how the hell he thinks I'll help you."

"Dad makes me put money in the jar if I cuss. And if I don't have money, I do chores." She frowned at her game, tapping at something to make it, I don't know, wobble or fly or whatever. "I do a lot of chores since I don't have a job since I'm a kid."

"Okay," I breathed. "Sure. Makes sense. Do you know your dad's phone number?"

She finally lifted her chin and pinned me with a dark eyed glare. "I don't know you."

"We seem to be at an impasse, kid. I don't know you, but I'm supposed to keep you safe? This isn't some fu—messed up eighties sitcom, okay?"

Mariska eyed me thoughtfully over the top of her game. "My dad made me watch some old show called *Small Wonder* one time. It was about a girl who's really a robot, and she lives with the family of the guy who made her. It was weird. And kind of dumb. It was made in the eighties." She looked back down at her device and shrugged. "I pretended to be a robot for a day or two after that, but I still didn't get the point. It was really boring, especially when my dad said if I was a robot, I'd have to eat microchips and oil for breakfast instead of banana toast."

"I... what?"

She shrugged. "Dad likes old shows. I'm really into this one super old show called *MythBusters*. Have you ever heard of it? It's like, super old."

"Oh my god. I can't be here right now," I muttered. There was one person I was sure could help me, but that certainty was born of sheer panic.

"Come on. We're going to go visit my... friend."

She sniffed, pressing a button that made her game go quiet. "Does your friend have juice? Because I really want juice."

"Speaking as a doctor, I need to inform you that you eat entirely too much sugar."

Mariska rolled her eyes. "I'm a kid. I'll burn it off with my exuberance. That's what Dad says, anyway."

Whenever I met Mal Benes, I decided, I was going to shake him just a little.

THE FAINT THUMP OF the Earl Demming High School Marching Band (Go 'Dawgs!) practicing for next week's homecoming game in the field behind the sheriff's office seemed to beat in counterpoint to the migraine pulsing behind my right eye.

"I understand that he's in the middle of something, but this is important."

"And Carver McCoy's dead cow isn't?" Cori Borse, the perpetual desk clerk for Belmarais, who'd been there since 1982, popped her gum gunshot-loud, making Mariska jump, digging her sharp little nails into my wrist.

"No," I ground out. "Mr. McCoy's dead cow is very important. I'll be sure to send him a condolence card later. But I'm having an emergency here."

"I'm not an emergency, I'm a Leo."

Cori's furiously working jaws slowed and her frosted blue lids lowered to half-mast as she shifted her attention to Mariska. "You done got some girl in trouble, Doctor Babin?" she asked with the slightest acid tinge to her voice. "I thought you were one of them guys who liked guys."

Jesus. "Gay. The word is gay," I muttered. "And I am. And Mariska is my guest for the moment. And also the emergency."

Cori's press-ons tapped out a slow, ominous beat on the old laminate desktop as she regarded me and Mariska with a curious, predatory tilt to her head. If my senses hadn't been so flatly quiet, I'd have thought she was a were, sussing us out. But no, just a nosy old gossip with backcombed hair that paid homage to Lita Ford in her heyday, and a dedication to gathering intel on every single person in the tri-county area ever since daytime TV got boring. "And this little lady isn't yours," Cori finally said. "But you think Sheriff Stone needs to get involved?"

Mariska sighed, her grip on my hand sweaty and slippery as she tried to wiggle loose. "I'm bored Doctor Babin. Can I go sit there? And can I have quarters for the machine? I want hot chips."

"You're five! You're not eating hot chips!"

"I'm ten!"

I narrowed my eyes, channeling my undergrad biochem professor's best *you little liar* glare. "Bullshit. Er. Corn. Bullcorn. You're seven if you're a day."

Mariska narrowed her eyes, finally jerking free of my grasp. "Eight."

"Six."

"You don't know how old your little girl is?" Cori asked, her gum once again cracking and popping furiously as she got into the swing of things, no doubt envisioning the months—no, years—of stories she'd get out of this little encounter.

"She's not mine."

I saw the moment the evil kicked in. Mariska widened her eyes and jutted out her lower lip, her body slumping as if her spine had just

HOWL AT THE MOON 57

stopped working. "But... Daddy. Daddy, you said you'd stop telling people that!" She gave a wet, rattling sniff and her chin started to wobble.

"Seriously?" I hissed. "You literally just called me Doctor Babin! You can't expect Cori—Ms. Borse—to think I'm your father."

Mariska turned her Louis Wain eyes to Cori. "Daddy told me to call him by his title when we met strangers," she lisped, twisting her fingers in the hem of her stretched-out t-shirt. "He said he had a rep'tation to uphold."

Cori's jaw worked that gum as if her life depended on it. "Did he now?"

"Oh my god," I groaned. "Mariska, I'm not going to reward this behavior with hot chips. Sit on that chair," I jabbed my finger at one of the faded green vinyl chairs lining the wall by the door, "and do not move until I say so."

Mariska rolled her eyes, dropping the facade. "Ugh. You're mean." The thwap-slap of her pink glitter rain boots gave way to the ringing thud of Mariska kicking the metal legs of the chair as she settled in for a good, solid glare at the back of my head and no doubt tried to develop pyrokinesis while I turned back to Cori.

"She's adorable," Cori murmured.

I don't think she was kidding.

"Look, can you at least let me wait in his office?" I asked, exasperated.

"Why?" Cori asked archly. "Are you trying to hide that little girl? Sweetie, where's your real daddy?"

"Cori, please?"

Mariska started singing some cartoon theme song—or maybe she was just making it up, I really don't know—pitching each word slightly higher than the one before. "Did you know," she warbled, "that puppies like green, green grass?"

The soft, genuine smile that creased Cori's cheeks was a surprise. "I remember when my Willy was that age," she sighed. "Obsessed with Pokemons."

"There's no s," I muttered. "Just Pokémon."

"There was more than one of 'em," she said, arching a brow. "Plural."

"It's like moose. One moose, seven moose. One Pokémon, seven Pokemon."

"Uh huh. And you went to medical school and all, huh?"

"Oh my god."

Mariska's song took a turn for the dark. The puppies no longer liked green, green grass apparently and were on to vengeance for not getting hot chips when they were absolutely starving to death in front of a mean, mean man.

I had to give her kudos for the internal rhyme structure, though, what with mean and green. The next verse should be a doozy, I thought. Probably rhyme sheen or maybe—

"Landry?"

I jolted at the sound of Ethan's voice, his tone amused and maybe a little worried. Or maybe that was just me hoping for an ally in that moment. "Ethan." I sighed. "I was just trying to explain to Cori that I'm in the midst of an emergency here and needed to see you."

"Sheriff, is it Pokémon or Pokemans? This one"—Cori nodded at me, her brows arched so high you could see the striation of the various blues of her eyeshadow—"says it's no s even when there's lots of 'em."

"Well," Ethan drawled, hooking his thumbs in his belt, and I swear to god I felt the annoyance wash over me like a hot wave of slime as he dropped into his *I'm just a simple country sheriff ac*t. "I reckon it'd be Pokemen, wouldn't it? Man is singular, men is plural? But as far as I know it's Pokémon, not men."

Mariska's laugh was sunshine-bright, the sudden lack of the drumming heel percussion making her amusement all the louder. "He's funnier than you, Doctor Babin."

HOWL AT THE MOON

"He brought his kid," Cori muttered, and though his smile didn't slip Ethan's eyes definitely took on a slightly startled sort of squint. "Said it was an emergency. We ain't babysitters here, Doctor Babin," she added in a more strident tone. "Just because you can't take care of your little girl don't mean I have to. This is a real job, you know! I don't just sit here and watch the YouTube all day."

"No," Ethan muttered. "She also gossips on messenger and orders shit to be delivered to the office from Amazon, so Ricky doesn't know how much she's buying."

I rolled my eyes. "Ethan, this is Mariska. She just showed up at the office and says her dad is—" I glanced at Cori, surprised her ears weren't sticking out like some old cartoon snoop, stretching to hear us better. "Her dad is detained in Colorado, and she decided to come visit for a bit. Apparently, Waltrip brought her but left before I could talk to him."

Ethan dragged his gaze from Mariska's bright smile, apparently unable to see the evil lurking in her eyes as she plotted the next step in making my day difficult. "Her dad's detained?"

"Mmm. Her dad. The one we were just talking about the other day?"

Ethan blinked at me. "Landry, have you been drinking today?"

Mariska slid down in the plastic chair, chin to her chest as she fixed us with a glare that would've been at home on any surly teenager's face. "He means my dad, Mal Benes. He's trying to be all sneaky or something."

"Mal Benes," Ethan repeated, gaze drifting back to Mariska. "I thought he had a son?"

"Nope," I said at the same time Mariska slid to the floor and folded her legs cris-cross-applesauce. "The report was wrong."

"I'm not a boy," Mariska said firmly, loudly. "Whoever told you that was lying."

MEREDITH SPIES

Ethan opened his mouth, then snapped it shut, his face flushing as he realized how deep he'd shoved his foot in his mouth. "My mistake," he murmured. "I'm sorry, Mariska. I misunderstood."

She didn't say anything, just tugged on the sparkly blue bracelet that seemed to be her favorite fidget.

Cori popped her gum, startling all three of us. "Sheriff, what report? I didn't see anything crossin' my desk about a kid. Hey, honey, you wanna not do that?"

Mariska had pushed herself to her feet and was scuffing the toe of her too-big boots against one of the peeling corners of vinyl tile, making it squeak a little louder each time. "Not really," she said, glaring at the dirty toes of her shoes.

"Why don't we go into my office." Ethan sighed. "Cori, I'm busy for the next hour, got it?"

She leaned back, folding her arms across her narrow waist and fixing Ethan with a disbelieving expression. "Hour?" she echoed. "What about that meeting with Sheriff Newburn and that community group from Lacey Creek? And the Citizens for Border Security Committee? They're sending a rep from Dallas just to meet with you!"

"The what?" I demanded. My stomach gave a slow lurch at the thought of Ethan being involved in any of those bullshit xenophobic groups that had sprouted like mushrooms in a damp autumn afternoon.

"Cori." Ethan sighed, weary and flat. "I told you I wasn't going to meet with either group. What the hell border security are they worried about? An invasion from Arkansas? The good people of Bossier City suddenly crossing the Red River to lay waste to Lindale?"

Cori sniffed. "You're not taking your position seriously, Sheriff. Border safety is a *national security issue*! You're on the front line, defending your people from the incoming hordes of foreigners!"

"Uh, quick question. What do you mean by *your people*?" I asked.

Ethan shook his head. "You know what she means. And you know what? I'm not late for the meeting. I just quit."

HOWL AT THE MOON

A tiny, whispered *holy shit* came from behind me, a quarter getting pressed into my limp palm a moment later. I could only watch, jaw agape, as Ethan yanked off his badge and service weapon, setting them both on a sputtering Cori's desk. "Call Skip and tell him his shift is starting early." He turned to me, a smile more relaxed than I'd seen in months curving his lips. "Lan, why don't we go celebrate with ice cream?"

"And juice?" Mariska chimed in.

Ethan nodded. "And you can fill me in on what the he—er, heck is going on," he muttered, practically frog marching me behind Mariska's skipping form as we left Cori squawking behind her desk.

"You just *quit*!" I gasped. "Ethan!"

"It's been a long time coming," he grumbled. "Priorities, Lan. Come on, I promised the little miss ice cream and I got stuck babysitting clan kids enough as a teenager to know you don't renege on promised treats without serious tantrums later."

"Ethan—"

"Come on," he said, smile glued firmly in place. "Mariska, do you like chocolate?"

"Pistachooooooo!" she yodeled.

At my muttered *oh my god*, Ethan gave me a nudge, opening his car door. "Did y'all drive here? Does she have a car seat? She's too small to be unsecured."

"Uh, yeah, Waltrip didn't leave one, but—"

Ethan closed his eyes and made a low, growly, sighing sort of sound. "Please tell me you didn't drive all the way here with her just unsecured in the back seat."

"I sat on a binder," Mariska volunteered. "He said it was so the seatbelt would fit me better. I didn't know they made binders that big." She held her hands apart to demonstrate the thickness of my five-inch binder I'd grabbed from the bookshelf in my office.

"Christ," Ethan sighed. "Okay, look, we keep a few car seats in the office for—" he paused and glanced at Mariska. "For just-in-case. Give me a sec."

I winced. "Are you sure you want to go back in?"

He shook his head. "Between Cori shouting at me and letting this little one be unsafe in your car, I'll take my chances with Cori."

"Okay, but then what? We get her ice cream, and then what?" My voice had taken on a frantic sort of reediness that stilled Mariska and made Ethan's eyes go wide. "We can't just move her into my place like nothing's wrong and okay I did do a pediatrics rotation in med school, but I have no idea how to take care of a kid in real life and—"

Ethan grabbed me by the shoulders and gave me a gentle shake, his smile small and a bit tense. "Lan, trust me. I can help keep a kid alive long enough to track down her dad, okay? Years of babysitting!"

I nodded slowly. The frantic gleam in his eye told me he needed something to distract him, something to focus on other than the explosion he just left in his wake at the department. "Sure. I trust you." I gingerly took Mariska's hand and gave Ethan another nod. "You go grab the car seat, we'll meet you at Dino's."

Mariska was fairly quiet (I'm assuming—she might just always be like that, but I had no way of knowing) as we walked the few blocks to Dino's, an old fashioned ice cream parlor that had been around since the forties. She took her time picking out her treat, something violently bright-hued that was allegedly bubblegum and cotton candy flavored, with sprinkles and a cherry.

"That much food dye can't be good for you," I muttered as she carried her paper bowl to the nearest table with the care and reverence one would expect for long-lost treasure.

"You mean you don't know?" she asked, digging in. "I thought you were a doctor."

"Cute," I muttered, taking a bite of my own, one eye on the door for Ethan. He finally arrived halfway through Mariska's technicolor sugar rush, giving me a wink as he ordered himself a banana split before coming to sit with us, a utilitarian gray booster seat under one arm. "Did you have to tell her you took it back and you're not quitting?" I asked, giving the seat a nod.

He snorted. "No, but I did have to sign a form saying I'd bring it back in forty-eight hours or the department would bill me for it."

"Maybe I can see if Reba's sister has one from when her kids were smaller," I said, mind spinning. "She's got a sister and two brothers, and a bunch of nieces and nephews so at least one of them is bound to have a car seat, right?"

"Maybe," Ethan allowed around a bite of his ice cream. "What flavor did you get, Mariska? It looks like unicorn poop."

She cackled at that, and they were off and running with gross out humor about what unicorn poop would taste like while I sank into panic mode.

Again.

My vanilla ice cream (the most boring flavor according to Mariska) melted into the cup while my brain switched into high gear. The panic spiral had receded slightly with Ethan's promises to keep Mariska alive, but my thoughts jumped around as I tried to figure out the next steps.

Find Waltrip. Kill him. Just a little. Then find Mariska's dad.

No, there were more immediate needs. Dinner for one. Clothes were another. Waltrip seemed to have brought zero luggage, and her clothes were in desperate need of a wash. Maybe I could ask Reba about that, too. Surely her nieces had some outgrown clothes? Or maybe give her money to run by Target for me while I was getting Mariska settled? There was also finding a way to charge her Switch which I hoped would keep her at least somewhat entertained. Then there was the car seat issue. Hell, I was going to owe Reba big time, I thought.

Then there was the promise I'd made to Hiller to be in Colorado in three days' time.

"We'll figure it out," Ethan promised, as if reading my panic on my face. He didn't know any of the questions but seemed to have all the answers. "You can make up the guest room for her. I'll make my famous chili mac, 100 percent kid approved, and we'll get in touch with Waltrip."

"REBA IS AN ABSOLUTE saint, and no one can tell me otherwise," I announced, hanging up my phone. "She's picking up some of her niece's hand-me-downs and swinging by Target for some other stuff and will be by around five."

Mariska glanced up from her tablet. "Did you tell her I don't want anything too boy? Like no football crap and stuff?"

"Why would she get you boy stuff?" I asked. "She knows you're a girl."

Mariska hesitated, lips pursed like she wanted to say something, then shrugged. "Dunno. Just checking."

Ethan emerged from the kitchen, face pink from the stove's heat, and sat down next to me on the sofa. "Tell her we're paying her back."

"I tried, but she refused." She'd be finding random five and ten dollar bills in her desk drawer for a while though, I decided, then remembered no, she wouldn't—we weren't going to have our desks much longer. I wilted against Ethan and sighed. "Today is so weird."

He grunted. "So, um, I guess I should've mentioned the job shit earlier, huh?" he murmured low enough that Mariska didn't call out his swearing.

"I knew it was getting stressful, but I had no idea it was getting that kind of messed up."

Ethan was quiet for a long few moments before speaking again. "When I joined up, it was because I thought it was the best way to help the clan, you know? Make sure a were like them was in a position to protect them. It's what my dad did and all. But I'm not my dad, and the longer I was on the force, the worse it felt. The way I thought things worked... Well. They don't. And I feel so angry and naïve for thinking I could change it."

"Ethan," I murmured, lacing our fingers together and giving his hand a squeeze as we watched Mariska pretending not to notice us. "I'm not mad at you for quitting. In fact," I said, glancing up at him to see his eyes were closed and brow furrowed, "I think it'll be good for you. And for us, if I might be so selfish as to add that."

"Oh? Why do you think that?"

"You weren't happy, and it sounds like they were trying to make you do things you're not willing to do. If you forced yourself, you'd be losing who you are. I'd rather have an unemployed grumpy werewolf boyfriend than one who went along with bullshit like that border security whatever just to keep employed."

He sighed, opening one eye to peer at me. "I don't know how to do anything else."

"Maybe we can join in whatever side hustle Reba's cooking up," I suggested. "Last text she sent, she wanted to start a pole dance studio."

He sputtered. "Can she pole dance?"

"It'll be a learning experience for all of us."

Mariska lifted her head and frowned, just a moment before Ethan did, both of them freezing. "Someone's here," Mariska whispered, and the sound of a cat yowling screeched through the open window. Ethan shot to his feet as Mariska screamed, throwing herself flat on the floor and covering her ears.

"Stay here," Ethan ordered. "Don't open the door, no matter what."

"Ethan!"

"No, Lan. Just please," he kissed me quick, then was already running to the door, "do it."

The sound of animals fighting—growling, screeching, howling, bodies hitting the side of the house—felt like it went on forever, but it was only a few minutes. Ethan's loud shouts joined the yowls and howls after just a moment and I knew he couldn't risk shifting, not when someone might see him. The yowling stopped and there was a sharp bark and a growl before Ethan shouted, *Get!*

Mariska whimpered softly, hands still folded over her head. "Hey," I whispered. "Hey, come on, he's okay. Let's get up."

She batted my hands away and scrambled to her feet, dashing at the tears on her cheeks. "I'm fine."

I nodded. "I know. Me too."

Ethan was back, shaking off debris and limping slightly as he came into the living room. "Close the windows," he ordered gruffly. "Make sure they're all locked."

I nodded, hurrying to do as he said. "Mariska, go sit in the kitchen," he added.

"But—"

"You can help me make dinner," he said. "I need to get changed first."

I waited for him in the hall outside the bathroom. "Where are you hurt?"

"Were got me," he muttered. "Not bad, just a scratch. But that wasn't a dog. Whoever it was, they had hold of Cullen's cat. She got away and high-tailed it back to his house, but the wolf didn't bother chasing her." He hissed as he eased his jeans down enough for me to see the deep scratch on his thigh. "He was waiting for someone. Probably you," he added, lifting his gaze to meet mine. "The cat must've startled him."

I huffed. "Or attacked him. That creature isn't a normal cat, I swear. Let me help you clean this up."

"I can get it."

"I'm still a doctor, Ethan. Let me put my student debt to work."

He huffed a soft laugh. "Alright then. Let me text Tyler first. I want another set of eyes on this place. We'll take shifts overnight."

I nodded, swallowing down the acid rush of anxiety. "Meet me in the bathroom. I'll get out my good bandages. Just bought a box with dinosaurs on them."

BY THE TIME I HAD HIM cleaned up, bandaged, and found a pair of his sweatpants that had made their way into my dresser, Reba was pulling up outside. Ethan made me stay inside while he went out to meet her and bring her in himself. "I appreciate the escort," she laughed as he led her in, "but I really do know how to walk up porch steps on my own."

"Oh, I was just heading out to check the mail for Landry when I saw you pulling up," he said, even though it wasn't a good excuse. "I'll be right back."

He shot me a glance, and I nodded. He was going to check the perimeter and would likely do it several more times during the night even when Tyler finally showed up. Mariska padded up, a faint stain of spaghetti sauce on her face as she shyly tucked herself against the door frame.

"Hey there," Reba said, crouching to get down on Mariska's level. "Landry said you forgot your suitcase, so I brought you a few things. Want to try them on?"

Mariska nodded slowly. "I like my *Sassy Dragon Princess* shirt, though."

"Well, my niece had one that she can't wear anymore but will look adorable on you. And I bet Landry can get that one there all cleaned up for you while you wear the new one."

I nodded. "Leave your dirty things outside the bedroom door, and I'll get 'em in the wash."

Reba and Mariska headed for the guest room I'd set Mariska up in, and I hurried back to the kitchen where Ethan stood, braced against the counter as he frowned at his phone. "Tyler said he'll be here soon," he murmured. "And he sent some stuff from Elio and Diz, things they found digging in Waltrip's personal files."

"Uh, do we want to see that?"

He made a face at me, turning his phone so I could see. "It's stuff about Mal and Shoot Well. He's been making visits up there since this past summer, apparently."

"Well, shit."

"Mmhmm."

Reba and Mariska made a noisy entrance then, Mariska showing off her new *Sassy Dragon Princess* shirt and a pair of leggings with a fluffy tulle overskirt that managed to be glittery and shimmery at the same time. "I grabbed her a pair of boots and a pair of sneakers," Reba said. "I wasn't sure which she'd like better but wearing rain boots all the time won't be comfortable, and a girl's gotta have options. Besides, with the spiders and wood scorpions we get out here, I figured best not to chance it."

"Thanks, Reba. Seriously, this is just above and beyond. Let me pay you back."

"Now you hush with that," she scolded, smiling as Mariska gave another spin and showed Ethan how her sneakers lit up when she stomped her feet. "I wasn't blessed with a little one of my own and getting the chance to spoil someone else's kiddo is a treat from time to time." She shot me a small, sad smile that disappeared quickly, before I could even begin to think of anything sympathetic. "Now, I better get my rear in gear. I need to swing by the feed store to check out their babies. Helen at the Rite Aid was telling me earlier that there's a real market for organic eggs."

"Ah... yay?"

She smacked my arm gently before heading to grab her purse from the hook by the door. "I figured that pole dancing wasn't going to work out, not when I can't install a pole in my garage without it being a whole thing. Chickens, though! I can sell the eggs and their shit—people pay a lot of money for organic fertilizer, too. Mariska, honey, you enjoy those clothes, you hear?"

"Thank you, Miss Reba! I love them!" Mariska bounded over and hugged Reba around the knees before darting back to show Ethan some made up martial arts move that made her skirt fluff out as she spun around.

"That little girl's got problems, Landry. She's upset about her daddy, and I know for a fact she's not related to you. If she was, I'd have heard by now."

I started to protest but just sighed. "She really is the daughter of someone I was kids with," I said. "And he's in a rough spot right now so I'm keeping an eye on her while things get sorted."

She stared at me for a long moment before shaking her head and sighing herself. "I know you're a good man, Landry, but I can't help but feel that you're in the middle of a bad mess."

"I'm fine, I swear," I lied.

"Hmph. I'm putting you down for two bottles of beard oil. Till the eggs take off, I still gotta work on my hustles, you know?"

"I still don't have a beard," I called as she shouldered her purse and started down the porch steps.

"You got time to grow one. I've seen your five o'clock shadow so I know you can do it. And your boyfriend's got a nice bit of scruff there. Tell him to grow it out and give him one of the bottles for the holidays."

"Alright," I laughed. "Thank you, Reba. So much. For everything."

She stopped, car door open, and glared at me. "Don't you get sappy with me, Landry Babin. Enjoy your days off and meet me back at work on Tuesday, got me? And check your damn texts. I'm gonna bounce some more ideas off you!"

"Can't wait."

"That was sarcasm. I know it." She jabbed two fingers at her eyes, then at me. "Watching you, Babin. Watching. You."

"THERE'S NO WAY I'M asking Reba to watch Mariska for however long we're gone," I sighed, throwing out the very suggestion I'd just made. Ethan watched me over the rim of his glass of sweet tea as I dithered. We'd been going over options for almost an hour as Mariska entertained herself in the living room, drawing and watching something on a kid's streaming channel I didn't even know I subscribed to.

Mental note: Check my billing later and make sure she didn't just add that to my line up for me...

"You're the one who brought that up, not me," Ethan murmured. "Tyler's looking like our best option."

"Ethan—"

"Nope." He set his glass down and shook his head. "You're not going solo on this one, Landry. It's not because I don't trust you or whatever notion you're spinning up in that brain of yours. It's because you're not at all familiar with how clans work, the protocols and expectations of entering clan territory. And, baby, I know you're pretty set on telling the world you're not a real were, but as far as a lot of weres are concerned, you're at least close enough to be a problem when it comes to showing up on clan territory."

"And you coming with me would help that?" I asked, aiming for arch but landing somewhere near exhausted.

"I'm the clan leader for this territory," he reminded me. "I come with you, and I can at least make nice with the local leader if need be."

"I don't think Hiller's planning on introducing me to the higher-ups." *God, I hope not.*

"Me either, but frankly I know how to kiss ass with weres if need be and I'm not gonna let you go into a strange clan's territory on your own, without someone on your side."

I wanted to argue but I knew he was right. Damn it. "So that brings us back to Mariska."

"Which," he sighed, getting to his feet to refill his glass at the counter, "brings us back to Tyler. I know he can be a fuckboy and kind of a pain in the ass, but he wouldn't let Mariska get hurt."

"But does he even *know* anything about kids?" I demanded, as if I had the first freaking clue outside of a medical setting. "Look, maybe I should just call Reba anyway. I mean—"

"Hey." Ethan said, cutting me off with a quick, soft kiss. "Listen. Tyler was raised in the clan, same as me. We both got stuck with babysitting duty for the little ones dozens of times over the years. He can do this. I promise you."

"Fuck." I sighed, resting my forehead against his shoulder. "Fine. Talk to him when he comes over later."

Ethan kissed the top of my head and gave me a squeeze. "It's the best option, Lan."

TYLER SHOWED UP JUST past nine. "Justin's on the move, apparently," he grumbled. "I got as far as Conroe when Elio called me. Verified sighting of Justin outside Dallas just this afternoon. He was in an unhoused encampment and the man who spoke with him picked up on his differences, thought maybe he was another were just down on his luck, so he approached him." He glanced at Mariska, who was hovering in the kitchen doorway like I hadn't been trying to make her go to bed for the past hour.

"C'mon, kiddo," Ethan cajoled. "Miss Reba brought some books you might like. How about we start one together?"

Mariska wrinkled her nose and pointed at Tyler. "He smells bad."

"Dude!" Tyler glared.

"She's not wrong," Ethan muttered. "Have you been rolling in something, bro?"

Tyler flipped us off with his hand low by his side, but it was an exercise in futility. Mariska giggled. "You're funny."

He grinned back at her. "It's all part of my charm. When did you get a kid, Ethan? Don't tell me all that fanfic you read in high school was right?"

"All that what now?"

Ethan's cheeks blazed pink as he turned his back on me pointedly. "Shut up, Ty."

"No, no," I urged, biting back a smile, "what fanfic?"

"What's fanfic?" Mariska asked, sliding off the sofa and shuffling over to join us in the foyer.

"It's when people write stories about shows or movies or books they like a lot," Tyler said. "Characters they want to see have other adventures that weren't in the shows or books."

Mariska turned that over in her head for a moment before looking up at me. "Can I use your laptop?"

"No, but you can have some paper and a pencil."

"That's for babies!"

"And my laptop is for grown-ups." It took a few minutes to find a blank notepad I could part with, and some pencils that actually had points because of course I didn't have a pencil sharpener that worked. By the time I got Mariska settled at the kitchen table writing what she said would be the best *Sassy Dragon Princess* fanfic ever. "Because they're all going to be zombies who eat the brains of their enemies, Doctor Babin. No, I don't know what CJD is. Is it like a grown-up thing?"

Tyler and Ethan were well into a low-voiced conversation. "Did you tell Tyler about Cullen's job offer?"

Ethan shook his head. "Thought I'd leave that up to you."

Tyler listened with a rather impassive expression as I told him about Hiller's visit and Cullen's offer. "I'm taking him up on it," I said. "Hiller, I mean. Cullen... I don't know."

HOWL AT THE MOON

Tyler let out a low whistle and shook his head. "Sounds like you'd be selling your soul on that one."

"Given my current job situation, it might be my only option."

Tyler glanced at Ethan. "And you think this is the best time for you to throw away your career? When your partner's gonna need your support?"

"Hey," I hissed. "Back off Ethan. I'm 100 percent behind his choice, asshat. And I don't need him to make me a kept man! I'll figure something out. Right now, my priority is her," I jerked my chin at Mariska, huddled over my coffee table with a stack of paper, "and this trip to Colorado. And yeah, it's also about the money he's offering but it's more than that."

Ethan laid his hand atop mine on the table. "It's okay, Lan. Tyler's not meaning harm."

Tyler gave me a look that begged to differ. "Right. So you're gonna do this freelance bullshit for Creepy McCreepface. What do we know about the clan in that area?"

"Clans," Ethan said, stressing the s. "They're not all weres up there." His voice was barely above a whisper. Mariska had finished a page and was scowling at it, erasing something with impunity. "Shifters have a bit of territory up there. Coyotes, if I'm recalling correctly. That's who Creepy McCreepface claims to represent."

"And that's not the same as a were," I reiterated Ethan's little lesson takeaway from the other day.

"Not to put too fine a point on it," Ethan muttered as Tyler snapped *I know* under his breath.

"There's more." Tyler sighed.

Ethan shifted uncomfortably. "What's happened?"

Tyler lowered his voice to murmur, "Damn it, I wish Waltrip would just call one of us back. He'd know way more than any of us right now. Last check in with his office—Elio, really—was yesterday morning. We figure it was a bit before he dropped Mariska off. Elio said he sounded rushed and was just checking in on some cases Elio and Diz are working and he'd be back by Monday.

"Diz did something fancy with his phone to track it, but the last place it pinged was somewhere near Coddle, which is a flyspeck on the map near the Texas-New Mexico border. But before that," Tyler paused. "Before that, he'd been back and forth to Colorado a few times. She didn't get the exact location but—"

"But we all know how to use context clues," I muttered.

"Diz and Elio did a sweep of hospitals and jails between here and Shoot Well, but no one matching Waltrip's description is being held at any of them," Tyler added. "They've been looking for him since this morning."

Inside, Mariska was singing her puppy song again and clattering around, racing up and down the hall to make her new shoes light up. "And Mal?"

Tyler shook his head. "They didn't have a thing on Mal, other than what Waltrip had. He's got no social media, probably uses a pre-paid cell phone, and the only public record he has is a driver's license issued when he turned sixteen and renewed on time every time since. His address hasn't changed since age eighteen." He shifted closer, damn near whispering now. "And he's listed on... Mariska's birth certificate. Under her birth name since she's too young to have it changed to her real name yet. Her mother is listed as Samara Goode."

"Oh... okay?" I glanced between the two of them, their expressions grim. "Fill me in here, y'all, because mind reading is not an ability I got from the Lycaon."

"Waltrip's notes said something about Samara Goode being the leader of some place called Penny Mine," Tyler whispered.

"Good for her?"

Ethan snorted softly, more frustrated than amused.

"Guys, you really need to just spit it out because I don't know what the hell the drama is about here."

HOWL AT THE MOON

"Are you guys talking about Dad?" Mariska demanded, her little voice much closer than any of us expected. She stood just a few feet away, inside the house and scowling. "When do I get to see him again? He said it'd be a day or two, but he hasn't even called!"

"He doesn't have my number," I said, which was the truth but also sounded awful considering he'd let his kid get brought to me without a means of contact.

"What about Mr. Waltrip? He said he was going back to get Dad." Mariska took a few steps forward, her shoes flashing blue and purple with each one. "Call him," she demanded. "He said he'd bring Dad back!"

"Mariska," I crouched to get closer to her height, to be less towering adult and more... squatting adult, I guess. It'd been ages since my peds rotation in med school, but I remembered the head nurse getting in our faces about making sure we got down on kid-level to make us less intimidating. "What else did Mr. Waltrip and your dad say about you coming to visit me?"

She frowned at me, eyes narrowed and shining with tears. "Dad's going to meet me here. Mr. Waltrip said he was gonna go get him."

"Why didn't you travel together?" Tyler asked, maybe a shade too aggressively because Mariska recoiled, folding her arms over her chest and baring her teeth with a small, rumbling growl at Tyler. "Whoa, okay then..."

"I don't like you," she said. "You don't know anything about my dad! He's not gonna leave me here! We're best friends! We got each other's backs!" she shouted, parroting something her dad said by the sound of it. "He keeps me safe," she added on a broken, jagged, tearless sob. "I don't like you!"

"Hey," I tried. "We're just wanting to make sure Mr. Waltrip is okay. We—Ethan and I—are going to Colorado tomorrow and you get to hang out with Ethan's brother ,Tyler." Tyler waved, giving a pained, too-wide smile. "He's a lot of fun and I bet he knows a ton of games to play while we're gone." At this, she stopped scowling and started looking suspicious. "And I just wanted to make sure your dad was waiting for us. I bet Mr. Waltrip just forgot to charge his phone, you know? And I'd hate it if we got all the way to Colorado and he and your dad were all the way back here, waiting for us!" I offered a small, friendly smile. "That's all."

She sniffed and took a few steps toward me, lowering her arms as she stopped. Before I realized what was happening, she gave me a hard shove, so I fell back on my ass and shouted, "I'm not a baby! Don't talk to me like one!" before running to the guest room and slamming the door behind her.

Tyler let out a low whistle. "This is gonna be such a great week..."

Chapter Five

Tyler waved us off in the morning with a half-awake, bleary-eyed wave. He hadn't been thrilled with suspending the pursuit of Justin (frankly, neither was I), but there had been no way we were taking Mariska with us, not when Waltrip and Mal had connived to get her out of Colorado in the first place. Ethan took the first shift driving, neither of us very chatty as we headed out of town toward 45.

"We have to stop for kolaches," I announced as we passed one of the many billboards advertising Old World Bakery and More. Ethan made an interested noise, signaling for a lane change and heading for the truck stop-slash-gift shop-slash-old-fashioned bakery that was one of a surprising many in Texas.

I ran in to grab us some pastries and more to drink, my medical brain kicking in and insisting I get some bottles of water to go with the caffeine I'd also stocked up on and returned to the car with a sausage kolache between my teeth, brandishing the rest of the bag at Ethan. "I got you poppyseed," I muttered around my mouthful.

He smiled, tired but true, and took the bag and one of the coffees. "I'm guessing you're not considering a pivot into nephrology?" he asked, nodding at the size of the drinks.

"Ha, no. Kidneys weird me out. Here, I got you too many sugars."

"A man after my own heart." Ethan doctored up his coffee as I devoured the rest of my breakfast then started on second breakfast (what? Kolaches are good!) and we got on the road again.

"Tired?" he asked as I took a deep sip of my drink. "I thought I felt you tossing and turning all night."

"Couldn't sleep so I read some of those files from Waltrip's stash," I admitted. "I had no idea Mal was brought into the cohort when he was only one. *One*! That's still a baby," I exclaimed.

"You were, what, four? Five?"

"Yeah... And that's a kid, but not a baby. Hell, at one, Mal barely had object permanence much less an idea of what was happening to him."

"Was it different from what happened to you?"

I shook my head, sighing. "Not really. It looks like they brought him into the cohort then just sort of... chilled on things a bit. There weren't any records of him being given medications until around age five."

"Like you."

"Yeah... And we were the only two who survived the first round of the drugs. The others..."

Ethan made a growling sound of disgust and anger. "Did Waltrip have records of the others?"

"Nothing I could find, but I'm sure they exist, at least in part. The Bluebonnet group is cruel and sadistic, but they still think they're scientists. They won't just toss records, especially if an experiment didn't work or had anomalous results." I wiggled my fingers in a wave. "I'm Anomalous Result One."

Ethan made a disgruntled sound around his poppyseed kolache. "And he was number two. Why didn't they try to keep him in the state if not the area? How were his folks able to leave without repercussions?"

"Waltrip didn't have anything about that," I said, "but if I had to guess? They figured out something was hinky and ran. They cared about him enough to get him the fuck out of dodge, no matter what Garrow offered to tempt them." Pain, a mix of fresh and old, stung my eyes and throat. Mal had had parents who loved him, who got him away from Garrow and the others, who kept him safe.

I'd been stuck with Cleverly, who I thought cared for me and loved me but... Well. But.

Ethan was quiet, too, and I knew his thoughts were on a similar track to mine.

The sound of his phone trilling startled both of us a few miles down the road, Tyler's name flashing on the screen. I pushed the speaker button, and before I could say hi, Tyler was off and running.

"Okay, guys, don't freak out, but I can't find Mariska."

"*What?*" Ethan swerved onto the shoulder, ignoring the blare of car horns behind us, as I scrambled to grab the phone.

"What the hell are you talking about?" I demanded. "We're literally an hour and a half on the road and you've lost the kid already? Christ!"

"Hey!" Tyler snapped. "It's not like that! Y'all saw her in bed before you left! I know you did."

He was right—I'd checked on her before Ethan and I left, and I know he peeked in on her, too. She'd been there at six, last we checked. "When did you notice she was gone?" Ethan demanded. "How long has it been?"

"After y'all left, I decided to grab something to eat and went to the kitchen and figured I'd make her something, too, for whenever she got up and—"

"How long?" Ethan repeated. "I don't need a blow by blow here, just a *time*!"

"Twenty minutes ago is when I noticed." Tyler sighed. "I realized it was too quiet in the house, you know? She was gone. Her scent is a bit faded, but I was able to follow it out the bedroom window and across the side yard."

"Shit," I hissed. "Where did she go? There's that fucking pond behind the neighborhood, and the swamp, and—"

"It stopped in the driveway," Tyler said. "Guys, have you checked the car?"

Ethan closed his eyes, breathing in slow through his nose and out through his mouth. "Lan," he said quietly.

"On it."

MARISKA WAS RESOURCEFUL, I'll give her that. She'd made herself cozy in the spacious trunk of my car with a bag of her new clothes, her tablet game thingy, a bag of snacks and a few cans of soda as well as a nest made of her fluffy purple blanket and a pillow from the guest room bed. She hadn't been surprised when I opened the trunk to find her, just squinty. She even let me yell at her for a good five minutes before she nodded and said, "Okay, I need to pee. Can we stop and pee?"

Guess how many times you can stop for a bathroom break between Broken River, Texas and Amarillo.

Go on. Guess.

The answer may surprise you.

If you're an adult with a relatively healthy bladder, the answer is maybe twice, if you bought a big drink at the first rest stop.

If you're an adult traveling with a grouchy seven-year-old who has been singing the theme to *Sassy Dragon Princess* at the top of her lungs and mainlining juice like her life depends on it, the answer is fifteen.

Fif. Fucking. Teen.

"You know, peeing too much is a sign of diabetes. Or a UTI," I remarked on the fourth stop in four hours.

"I'm little," Mariska snarled. "Back off."

"Maybe cut back on the juice."

"The water tastes gross. Like a swimming pool."

Ethan sighed and merged back into traffic. We'd left the house at six that morning, and it was early afternoon now, but traffic was heavy the closer we got to the bigger city. "I told you your filter was bad," he muttered.

HOWL AT THE MOON

"My filter is fine. She's just complaining to complain."

Mariska slurped her juice loudly, making a point I assumed. The next five hours went about the same though with fewer stops after we pulled into one rest area where Mariska found five spiders in the bathroom.

And brought them back to the car to show me.

After that, I handed her the empty bladder buster sized cup and told her to make do if she needed to pee before we got to Amarillo, where we'd planned to stop for lunch.

No one wanted to listen to podcasts, and I told Ethan I loved him but I'd cancel his Spotify if he tried to play hair metal for the next three hours. Mariska's suggestion of a Disney sing-along was met with silence.

"Fine," she sniffed. "I'll sing by myself."

Cue *Sassy Dragon Princess* theme on a loop.

"Hey, Lan," Ethan murmured around hour six. We were nearing Amarillo and making decent time, but even I knew trying to power through to Colorado in one long drive was a bad idea with a kid in the car. "I think I need to pee. Hand me the cup."

I glanced at him to see he was smirking as he navigated around a slow-moving hay truck. "No."

Mariska snorted in the back seat.

"Damn it," I said a moment or two later. "You jinxed me. Now I need to pee."

Ethan was already signaling to exit the freeway. "I knew you did. Unlike you, some of us got psychic powers when we became werewolves."

"Seriously?" Mariska squeaked. "That's so cool!"

"He's being silly," I said. "There's no such thing as a psychic werewolf."

"No?" Ethan asked, all faux innocence as he followed the sign for a Love's Truck Stop:

Open 24 Hours! Hot Food! Cold Drinks! Showers! Pull-Ins!

"Then why do I know you're thinking you want to get dinner?"

I mock-growled. "Damn you! You know my weakness for gas station hot dogs!"

"Grandma says those are made of lips and assholes," Mariska piped up helpfully.

Ethan and I both burst into laughter, her unexpected and very frank statement in that sweet child voice funnier than it should be. "You get to see your grandma a lot?" I asked as casually as possible.

Mariska was quiet for a long moment. In the rearview mirror, she was glaring at me before her expression softened and she seemed to accept I was just making conversation. "Sometimes we see her like every week, other times it's not for a month or two because of Dad's work. She lives in Denver though, and it's so cool because she's near the museum there, and one time she took me to see where they dig up dinosaurs at the Morrison Ridge place. Do you know what the Bone Wars are, Doctor Babin?"

"No," I fibbed. "What are they?"

She leaned forward. "Are you sure you went to college? Dad said he learned about it at college when he was studying geology."

"If you don't want to tell me, that's fine," I said over Ethan's chuckle, elbowing him as he braked at a massive intersection.

"Ugh, fine. I'll educate you. Okay, so there were these two guys, Marsh and Cope."

By the time Ethan got to the travel plaza, I was about to have an accident and Mariska had gone through the Bone Wars, her own feelings on brontosaurus, and a short narrative about her dad's driving and how he cusses at trucks who don't understand what steep incline means. I left her and Ethan debating the merits of Princess Sparkle Toes versus Princess Sassy Britches or whatever those creatures were called. I made a beeline for the men's room and nearly wept with relief to find it clean and empty. Which could not be said for my car when I returned. "How the hell did glitter and crumbs get all over the back seat in the five minutes I was gone?"

Ethan shook his head, thousand-yard stare firmly in place. "Remind me after this is over we need to have a serious talk about if we want kids one day."

"Er, are you for or against?" I asked, buckling in while Mariska sang at top volume to the *Sassy Dragon Princess* theme song.

"I'll let you know in a week."

I snorted. "You get hold of Tyler yet?" After we'd found Mariska and took her to the first of many rest stops, we'd made arrangements with Tyler to meet us the next morning in a small town called Boise, Oklahoma (like Boise, Idaho but with wheat instead of potatoes, and way less tourism.) We'd pushed to meet sooner but between two flats and having to drop off something for one of his actual tech clients, Tyler wouldn't be able to make it before eight a.m. at the soonest.

It wasn't ideal and would slow our trip down by at least half a day, but there was no way we could take her to Colorado with us—there was a reason Mal had done so much to get her out of there, and given what I was going there to do, there was no way taking her back was a good idea.

"Yeah, and he's pissed but nothing else to be done. We'll stop for the night and get shit settled in the morning."

Mariska's plaintive cry came from the back seat. "Doesn't anyone care what I want?"

"Hey, you want input on the trip, you don't hide in the trunk," I sniped.

"Well, you were gonna leave me behind!"

"There's a good reason for that," Ethan put in. "Now buckle in. We have a few more hours to go and I'm sick of being in a car."

ETHAN MADE A FACE AT the hotel before us. "I thought you made a reservation," he muttered.

"I did! Online, it looked nice enough! Midrange, nothing fancy, but not... this." I frowned. "It must've been an old picture."

"I bet they take cash and do by the hour arrangements," he muttered. "Call it a hunch."

"Hunch, huh? A professional one?"

"Not anymore."

Ethan hadn't been wrong. The place didn't blatantly advertise charging by the hour, but it might as well have.

A sign taped to the bullet-proof glass of the check-in window urged us to: Ask about our closed circuit TV rooms.

"I'd rather not," I muttered.

"What's closed circuit TV?" Mariska asked. "Oh, a vending machine! Doctor Babin, can I have quarters? They have gum! It's strawberry flavored!"

"That's not gum," I muttered. "If you promise me you'll never touch anything in this place, I'll buy you six packs of gum when we get to Denver."

"Sugared or sugar free?"

"Sugared."

"Deal."

Ethan let out a low whistle and gave me the ghost of a leer. "Landry, I do believe we found ourselves one of those voyeur hotels," he whispered in my ear.

"Dear Penthouse..."

"I don't think people send in letters anymore. I think they just post it to TikTok or something."

"Okay, grandpa."

He shot me the finger, smiling to himself, and approached the desk to see about getting us a room for the night. The chances of this place being bugged or under surveillance by anyone other than the voyeurs in room four were slim to none.

Ethan came jogging back, dangling a very retro-looking plastic key tag from his fingers as if he were afraid to fully touch it.

"I hope I still have hand sanitizer in the glove box because this thing is sticky, and I don't want to think about why."

"Oh, god..." I fished out the sanitizer for him and he doused the key chain and his hands liberally.

"The clerk said the listing is legit, but the management is using an old pic. The place used to be a Super 8, but new management had grand plans, apparently."

"We can drive on," I suggested. "The next town's not that far."

"Also not exactly a hotbed of motel options. I checked." He sighed. "There's a rodeo in the area so most of the nicer places are full up."

"Well, sh-oo-t," I muttered. "Okay, let's get this over with."

We were in room six, around the back of the homage to brutalist architecture on the edge of town. Hotels like this one weren't uncommon up and down the freeways, at least between Texas and Mississippi, so I wasn't too surprised to see they ran west, too. They looked innocent enough from a distance, unless you knew what you were looking for. The promises of the CCTV, special day rates, the intense security gates, and bullet-proof windows...

I was on the verge of telling Ethan I wanted to take my chances. "Let's not linger," he said. "I don't think we were followed, but this sure as hell ain't where I want my body to be found in the event we were."

"Same."

"Oh my gosh," Mariska whispered loudly. "Guys, I think this place is gross. I'm not going in. Take me home."

"We have to stop for now," Ethan explained patiently. "Let Landry rest, and I need to make some calls. And you can nap."

Mariska and I both turned similarly horrified expressions toward Ethan.

"Or at least stand inside in the air conditioning and don't touch anything."

We hurried—not ran, but pretty close—to the room, all of us gagging on the smell of cleaner and mildew and worse. Ethan locked the door behind us then dragged the particleboard dresser in front of it, frowning at the curtain-less window. "There's not much we can do about it." I sighed. "Unless you want to prop one of the mattresses against it, but I feel like that'd draw more attention than not."

He grunted, considering it. "I'll chance it. Shut off the light and check for the CCTV camera while I do this."

There were two, at least as far as I could find. One in the smoke detector overhead, and one tucked in the corner of the mirror, both facing the bed, of course. I'd been able to use the light on my phone to pick out the glinting glare of their tiny lenses, but I had a sneaking suspicion there were probably more.

Mental note: do not go to the bathroom here. I said as much to Mariska when she side eyed the toilet with the dark orange streaks and suspiciously beige water.

"Yeah, no, I'm good," she muttered. "I'll just get one of those UTI things you said earlier."

"Might be easier to treat than whatever you'd get from using that toilet."

Ethan had managed to upend one of the beds and prop it, so it blocked the window but left a discolored, disgusting patch on the floor where the carpet hadn't aged at the same rate, but the mildew had sure been good at its job.

"I might vomit," Mariska announced.

"Might improve the place," he muttered. "Fucking hell. Alright, I'm gonna try to get hold of Waltrip. You..." he glanced at the other bed and grimaced. "Lay down for a bit?"

"I wish this whole not quite human thing came with the ability to levitate," I grumbled, tugging the comforter and top sheet off the bed.

HOWL AT THE MOON

"Get the pillowcases too," Ethan murmured, gingerly holding the room phone near—not against—his ear.

I nodded, shucking them as well, then laid the blanket from the car and the sweater I'd brought in case it was chilly on one side of the bed for Mariska. "Don't move from this spot, got it? Unless the room is on fire." She nodded and very carefully climbed onto the 'safe' spot, leaving me on the gross side of the mattress. "What the hell, I need a detox shower after this, anyway." I sighed and crawled into the bed. I was already drifting when Ethan started talking, slipping into a chunky sort of dream state where his voice wove around with memories of the evening made hazy by my brain trying to fill in the gaps between what happened and what I didn't know.

"Want the good news or the less good news first?" Ethan murmured when I woke up several hours later.

"You look like a Fraggle on a ket bender," I grumbled, reaching out to tug on his bird's nest hairdo. "You get any sleep?"

"A bit. You get to drive today."

I grunted in acknowledgment. "Good news first I guess."

"Good news A or B?"

"Ethan, I love you so much. But I swear to god, if you make me play some sort of Sphinx riddle game right now, I am going to have to murder you just a little."

He had the gall to chuckle! The absolute nerve of that man! "Well, I heard from Waltrip. He called about an hour ago."

"Oh, thank god." I sighed, starting to sink back into the bed before remembering we were on a giant Petri dish. "What did he have to say for himself?"

"He's going to meet us here in a few hours."

"And the bad news?"

"Waltrip is gonna meet us here in a few hours."

"Ha. Fuck, okay then let me find coffee and—"

"Um, don't. I found a dead roach in the coffee maker this morning and a live one in the shower."

I stared at him for a long moment, then sighed. "Let's get the kid up, burn all the things that've touched the bed, and go to McDonalds. This feels like I need hash browns."

Chapter Six

"Dad says fast food gives you heart problems," Mariska announced—loudly—in the line to order at McDonalds. "You're a doctor, shouldn't you know that?"

"To be fair, all of my patients are dead, so I don't give them much in the way of health advice."

The man in front of us took a big step forward, shooting us a concerned glance over his shoulder.

"Besides," I added, "moderation is fine. Don't eat it all the time, just sometimes."

Mariska frowned, clearly thinking I was full of shit.

"Besides, hot chips and cotton candy taffy aren't that great for you either."

She opened her mouth to argue, then scowled, snapping her teeth together and looking away.

Ha. Score one for the adult. We got our order and started back to the hotel, Mariska's attention shifting from her favorite junk foods to Waltrip's arrival. "He was nice when I got to ride with him, but he doesn't talk a lot," she informed me. "So I had to keep up both ends of the conversation!"

"You're pretty good at that."

She nodded. "Dad says so, too. He says I could talk the hind end off a donkey, but I don't think that'd really happen." She stopped, one arm elbow deep in the bag of food, and wrinkled her nose in thought. "If a donkey's butt fell off, how would it stand up?"

"With great difficulty."

"Huh. I'm eating my hash browns now."

"Are you gonna save me and Ethan any?"

She shrugged. "Depends on how fast you drive."

Waltrip was waiting for us when we got back to the hotel.

"Hey!" Mariska cheered, bouncing into the room like a rabbit on a sugar high. "I saved some hash browns for you and Ethan even though Landry said they were bad for you, but they're made with potatoes and potatoes are a vegetable so how bad could they be?" She stopped her rollicking tour of the room and frowned, her bubbly mood suddenly gone. "Where's my dad?"

Waltrip, who had been silent and wide-eyed until that moment, cleared his throat. "He's not with me right now, Mariska."

"You promised," she said, her voice flat.

Ethan and I exchanged a look. I'm not getting involved. Nope, me neither.

"I really wanted to bring him to you, Mariska, but I need a little help. And Ethan and Landry are going to help me. That's good, right?"

She stared at him, her scowl firmly in place as she turned this over. "Fine. But you don't get a hash brown. People I'm mad at don't get hash browns."

Mariska got settled with her food as I doled out the rest and got her sassy dragon pony whatever rainbow abomination show going on her tablet. I joined Ethan and Waltrip at the tiny table slash desk near the window, giving ourselves an illusion of privacy.

"So some not great news," Waltrip began.

"Is it about how you just dropped a kid off at a stranger's office like she was an order from Amazon then disappeared like a douche canoe? Because that seems like it should be top of your list for shitty things to tell people."

Waltrip took a deliberate bite of his breakfast sandwiched, chewed, and swallowed before replying, "Well, given that my other options were to leave her on her own or let her stay with her dad who was being

HOWL AT THE MOON

stalked by shifters and a were, I'd say I made the best of the hand I was dealt."

"You didn't even stay long enough to tell me what was going on," I hissed. "You were too busy playing spy or some shit, not answering your phone and—"

"And," Waltrip murmured, leaning in close as if Mariska wouldn't be able to hear us, "there's other shit going on that has nothing to do with you, her, or Mal."

"Seriously?" I snapped. "You could've at least gone with *oh my phone died,* or *I had no* bars or something. Not adding in a fresh layer of fuckery."

Ethan pushed my coffee closer to my hand. "Landry, we can tear him a new one later. Now," he nodded towards Mariska, "isn't the time."

I scowled, grabbing my coffee and pretending it didn't scald my tongue when I took a swallow. Petulance hurts but sometimes I was willing to pay the price.

"What's the bad news?" Ethan asked, redirecting Waltrip's attention.

Waltrip cleared his throat. "Tyler's not coming."

Mariska perked up. "I get to come with you?"

Ethan ignored her, leaning in and lowering his voice to add, "He's getting Justin. He's found him, and if he leaves right now—well, an hour ago—he can intercept him, get him away from the other lab before it's too late."

"It's not ideal," Waltrip groused, "but there's not much of a choice. It's not safe, on any level, for her to be left alone, and sending you in on your own, Landry, would be like slathering a sheep in barbecue sauce and turning it loose in a wolf's den." He smirked. "No pun intended."

"I feel like it was very intended," I muttered. "What about the IC? Can't we just let them know something's fishy and let them handle it? I know Cullen said they—"

"The IC," Waltrip said flatly, though his eyes flared with something like fear. "What do you know about the IC?"

"Apparently more than you'd like us to," I said, widening my eyes. "What do *you* know?"

Waltrip's lips pressed into a thin line of annoyance as he glanced between me and Ethan.

"The IC isn't everything it claims to be, in some ways. And in others it's more."

Ethan snorted. "Vague, yet unclear. Awesome."

Mariska was done with her food and slumping in the chair. "I'm bored," she announced. "Are we leaving yet?"

Waltrip darted her a glance and seemed to soften a bit before sighing and shaking his head. "There's no good way to do this. Look, I've been doing a bit of freelance stuff for the IC," he paused and looked over at me. "I saw that flinch. They rook you in, too?"

"Something like that," I admitted.

With a shake of his head, Waltrip pressed on. "I need to meet some contacts today. Sooner rather than later really, but I want y'all to stop in Denver for the night. Get a hotel room, somewhere safe. Don't head to Penny Mine until you hear from me, got it?"

Ethan and I exchanged wary looks. Ethan replied, "Why?"

"Safety in numbers." He bared his teeth in a grim smile. "Penny Mine's clan leader is... determined. She wants what she wants when she wants it, and she's not going to let someone slow her down."

"What the hell does that mean?" Ethan asked. "What are we walking into?"

"Samara wants to restore her clan to their former glory," Waltrip said, pushing himself away from the desk he'd been leaning on and walking toward the door. "Shoot Well isn't gonna let that happen without a fight. Wait for me, alright?"

"Hey, Mr. Waltrip," Mariska piped up, getting to her feet and taking a few cautious steps toward him. "Did you mean it when you said we were gonna get my dad? I know you said it but sometimes people say things and..." she shrugged. "I'm not little. You can tell me."

Waltrip's smile was unconvincing. "He's okay. You'll get to see him real soon."

Mariska nodded but the look on her face reflected what I was thinking: Waltrip had no fucking clue.

COLORADO IS CLOSER to Texas than people usually realize. Or maybe that's just me. Ethan assured me it'd be just the rest of the day we'd be on the road, but I had my doubts.

Tyler had taken to calling regularly, sounding contrite each time. "Where y'all at?" he asked when Ethan put him on speaker around midday.

"Just passing through Gunmetal, Colorado," Ethan said. "City on the move, city of industry."

Tyler was quiet for a moment, then sighed. "How's Mariska doing?"

"I'm fine," Mariska called loud enough to be heard over the road noise. "I think I have cooties of the face now! They made me sleep in a hotel with CTV! Doctor Babin said we'd all need penicillin when we got home!"

"CTV?" Tyler asked dryly. I could almost hear the smile in his voice. "Ethan, you do know some places aren't appropriate for kids, right?"

"Shut up," Ethan grumbled. "Did you get my text? About Waltrip?"

"Nah, I just thought I'd call to hear the melodious sounds of your mellifluous voice this fine morning. Hey, asshole! Zipper merge! Did you fail driver's ed or did it fail you?"

"Swear jar," Mariska sing-songed, drawing on a notepad Ethan had found in his glove box.

Tyler snorted. "I'll get right on it. Hey, take me off speaker, Ethan."

I popped the phone out of the dock and switched off the speaker, before telling Tyler it was me.

"Talk to me, Goose," I ordered, and Tyler snorted.

"I just got off the phone with Diz," he said. "I told her everything Ethan passed along earlier, and she did some digging. Mal Benes hasn't been to work in about a week."

"How the he—heck did she find that out?" Mariska gave a little hum of satisfaction in the back seat, pleased with my word choice.

"He works for a pretty big ranch and when he didn't turn up the first day, it caused some stirring. There's been a lot of chatter between the ranch employees via social media messaging and very easily hackable phones about his whereabouts."

"Anything useful?"

He made an *eh* sound and swore under his breath at another driver again before saying, "Maybe. Most of the ranch hands are also weres, apparently, and there's been some rather tense speculation about those assholes from PM, which I'm assuming is Penny Mine, and some missing shifters."

I closed my eyes and sighed. "The ones I'm supposed to examine," I muttered. "Shit. I'll owe you, Mariska," I added at her little throat clearing sound. "Okay. Anything else?"

"Nope," he said, popping that P hard.

"Shhhhh-oot."

"Nice catch," Tyler chuckled.

"What about Mal? Do you think someone's detaining him? Or maybe he's hiding out somewhere safe?"

Behind me, Mariska stopped humming.

"Nothing. Diz was able to dig around some and find security camera footage of him at the feed and grain about a week ago, and he shows up a few times walking past the doorbell camera on the ranch's main house, but there's been nothing on him, either.

HOWL AT THE MOON

"Crap."

"Pretty much." He sighed. "You two going to be safe?" he asked quietly. "Or am I going to need to come find your bodies in a few days?"

"Time will tell," I muttered, and that made Tyler laugh, though it sounded a bit manic. "What about you?"

"Ah. Yeah, yeah. I'm fine. Going to be fine. Maybe. I mean. Yeah."

"Tyler." Beside me, Ethan shot me a sideways look that said *what the hell is my brother doing.* "What's going on?"

"It's been a year, and this is the closest I've gotten. A rogue were outside of Dorian Springs talked to Justin yesterday. He's definitely headed for that place we talked about."

"You've thought you were close before."

"Fuck, Landry. I know. But, he can't go there. He just can't. The guy I spoke with said these guys have been recruiting for months. People go in, but nobody comes out."

"How very Willy Wonka."

"Yeah, well I don't think there's a chocolate fountain or fizzing lemonade. He's going to get himself killed."

Ethan made a soft huffing sound and glanced in the rearview mirror to where Mariska was not even pretending to be ignoring us.

"What about them?"

"Looks like Justin might be heading right to their loving arms," he said on a sigh. "Diz's research kicked up some indications this group is real keen on Justin. They don't mention him by name but he's described a few times on these chat sites. Got a bounty on him, live only," he hastened to add. "I don't want to let this go too long, Landry. If they're out there already starting to work again..."

"Yeah. Yeah, I know. Fu... Fudgesicles. Okay. Let me know what's going on, alright?"

"Will do. Tell my brother to bring me back a postcard."

"Will do," I mimicked. Once I'd disconnected, I shot Ethan a glance. *Later*, I mouthed. He nodded.

Behind us, Mariska turned up the volume on her tablet and started rummaging in the bag of snacks. "Doctor Babin, can I eat some grapes?"

"Sure. Go nuts."

ROAD TRIPS CAN TEACH you a lot about yourself and whoever you're traveling with. For example, Ethan and I learned we both love mountains from a distance but would rather be exsanguinated with a dull spork than drive in them. And I learned that Ethan would listen to the same ball game on four different radio stations and not think that's a problem. And he learned that Mariska will absolutely make a disgusting mess of the car if he doesn't pull over when she asks him to.

For the record, the number of grapes a seven-year-old can eat before it becomes too many is somewhere around forty.

Outside of Denver, we stopped for the night. It was only another hour or so to Penny Mine and Shoot Well, but Waltrip hadn't called. And we were tired. And needed a shower. And laundry facilities.

"I don't know how you got sick all over every piece of clean clothing you have," I muttered, eyeing the duffle bag we'd found for Mariska to use. "That's both disgusting and impressive."

Mariska muttered something that might have been one of her forbidden swears, but stayed leaning against the window, eyes half-closed and hating grapes.

Ethan pulled into the parking lot of Big Horn Valley Inn, a hotel that looked infinitely less Chainsaw Massacre than the no-tell motel we'd stayed in the night before. "Wait here. Lock the doors."

"Oh, gee, and miss my chance to absolutely get murdered? Ethan, you take away all my fun."

He rolled his eyes at me and made a point of staring until I activated the door locks. As he walked away, Mariska made a very unhappy noise and flopped to the other side of the back seat. "I think I'm dying of grape overdose. The only cure is hot chips."

"Speaking as a doctor—"

"Your patients are all dead!"

"So, I know what I'm talking about when I say that eating a diet that's 90 percent junk food isn't the best idea."

"I ate grapes. That balances it out."

"That's not how it works."

"We'll see," she sing-songed, and went back to slumping sideways while we waited for Ethan's return.

My phone buzzed as Ethan trotted back from the lobby. It was Reba with a new suggestion:

Reba: Two words, Landry: Bedazzled. Koozies.

Me: That can lead to an infection.

Reba: You're a strange man. And koozies! Those things you put your beer in on a hot day!

Three pictures followed, all of bedazzled... koozies. I really hated that word. It sounds like something that should be very private or at least behind a pay wall. I was just sending as much back to Reba when Ethan got back into the car with a smile of relief. "Room 285, second floor. And they have a card-operated laundry room so we can clean up the Grapes of Wrath back there."

Mariska moaned loudly. "No more grapes. Please."

"How about a bath, clean clothes, and bed?"

She nodded, and Ethan and I both pretended not to hear her mutter *and hot chips too*.

Getting into the room was a relief. Two beds, carpet that was more carpet than dirt, no hidden cameras thank you very much, and it all had that hotel smell, a combination of soap, industrial cleaner, slightly burned coffee, and the cigarettes no one is supposed to be smoking in there but do, anyway.

"I'll get this going," Ethan announced, grabbing up our dirty laundry. "Lock the door."

"Yes, Dad," I muttered, earning a stink eye from my boyfriend. Mariska was sprawled on the bed in one of my t-shirts and her one clean pair of leggings that somehow miraculously survived the fruit-based carnage, giggling at the exchange. "You think that's funny, huh?" I asked, closing the door behind Ethan and, yes, locking it.

"You and him are weird but funny. I like you two. Can I call you Landry instead of Doctor Babin?"

"Er, sure. I mean, it is my name."

"Dad said I should call grown-ups by their titles unless they tell me it's okay."

"You called Ethan Ethan right off the bat."

She rolled onto her side and shrugged one shoulder. "Don't tell Dad." After a brief hesitation, she asked in a very small voice, "He is okay, right? My dad? I heard what you were saying on the phone and I'm not dumb. I know my dad wouldn't have sent me off unless he was scared. Before he called Mr. Waltrip that last time, some people had been being weird in town when we went."

"Weird how?" I asked, sitting on the bed opposite hers. "Did they hurt your dad?" Nervousness clutched at my belly—I didn't know Mal, but I couldn't deny a connection, whether I liked it or not. The idea of anyone being hurt (well, almost anyone because there were a few people I definitely wouldn't mind getting five across the eyes) wasn't something I relished, but the idea of someone with this odd thread between us being hurt made me especially uneasy.

Was it selfish? Maybe. Maybe it was me having anxiety over everything that happened the year before, over everything that happened from my childhood onward.

But I wanted to think it was more than that, that I was worried because I somehow cared for this stranger that shared my super villain origin story.

HOWL AT THE MOON

"No," she drew out, poking at the fringe on the comforter. "They wanted to talk to him. They offered him a lot of money I think."

"For what?"

Yes, I was lightly interrogating a child. Very lightly. Like, it'd hardly count if anyone from The Hague asked about my interrogation techniques.

She shrugged. "I dunno. They asked about me but..." She glanced up, her expression tight and unhappy. "They used the wrong name. So, Dad just said I wasn't there. He used my wrong name too, but later said he was super sorry, and he cried a little on the way home. I know my dad didn't mean it, so if he was pretending I wasn't me then I think those people were really bad. Because he's never done that before."

"Oh, Mariska, I—"

She shook her head. "No. Don't. You don't know, okay? But Dad does. And if he did it, it was to keep me safe! The guy was really weird and kept asking Dad about flowers and didn't he want answers. Dad told him to"—Mariska paused and mouthed the word fuck—"off. I thought we were gonna leave but Dad kept shopping forever and we finally left after like two hours."

He was waiting for the 'bad guy' to leave... "What flowers?" I asked, the realization suddenly clicking. It had to be Bluebonnet—unless Colorado had roving bands of BBEGs who were super into flowers and randomly assaulted people in feed and grain stores.

"Bluebells?" She wrinkled her nose. "Blue something."

"Bluebonnets?"

Mariska yawned widely, her little jaw popping with the effort. "That sounds right. Dad said they're a lupine, and that was funny in context, but then he didn't tell me the context, so I don't think it's that funny."

She lost interest in the conversation after that, finding the hotel's cable offerings far more interesting especially as there was a *Sassy Dragon Princess* marathon on Cartoon Network.

Yay.

Ethan texted to let me know he would be a while—apparently several other guests had aspirations to clean laundry also, and he was loath to leave our things where strangers could suddenly develop a yen for our wet jeans and vomit-smelling t-shirts. There was also a string of texts from Reba back-burnering the koozies—apparently, she'd need more stick on jewels than she felt comfortable keeping in the house around her pet rats—and instead plotting out starting Broken River's first ride share company. Called Reba's Rides, of course.

And below that thread was a text that just felt gross.

Creepy McCreepface: I told you that we expected you here in two days' time. It is now 6 p.m. on the second day.

Creepy McCreepface: Your unprofessionalism is telling.

Me: I'll be at the location tomorrow morning by nine.

Creepy McCreepface: Eight.

I glanced at Mariska, already dozing on the bed. I needed to feed her something that wasn't grapes or hot chips. Did the hotel have room service? Maybe there was a store nearby. If she was anything like I'd been at that age, even with a full stomach and clean, comfortable bedding, she would not want to sleep due to nerves, being in a strange place.

Me: Nine.

Creepy McCreepface: Nine. Without your plus one. This is a job, Doctor Babin. Not a vacation.

I flipped off my phone instead of sending my thoughts. Mariska giggled, and we both pretended she hadn't seen me do that.

"Feel like dinner?"

She nodded. "Hot—"

"No chips. What does your dad feed you?"

"Stuff... food..."

"Like?"

HOWL AT THE MOON

Mariska shot me a calculating look and apparently decided it wasn't worth the argument because she sighed and flopped onto her back. "Vegetables, fruit, noodles, chicken, fish, boring stuff. He said I can only have mac and cheese if I have half a plate of green stuff with it."

I thought of my own tendencies to just throw things together after a long day at the office or grab takeout from the grocery's deli counter. I really had no room to lecture about eating healthy, but I was the adult in the room so I had to at least pretend like I enjoyed a nice plate of broccoli now and then, right? "Well, let's find something vaguely healthy then."

"Ugh, salad?"

"Do you like salad?"

"Depends. Does it have croutons, cheese, and ranch dressing?"

Damn, I hoped so. "Let's see what's around here first, okay?" Mariska moved to sit beside me on the bed and we scrolled through options on my phone, settling on a Greek place that delivered. She'd never had dolmade and liked the idea of eating grape leaves.

Given the way she looked so fiercely excited at the prospect, I could only guess it was her way of seeking vengeance for the way the grapes had upset her stomach earlier. Ethan texted me back his order when I asked, and before the wash cycle was even done, I'd ordered and paid for probably too much food to be delivered within the hour.

Mariska had just settled into the epic *Sassy Dragon Princess* arc where Bumblefuzz discovers he's got magical powers and the power of friendship (and a few catchy musical numbers) can save the kingdom of Dragonsvanya from the evil wizard Snicklefritz when a heavy knock fell on the door. We both sat up and stared at it as if we could see through it, jumping when the knock fell again.

"Get in the bathroom," I whispered. "Don't come out, no matter what, okay?"

She nodded. "What if they kill you? I'll be easy to find. I'll get under the bed."

Before I could voice my disgust at that idea (it was a clean room, but it was still a hotel room after all), she was rolling under the far bed and whoever it was, was knocking a third time. I padded to the door and peered out to see a man in a white shirt, holding what looked like a paper bag in one hand.

It was too soon for food.

"Doctor Babin," the man said just loud enough to be heard through the door, "I can hear you on the other side. Please open the door."

Mariska muffled a squeak under the bed.

Shit.

"Put your hands where I can see them," I ordered, wincing at how ridiculous I sounded. The man rolled his eyes but did as I asked. Taking a deep breath, I opened the door and stepped back. He stared at me, hands still raised, paper bag dangling from his fingertips.

"It's a cookie. For Mariska."

She rolled out from under the bed and was on her feet with a swiftness and grace that would make even the most expert gymnast jealous. "Mr. Dunnigan! Hi!"

He raised his brows at me as Mariska ran across the room and flung herself at Mr. Dunnigan, hugging him around the waist as he patted her back. "So can I come in, or do you need more proof I'm not the bad guy here?"

"Kids aren't always the best judges of character." He was moving into the room, anyway, nudging Mariska ahead of him and handing her the cookie. In the corridor, by the elevator, two large blond men stood, ostensibly looking at their phones but their entire demeanor was screaming bodyguards. "Can we sit?" Dunnigan asked, drawing my attention back to him.

I shut the door and locked it again. "You tell me."

"Mr. Dunnigan is cool," Mariska said around a mouthful of what looked like oatmeal raisin cookie.

Apparently, she wasn't mad about all grapes, just the fresh ones.

HOWL AT THE MOON

"He owns the ranch! Dad works for him! What're you doing here?" she asked, turning back to Dunnigan. "Is Dad at home? I want to play with the baby goats. Can I?"

Dunnigan smiled down at Mariska and gave her braided hair a tug. "I wanted to talk to Doctor Babin here for a minute, if that's okay? I've heard good things about him from your dad and some other people, and I couldn't wait till he got to town tomorrow before introducing myself."

My senses, which had been on a sort of low alert level for days thanks to traveling with Ethan and Mariska, were slowly opening up. I wasn't afraid, just very... wary. Dunnigan was definitely a were, and without knowing anything about him, I could tell he was in charge. Ethan had the same sort of self-assured vibe, the one that low-key said leader even without him saying a word.

He held out his hand and gave me a tight, businesslike smile. "Nate Dunnigan. I own Shoot Well Ranch. My family's been in the area for over a century now."

"Doctor Landry Babin." I shook his hand and was relieved to find he didn't do that macho man must crush bones thing like so many wannabe alpha types did. "What the hell are you doing here?"

"He's dad's boss!" Mariska piped up helpfully. "He's got goats! And sheep! And he lets me watch *MythBusters* with his kids sometimes when Dad's working after dinner, and one time he let me help with the chickens, but I got stuck in the brood box." She shoved the rest of the cookie in her mouth and turned to Dunnigan. "We ordered Greek food! Have you ever eaten leaves?"

"Ah, yes, I sure have. Cynthia and I went to Crete for our honeymoon, and I got to try them there."

Mariska nodded thoughtfully. "I hope they taste purple. Like juice."

"She's in for a world of disappointment." Dunnigan chuckled as Mariska flung herself back onto the bed, all was right in her world for the moment as a familiar face joined us for the evening.

"What the hell are you doing here?" I asked again. "And how do you know my name? Have you been following me? Show me your torso."

"I'm sorry," he laughed uneasily. "What?"

"You knew where we were and who I am. How do I know you're not bugged?"

"You're one paranoid little shit," he muttered.

Mariska was very quiet and still. Something in me was pushing outwards, a pulsing sort of tension, that bone ache and heat that had come over me at the lab almost a year ago, and I'd felt echoes of sometimes when Ethan and I 'practiced' my (lack of) shifting.

Dunnigan unbuttoned his shirt and lifted the plain white tee underneath, showing his bare chest and stomach, then turning to show me his back. He dragged the collar down to show me the slope of his shoulders. He had no wires or anything, just some old scars and the usual signs of a man who'd worked outside much of his life. "Satisfied?"

I nodded. "But that doesn't answer my questions."

He heaved a put-upon sigh. "I'm here because Cullen contacted me. I'm the head of the Shoot Well clan."

Even hundreds of miles away, Cullen was finding ways to chap my hide. "Cullen. Cullen contacted you."

Dunnigan gave me a sheepish, stupidly charming smile and a shrug. "Said he got your location from a Tyler Stone, and I thought the name sounded familiar and turns out I've met his brother Ethan before, way back in the day when their daddy was still clan head for your area." He chuckled softly, a *what can you do* sort of sound. "Cullen thought maybe it wouldn't be a bad idea to let the clan know other weres would be in the area. And... I'm Mal Benes' boss, and I'm concerned about him."

Mariska hit mute on the television. "Is Dad okay? Landry said he was, but I think he's lying."

Dunnigan met my wide gaze with one of his own. "Your daddy's gonna be fine, lil' bit. I just wanted to let Doctor Babin here know we were keeping an eye out for you three. Ever since you got to Colorado, the clans have been so excited about your arrival that they just couldn't help passing the word."

You're being watched. The clans between Texas and Colorado all know you've been passing through...

"So, you're all playing telephone," I said lightly, practically hearing the dings of my blood pressure creeping up like one of those midway games where you test your strength against the machine.

"More like some folks back home—your home, that is—were concerned about their clan leader taking off with little to no notice. And Mr. Cullen's been real helpful with the IC communication and figured maybe it wouldn't be a bad idea to give us a head's up about any potential trouble." He glanced at Mariska and lowered his voice, even though we both knew damn well she could hear us if she wanted to. "Cullen didn't say too much more than just you guys were coming into the area and weren't a threat. But he said you'd been talking to Travis Hiller. That true?"

"He's the one who pushed for me to come out here."

Dunnigan made a displeased sound in his throat. "Hiller was part of Shoot Well up until a few years ago." He glanced up at me from below beetled brows. "He started working with Samara Goode just around the time she decided to break the treaty between us and them."

"So, he turned coat on his own clan? Why?"

"Power. Greed." Dunnigan shrugged. "He was crazy as a shit house rat to start with." Another glance at Mariska, who was staring at us both open-mouthed. If her ears could've quivered... Dunnigan putting his stocky body between her and I, keeping his ba⁄ olent," he mouthed.

Oh. Goody.

Chapter Seven

To say Ethan was annoyed when he returned to the room to find not only two massive weres nearby, but one inside with us would be the understatement of the century. The shouting is what alerted me to his return; I opened the room door to find him with one of the guards pressed to the hallway wall, Ethan's forearm across the other man's throat while the second guard tried to get Ethan in a headlock. "Stop! Ethan! It's okay! Stop!"

"Stay out of it, Landry!"

Okay, wow... Talking about that later.

Dunnigan stepped into the hall. His very presence seemed to command the two men. The one Ethan had pinned went soft, no longer struggling, while the other released Ethan from his grasp. After a moment, Ethan let go. "Who the hell is this?" Ethan demanded.

"Nate Dunnigan," he introduced himself.

"He's dad's boss!" Mariska piped in helpfully from the doorway, blissfully unaware of the two weres sizing one another up in the corridor.

"So, this is kind of hot in a very uncomfortable way, and I promise I'd be swoony if things weren't so fraught, but maybe we should take this into the room and sort out what the fuck?"

"Swear jar," Mariska said, heading back into the room and the damned dragon princess things.

Dunnigan and Ethan stared one another down a moment longer, then by some unspoken agreement, nodded and turned to stride ; the room.

"Seriously," I muttered, stopping Ethan as he passed, "did y'all do one of those subsonic growly things like cats do, or was that pure coincidence?"

"What the hell are you talking about?"

"Like cats can do this thing humans can't hear but they communicate and—"

"And." Ethan sighed. "Get in the room, Landry. Here," he grabbed the plastic bag of laundry one of the guards was holding. "Take this and just... go."

Ethan sat on the edge of the bed, arms iron-hard over his chest. The food had finally arrived, and I'd doled it out as best I could, pushing some of the spanakopita on the guards. "Go on, I ordered way too much."

Dunnigan gave them a subtle nod, and they accepted the paper napkins with the little phyllo triangles. Mariska was inhaling the dolmades, quickly over her disappointment that they did not taste at all like grapes, but Ethan pushed aside the plate of souvlaki he'd ordered and Dunnigan refused the gyro I tried to offer him. "Really, there's no way we'll finish it," I started but Ethan huffed. "What?"

"He said no, Landry. Let it go."

"Your *companion*," and neither of us missed Dunnigan's emphasis on the word, "is just being polite, Mr. Stone."

"Cut to the chase, Dunnigan. You're not here as the welcoming committee."

"Christ," I muttered.

Dunnigan was nonplussed. "You're right. And if Cullen hadn't gotten in touch, we'd have sat back and let this play out, so long as it didn't interfere with Shoot Well's business."

"The dead shifters were allegedly killed by weres," I said. "I'd think that'd be Shoot Well's business."

Dunnigan shrugged. "We care in that it is a needless loss of life, but they're not our clan. Not my responsibility."

HOWL AT THE MOON

"But a were killed them."

Dunnigan gave me a thin, unamused smile. "Allegedly, remember?"

"If my clan was on the hook for murders, I'd be a damn sight less calm about it," Ethan muttered. He was stiff beside me, not looking at me. I wanted to shake him, to tell him to snap out of it, trust me, but I forced myself to sit still, folding my hands on my lap and squeezing my fingers together to keep from reaching for him.

"Your clan." Dunnigan tasted the word and found it lacking. "Our world isn't so big that we can ignore our neighbors. Your clan is fussing about your absence."

Ethan's ears went chili red. "My clan is none of your business."

"Of course not. But what is my business is if we get disaffected weres looking for a new home. Or if a clan starts to fall apart. Or in-fight. Then that means I gotta be on high alert. That means I gotta decide if I'm going to send help or send warnings."

"Are you threatening my clan, Mr. Dunnigan?"

"Ethan..." I glanced at Mariska, who was watching the entire exchange with overstuffed cheeks and wide eyes. "Not here."

"I'm not threatening your clan. I'm warning you, specifically. Get yourself in order, Stone, because if I'm hearing about dissension in your tiny clan hundreds of miles away, you know I'm not the only one. I'm not so high and mighty that I should be hearing, either. My clan is a good size, and we have a nice bit of territory, but we keep to ourselves. We don't want a fuss with anyone or anything. Between the shifters riling up and trying to renege on the treaty, and then you, the head of a clan that sounds like it's looking to boot you out as leader, showing up with intent to come onto my territory? Well. That's a warning."

"He's not." Both men looked at me like they'd forgotten I was there. "He's not coming onto your territory. We're here because Hiller hired me to examine the bodies of dead shifters. If anything, we're going on shifter territory."

Dunnigan exchanged looks with his men, who then wordlessly stepped outside the room no doubt to take up post in the hall. "And that's the other problem. The bigger one, really. You're here to check out these bodies. Bodies Samara Goode claims were done in by a were and is looking to blame my people over."

"You talked to Cullen. You know him."

Dunnigan nodded slowly, eyes never leaving my face. "After the IC approached us over the summer, Cullen became our point man with the organization. We haven't made a final decision yet."

Ethan grunted. "Landry's not doing this for Hiller."

"Way to steal my thunder," I muttered. "Cullen, ah, encouraged me to accept Hiller's offer since the IC can't get close to the Penny Mine clan. They've heard rumors, I guess, and they know that Samara is up to something but want someone closer to see."

Dunnigan glanced at Mariska and, after a brief hesitation, seemed to come to a decision. "Mal's there. At the Penny Mine compound."

"Dad's there? I'm going with you tomorrow," Mariska said. "He said he'd come to get me but hasn't yet, so let's go get him, okay? Let's go see him. How far is it? Can we go now?"

"How do you know?" I demanded.

Dunnigan stood, holding up his hands to silence us. "I don't know about anyone else, and I only know about Mal because he's worked for me for over a decade now and..." he twisted his lips, trying to figure out the words. "I know."

"Know what?" Ethan asked.

Dunnigan stared at me, repeating slowly. "I. Know."

"About... about his childhood," I murmured. "What he is."

"He's my dad!" Mariska shouted. "That's what he is! Why won't you let me see him? Is he dead? Tell me!"

And Mariska finally broke. Her little body folded in on herself, face crumpling as sobs racked her so hard, she shook. Dunnigan awkwardly reached to soothe her, but I growled, the sound rumbling in my chest and startling us all. Dunnigan drew back and Ethan's eyes widened. Mariska, after a gasp, shocked the hell out of me by throwing herself at me, just leaping from her spot on the floor and pushing me back, throwing her arms around my neck and sobbing against my shoulder. "Tell me," she repeated. "I want my dad!"

Dunnigan gestured for Ethan to follow him, but Ethan shook his head. "She needs to know."

"It's not pretty."

"She deserves to know. I'm not gonna keep lying to her," I put in.

Mariska sniffed wetly and oh, gross, my shirt was wet and a little sticky when she lifted her head. "I thought you were Dad's friend," she accused Dunnigan. "Why are you being like this?"

Dunnigan sighed, scrubbing his hands over his face and muttering something under his breath before he finally said, "Mal put in his notice a few weeks ago. I told him that wasn't necessary, but he insisted. He said he was gonna bring trouble to the ranch if he stayed. He was worried—someone had been following him whenever he left the ranch, he said. I didn't think much of it to be honest. The shifters get froggy now and then, try to intimidate some of the non-weres who work for the ranch, act like toughs and hope they drive off our employees. There's not much they can do, see, thanks to the treaty. Making it hard to run my business is about the extent of their imagination."

"Until recently," I murmured.

"Yeah. Until recently. Mal was worried. He'd been approached by someone at the feed and grain who knew about his past and offered him a shitload of money to run some tests or something. Said they knew he had a kid. He was pretty sure his ex put them on to him, but I'm not so sure."

"I told you about that," Mariska reminded me. "The guy used the wrong name..."

Dunnigan's expression morphed from barely checked irritation to open concern. "He approached Mal when y'all were together?"

Mariska nodded. "Dad was real upset."

Dunnigan sat back down. "I know we've got no reason to trust one another," he started, and I snorted.

"Putting it mildly."

"Don't take Mariska to Penny Mine."

"Daddy's there!" She wiggled away from me and stalked to Dunnigan. "I thought you were his friend!"

"I am." He sighed. "Mariska, it's dangerous there. There're bad people—"

She threw her hands up. "So that means I need to go help him! If bad people have him, I need to get him!"

"Mariska," Ethan tried, "that's why Landry and I are going there. To help your daddy."

I opened my mouth but, at a warning look from Ethan and Dunnigan both, closed it. They were right—it was better not to bring up the rest of the details now. Not when Mariska was already on edge. "Mariska, it's dangerous for you, too. You're a kid, and I know you're strong and quick and smart, just like your *Sassy Dragon Princess*, but sometimes it's better for grown-ups to deal with a bad situation."

Mariska's growl was small and would've been cute if she hadn't flashed sharp teeth with it. "So what? I have to stay by myself?"

"I was thinking," Dunnigan offered, "that you could come visit the ranch."

"Home," she muttered. "You mean go home. But I can't live there without Dad! I don't know how to pay bills!"

I bit my lip to keep from laughing at the twists and turns of her thought processes. "I don't know about that," I told Dunnigan. "Mal entrusted her to me while he's... indisposed."

"I've known her since she was born," Dunnigan said. "She's lived on the ranch her entire life."

Mariska looked between the three of us and seemed to grow very tired, very fast. She shuffled to the other bed and climbed onto the mat-

HOWL AT THE MOON

tress, fussing with the tiny hole in the knee of her leggings as she spoke. "I just want Daddy back. I want to go home. I want to see the goats. I want to play in the pool. I want my room and my things, and I want to eat pancakes even though Dad always burns them and—"

"And," I said, breaking into the ramble. "We're going to keep you safe, Mariska. I promise."

"Did you know I'm super-fast and I bite?" she asked with some sass in her tone, folding her arms over her chest and glaring across at me. "I can help!"

Ethan and Dunnigan exchanged mutual looks of frustrated leadership before Dunnigan sighed and shook his head. "Look, I can't tell you what to do, but I can tell you this much: My clan has no desire for another battle like what happened thirty years ago, got me? Samara is pushing hard, trying to provoke us, but we're not taking her bait." He shifted his gaze to me, assessing me coolly. "I can figure why she asked you out here and likely what you'll say to her, but I need y'all to know that we're not gonna engage."

Ethan blew out a heavy breath through his nose, closing his eyes for a moment before he opened them to fix on Dunnigan. "You saying you won't offer aide if we're in need?"

"I'm saying," he murmured as he headed for the door, "that you're on your own, unless we have a damn good reason to intervene. You're gonna be on shifter land, Stone. Outside of my clan's territory. If we come in, metaphorical guns blazing..."

Ethan nodded. "Understood."

"Wait, so you just came out here to piss on our legs and then tell us we're fucked?"

"Swear jar!"

Dunnigan scowled. "Ask your partner, hoss, and he'll tell you the fact I came out to see you myself is a damn fine courtesy. You're not exactly subtle, you know? And me being seen coming out here—you can be damn sure it was noticed—means anyone who feels froggy is gonna think twice."

Ethan laid his hand on my shoulder, squeezing gently. "He's right, Lan. He can't offer us protection, but this? It's letting any other clans or rogues watching know he's aware we're here and that if something happens to us, powerful eyes are on us."

"It's the best I can do," Dunnigan said quietly. "If y'all aren't gonna let me take her back to the ranch, the best advice I can give you is get in and out fast as you can. Do what you gotta do, get your money, and run. Keep her as far from Samara and Hiller as possible," he added.

Mariska padded over, frowning deeply. "Are you leaving?"

"Gotta get back to the goats, girlie." He glanced up at us and added, "Maybe y'all can come by when you're done."

Mariska bounced on her toes, dancing back toward the bed. "Yes! Landry, the goats are sooooo cute! Yes!"

Ethan and Dunnigan did some big quiet guy eye contact-head nod-hand shake thing before Dunnigan gave me a tight-lipped smile and nod of my own, slipping out the door to join his guards, leaving us kicking our heels in uncomfortable quiet.

THE EVENING UNSPOOLED in fits and starts, the heavy quiet giving way to Mariska asking questions about the food Ethan and I were picking at, then why the news had chyrons, why we lived in Texas. If I didn't know any better, I'd have thought she was drawing us out on purpose but given her meandering topics and her lack of interest in many of the answers, I think she just wanted to fill the silence.

Whyever she did it, it worked to get us unbent a bit, and Ethan was busy explaining to her how a piston engine worked (I have no idea how they got on that topic, and it was all kind of white noise to me, to be honest) when someone knocked on the door again.

HOWL AT THE MOON

"Swear to god," I muttered, motioning for Ethan to stay seated. "If Dunnigan is back to convince us to let Mariska go with him..." Peering through the peep hole, I could see the back of someone's head, their blond hair thick and short.

"Yep, Dunnigan. Or one of his goons, anyway," I announced.

"Landry, wait—"

Ethan's words were cut off on my sharp shout of shock. As soon as I opened the door, the man spun around and drove his fist into my belly. Mariska screamed, but I was too stunned to check on her. My breath whooshed from my lungs as the man struck me again, pushing me back into the room. Another man followed him, this one stockier and shorter but no less powerful. He slammed the door, shouting at me to shut up as Ethan leaped toward him. Their bodies crashed against the door, wood cracking as the man shouted and Ethan growled. Mariska screamed again, her shrill panic snapping me out of my own startled silence. The man throttling me had pushed me back onto the bed, one knee beside me as he struck at my face and chest.

Mariska had gone quiet, but Ethan and his opponent were snarling and cursing and I knew, without seeing him, that Ethan was about to shift.

But these two attacking us... They weren't like him. They didn't have that *smell* to them like a were. Didn't set my alarm bells ringing like weres did (no, these guys had their own special alarms). "Wait," I shouted. "Ethan! They're... they're not like you!"

"The fuck," the guy on top of me spat. "Shut up, asshole. You keep running your mouth, you're gonna be spitting teeth in a minute!"

Ethan threw the man who was trying to choke him, spinning to lunge for us. The man he threw, though, was fast, rolling to his feet and leaping to catch hold of Ethan around his neck. He moved fast, swinging around to drop to the floor as Ethan fought, his hand lashing out and striking Ethan's thigh. Ethan howled—an honest to god howl—and the man shouted, recoiling. Blood bloomed on Ethan's leg, the flash of metal in the other man's hand sending cold spikes of panic through my veins. Something inside me snapped, a familiar but strange pressure pushing at my bones and skin. It hurt, like stretching to fire but also being on fire, like my bones were cracking from the inside out. I snarled, my voice thick and rough, lashing out with one hand to strike at my attacker's face.

Claws raked his skin, and he shrieked. My hand was different. Mine, but changed. Something between a wolf's paw and a human hand, curved and thick, darker, with crescent moon claws where my nails should have been. The man atop me fell back, blood pouring from his face. "You fucker," he panted. "I was gonna let you live but—"

I grabbed for the first thing I could reach, ripping the alarm clock from the wall and swinging it hard at his face. He dodged but didn't pull back, moving just enough for me to get a leg free. I drove my heel up into the soft part of his torso, kicking him back onto the floor. His friend was there, grabbing for him, eyes wild and panicked. "Come on, come on," he panted. "Let's go. This isn't worth it." He was staring at me, my hand still changed. Ethan was heaving for breath, eyes squeezed shut as the men stumbled, bleeding, from the room.

Someone had called 911. The cops arrived while Ethan and I were still on the floor. Mariska was nowhere to be found. "She's gone," I hissed as the sound of people running down the hall thundered toward us. "Mariska? Mariska, honey, come out!"

Nothing.

"Don't," Ethan breathed, leg seeping blood through his fingers.

"Ethan!"

"Mariska isn't a normal kid," he muttered. "We'll find her. Get rid of the humans and we'll find her."

The police were less than thrilled to be there. Nothing had been stolen, no one had seen the men breaking in or leaving, just heard the shouting, and us—bleeding and in a battered room with a broken door.

HOWL AT THE MOON

"Look, *if* this room got broken into, the chances of us finding the guys are low. The management claims the cameras aren't working on this floor or the third and sixth. If no one saw them, there's not much we can do other than take a statement."

"We've got your descriptions," the second officer added. "And your numbers. You can call the precinct in about three days to follow up if you don't hear from us sooner."

Ethan laid a hand on my wrist, quieting me when I opened my mouth to snarl at them. "Thanks. We'll do that."

"We can give you a lift to the hospital," the first one said, eyeing Ethan's bloody thigh. "Or call an ambulance."

"It's not as bad as it looks," he lied. "We'll be okay."

Next came management, on the cops' heels. We were cordially invited to get the fuck out since they didn't want trouble. I had a sneaking suspicion the fact Ethan and I were holding hands and obviously a couple didn't win us any points, but I was too tired and afraid to fight it. Ethan and I grabbed our—and Mariska's things—as the manager waited by the door. I bent low, pretending to check for missing items under the bed and then checked the bathroom and closets.

No sign of Mariska.

Fuck, fuck, fuck!

"Ethan," I muttered, helping him limp to the car. "What the hell are we gonna do?"

"There's a clinic," he replied. "It's a specialty one, so to speak. We can go there, get my leg looked at."

Dropping our bags. I realized my hands were shaking. "What the hell just happened? Who were they? They weren't there to rob us. Do you think they were there for Mariska? We can't just leave, Ethan! And how the fuck do you know about a clinic?"

He was pale, shaking, but sweat spotted his face and throat. Despite his obvious pain, he tried to act like this was fine, like nothing was happening as he leaned against the car and shrugged his shoulder. "I texted Cullen while the cops were talking to you. He said it's about ten minutes from where we are and to ask for Doctor Lafayette."

"Fuck. But Mariska—" The thought of her alone, or worse *not* alone, made me sick. Nausea nearly sent me to my knees, the thought of her needing help overwhelming. Swaying, I caught myself on the car before I could fall. "What if they were there for her?" I demanded. "What if this was some ploy by Dunnigan? What if he—"

"It wasn't him," Ethan insisted through gritted teeth. "They weren't were, but they weren't human either." Quietly, he added, "Lan, I think they were like you."

Whatever response I could have formulated was lost in the soft sound of padding feet. Ethan jerked his head up, eyes going wide, and a relieved slump hitting his shoulders. Mariska was dirty-faced, her knees scraped and hands grungy as she sloped closer, her gaze frantic as she clung to the ragged bushes along the side of the building. Even from yards away, I could tell she was breathing hard. "Mariska," I gasped, bolting toward her. She froze, her body caught between a crouch and a lurch, then seemed to realize it was me. She made a startled, sharp noise like a bark and flung herself at me as I got close. "Where were you?" I demanded. "I looked everywhere and—"

"The window," she said, looking equal parts upset and proud. "I went out the slidey door window thing onto the balcony. When the cops were there, I climbed down the tree next to the railing. I almost fell!" She showed me one scraped palm with a sort of amazed excitement in her tone. "But I got to the bottom and thought what if they arrested you and I didn't know how to get to Shoot Well from here, so I thought I'd take your car."

I carried her back toward Ethan who looked worse than before. "How the he—heck were you going to do that?"

"I was gonna watch a YouTube about hot-wiring it."

"Oh my god."

Ethan stood straighter as we neared. "Where was she?"

HOWL AT THE MOON

"She decided she was a monkey shifter and climbed out the window."

"What did those guys want?" she asked quietly. "Are we in trouble? Did Dad get mad I'm with you?"

Ethan winced as he moved aside so I could open the door. "They were just mean men, hon. They didn't want anything more than to scare us."

Mariska looked like she wanted to say something more but kept her lips pressed tight.

"Here," Ethan said when I slid into the driver's seat. "Cullen texted directions."

I nodded. "Hold tight, okay?"

He smiled wanly. "Remember when I said we should go out more, take a trip or something? This isn't what I had in mind."

Chapter Eight

The clinic was discreet without being secretive. Set at the end of a strip mall situation with one end anchored by a three story complex with a huge sign reading *Office Space for Rent! First Month Free! Medical Office Set Up Available!*, High Top Medical Center was in a more modest two story situation at the other end, beside a Mexican restaurant whose smell made me wish I'd waited to eat dinner because it smelled *good*. Ethan insisted on walking himself in, refusing my offer to run in and ask if they had a wheelchair or even crutches available. I carried Mariska, nudging him aside when we reached the desk. "Is Doctor Lafayette in?" I asked, breathless and probably a bit too loud.

The receptionist swept an assessing gaze over us and, without looking away, called over her shoulder, "Marty!"

Somewhere in the back rooms came an answering, *"On it!"* There were a few people in the waiting room, most staring at us as we stood bloody and dirty at the counter, but we were soon hustled past them into a large exam room at the end of the clinic's main corridor. Marty turned out to be a middle-aged nurse with a kind, round face and ruddy cheeks who scooped Mariska from my arms effortlessly and set her on the table. "Well, look at you, hon. What happened here?"

"I fell out of a tree," she said, darting a glance at me to see if I would call her on her half-truth. Instead, I offered a small nod. "But Ethan's bleeding! Look!"

Marty turned to Ethan and his expression crimped into sharp concern. "Did you fall too?" he asked dryly.

"Ah, no. I... got cut," he settled.

HOWL AT THE MOON

Marty nodded. "Well, good thing our kind heal quickly. Doesn't mean it won't hurt like a devil though. Doctor Babin, right?" he said, pointing at me. I nodded—we figured it wouldn't make much sense to give the clinic fake names, not when we were apparently already a known commodity here in Colorado were and shifter territory. "Why don't you go with Mariska to room three, right down the hall, and we'll get Mr. Stone here sorted."

I didn't want to leave Ethan, but Mariska was already climbing into my arms again as Marty cleared the exam table for Ethan to lay on it. "Ethan..."

He smiled thinly and nodded. "I'll see you in a bit. Wait for me in the waiting room?"

Marty shooed us out of the room and told us we'd be seen in a few minutes, watching us until we went into the brightly painted room three.

"It looks like a daycare vommed in here," Mariska muttered, staring at the bright walls and generic cartoon characters painted in scenes of medical happiness, getting bandages with a smile and positively gleeful over a booster shot. A basket of toys sat in one corner and a magazine rack hung from the back of the door bearing issues of kid-friendly periodicals mixed with pamphlets about puberty and ear infections and a few more serious ones about screen addiction and teenage depression.

"This place," she asked in a near-whisper, "they see people like us? Like... with shifter parents and stuff?"

I nodded. "So I hear."

She shifted, the paper on the table crinkling with her movement. "Dad would take me to the doctor in Denver sometimes, when I needed my shots and stuff. We'd stay with Grandma at her old people condo. All her neighbors are grandparents, and they don't let kids live there. It sounds kinda boring, but Grandma says sometimes it's nice to be old with other old people."

"Did the doctor your dad took you to see kids like you?" Were there doctors who specialized in weres and shifters? Or was this clinic an outlier? Was there some arrangement made with humans, maybe the IC paying them off or a protection racket with the local clans? Too many thoughts tangled up in my brain, but the one that stood out the sharpest was the one telling me weres and shifters needed medical help like any other group, and there had to be a way for them to access it.

"He said I had to be careful." Mariska shrugged. "The doctor always said my temperature was too high and one time he made Dad talk to a socialist."

"I... what?" I laughed. "Do you mean a social worker?"

She shrugged again. "Dunno. Had the word social in it. They wanted to talk about why I always had a fever and my heart is always so fast. They asked him if I lived with drug users and stuff. I told them Dad took pain killers for his head sometimes and allergy drugs, and that made the social lady all weird. We never went back to the doctor after that, but the social lady came out to the ranch a few times to visit with me."

I didn't have time to question her further, barely formulating the realization that of course weres and shifters would have different metabolisms, no shit Sherlock, when the door opened and Marty stepped in, closing it behind him with a smile. "Doctor Lafayette is with Ethan right now. He'll be going up to radiology soon to make sure there wasn't anything left in the wound but it's looking good so far. He'll get cleaned up and will be good to go soon." He pulled open a few drawers, gathering supplies while he spoke. "I'm not sure how you knew we were here—you're not one of the local clans or rogues—but you did the right thing coming here. You knew to ask for Doctor Lafayette," he added, cutting me a questioning look as he gently lifted one of Mariska's hands to start cleaning the scrape.

HOWL AT THE MOON

123

"We have a... Hm. An acquaintance," I settled, knowing Cullen would hate to be called my friend even in passing. "He suggested we come here when he heard Ethan was hurt."

"What's your friend's name?"

"Why does it matter?"

"This is gonna sting, sweetie," he warned Mariska, and for a few minutes everything was about her wounds, which was fine by me. *How much can I tell this guy without it becoming a problem? What's safe to let slip? Do they know Ethan's a clan leader, or should I play dumb?*

Finally, Marty had her settled with bandages on her knees and a glittery rainbow sticker on her arm. "The thing is," Marty said, washing his hands now, "I know she's not your kid. She's got the smell of a shifter on her but you... You're not human, but you don't give me a full wolf vibe, you know? Your man in there, though." Marty let out a low whistle, shaking his head as he shut off the water and turned to face us. "He's as were as they come. Now, I shouldn't even be treating this one here without her parent present, but I'm not about to turn away an injured pup. Where're her parents?"

"My dad's in Shoot Well," Mariska piped up. I winced as Marty's brows lifted.

"Shoot Well, hm? Well, you're not one of their clan," he said to me. "Who told you about us?"

"A guy called Cullen. He's—"

"With the IC." Marty sighed. "Lordy. He's been here. About a year ago. There aren't a lot of clinics like ours. Ones that see non-humans as well as humans. Lafayette's the only doctor for about a hundred miles who has any idea how to treat folks like us. What kind of doctor are you, then?"

"He sees dead people!"

Marty chuckled, but I nodded, smiling a little at Mariska's endorsement. "I'm a pathologist. I work for the state medical examiner's office back home." Technically still true.

Marty clicked his tongue. "Too bad. We need more were and shifter medical sorts. We're pretty thin on the ground. Mostly because most of our communities aren't well off enough to have access to the right kind of education that'll lead to med school or nursing or even things like PT and phlebotomy, but listen to me on my soapbox here," he chuckled. "Your man's gonna be done soon so if y'all want to take up a seat in the waiting room I can find some juice for the little miss here and there's coffee and tea out there too."

We nodded and Mariska jumped down from the table, letting Marty lead her into the seating area with me trailing behind. It didn't take much longer for Ethan to be brought out. His jeans were stiff with dried blood and a white bandage was visible through the gash in the fabric. He was limping but able to walk on his own without assistance. The nurse with him handed off a thick sheaf of papers and a white bag that I knew would contain samples of antibiotics and probably pain killers. "Hey," I breathed, standing as Ethan drew close. "Everything okay, I take it?"

He rattled the bag and smirked. "I got party favors. Take the big ones every eight hours, the little ones as needed."

"And keep the wound clean," the nurse reminded him. "And try to stay off that leg for a day or two." In a lower voice, she added, "you might heal faster than most, but you still need time, especially with one that deep."

Ethan winced. "Will do."

"And come right back here if there's any sign of infection, you hear? We have an after-hours clinic for..." she stopped herself. "Well. Call the number on the paperwork if there's something you need and we're not open, got me?"

He nodded, and we made our way back to the car, Mariska showing off her sticker and telling Ethan how she was brave because she pretended to be a Sassy Dragon Princess. We got into the car and Mariska, chattering a mile a minute, grabbed her tablet to bring up some game she suddenly just had to play while Ethan and I got settled.

"Seriously, you okay?" I muttered. "How bad is it?"

"Narrowly missed some major vessels," he replied quietly, "and cut the muscle pretty bad. It's already knitting but..." He made a face. "Not as fast as I'd like."

It was all suddenly too much. One damn thing after another, starting with everything last spring. It weighed on my chest like a mountain, pressing the breath out of me even as I sat there in the early afternoon sun under a clear blue sky. "We should go back," I blurted. "Tell Hiller to fuck off, just go home. Get hold of Waltrip and explain—"

"No!" Mariska wailed. "We have to get my dad! He needs our help!"

"Landry," Ethan sighed, "I'm okay. We're gonna be okay. And we're already here. There's shit going pear shaped, and we're not gonna fix it ourselves, but we can help. Whatever's happening in Penny Mine and Shoot Well, Mal..." He reached out and cupped the back of my head with his large hand and gave my neck a gentle squeeze. "Landry, we got this."

"Please," Mariska whispered. "Please, Landry. My dad..."

"This is a whole fucked up new path we're on," I said, closing my eyes and leaning into his touch. "I don't like it."

He nodded. "I'm not a fan either."

We were quiet for several long moments before I finally nodded and opened my eyes. "Okay. Let's get on the road then. Text Waltrip though."

"Got it. Hey. Are *you* okay? I mean, from the hotel..."

"Uh, yeah? Shaken. Maybe bruised a bit. My hand..." I glanced at them, looking almost normal on the steering wheel save for some reddening around the knuckles. They ached in a way I hadn't felt since my surgical rotation in med school, but they looked... fine. Nothing like what I'd seen in the hotel room.

"What about your hands?"

Ethan didn't see. He didn't know...

"Just a little sore from hitting the guy," I admitted. "Okay. Let's get this show on the road."

Chapter Nine

We weren't exactly flush with extra funds, but Ethan didn't fight me much when I suggested getting another room, even for a few hours, so he could rest and we could wait for Waltrip to show his face again. I found a motel just a mile or so from the clinic and got us a room.

Mariska was subdued, watching her tablet in silence as Ethan drowsed on the surprisingly comfortable bed. I sent Waltrip a text as we loafed.

Me: Where are you?

No response.

Okay, he's busy. He was meeting up with someone so give him some time.

Me: We moved hotels for now. Tell you deets later. Address in next msg.

I sent him the hotel name and our room number with the street address and waited.

"Maybe we should get something to eat that's not fast food," Ethan suggested as he surfaced from his uneasy nap. "There's a grocery store across the street."

"I'll go. Will you be okay with Mariska?"

She lifted her head from where she'd slumped on the other bed. "We're going out?"

Swear to god, she was a golden retriever in human form sometimes. Though considering she wasn't quite human herself, that might not be far off the mark.

"I'm going out, you're staying here to keep an eye on Ethan for me, okay? Make sure he doesn't get up."

Ethan rolled his eyes but didn't argue, and Mariska sat up straight, her shoulders set in a determined pose. "No more grapes," she said as I headed for the door. "But can I have an orange?"

"Oranges. Check. No scurvy on this road trip."

One trip to the grocery store, two oranges, one apple, and three sandwiches later, still no word from Waltrip.

"What should we do?" I asked Ethan quietly as Mariska, sucking the juice out of an orange slice, drew horses on the hotel stationery.

Ethan sighed. "Looks to me like our options are wait longer which means you gotta get in touch with that Hiller guy and tell him we're going to be late, or we go on ahead without Waltrip and wing it."

My head throbbed in warning of my impending migraine. "Or we just say fuck it all and go back to Texas."

Ethan's unamused look told me where he stood on that option.

"Okay. Okay. Let's get cleaned up then and check out. We'll take turns messaging Waltrip, though, so he knows where we are."

"I'm gonna shoot Cullen a text and double check Dunnigan's story. Just in case," Ethan murmured as I passed him.

In case he was in with Penny Mine after all. In case he had his own pile of dead bodies behind him. In case...

It wasn't ideal. It was so fucking far from ideal that ideal would need a passport to visit. But it was the best of two bad options. "Hey, kid, go wash your paws and face. We're about to hit the road again."

IT TOOK ABOUT AN HOUR to get to Penny Mine itself, then another half hour to find our way to the coordinates Hiller had given me just a few days before. The place was unassuming—it looked like about half the sprawling, old ranch houses between Texas and the west coast. Not the flashy, magazine ready numbers but a working, living ranch house that had been around for decades and added on to here and there, in need of paint and maybe some shingles. It was visible from the road, down a long and rutted dirt drive past a barb wire fence with an open steel tube gate.

What gave me the heebie jeebies were the scattered outbuildings, obvious later additions judging by the lack of age to their appearance, and the huge pole barn that looked practically new. I wouldn't have been shocked to see a price tag stuck to the door that, from the distance down the drive, looked to have a heavy chain across it.

Yeah. Not weird at all.

I steered down the drive, wincing with each jolt that rattled my car. "Sorry," I muttered as we hit a particularly violent dip. "I'll get your tires realigned when we're back home," I said, patting the dashboard soothingly.

"Forget the tires. What about my spine?" he grumbled. In the backseat, Mariska made a tiny little *whee* noise as we hit another bump, followed by a dire sounding *oh no*.

"Are you going to be sick again?" I demanded.

"No, but I think I don't need to pee that bad anymore."

"Oh my god..."

"False alarm," she chirped. "But I do really need to go. You shouldn't have let me have all that juice!"

Ethan sighed. "Throw in detailing and I'll shut up about my back."

I slowed down even more as the drive made a rather tight curve, then flattened. A wide spot in the scrubby grass that had been beaten down and worn away was either a parking spot or I was about to commit a major faux pas.

The front door opened as I shrugged and shut off the engine—let them have me towed. So long as I got this day over with. Standing on the porch, looking entirely out of place with his expensive suit and fiercely styled hair, was Hiller, peering down his long nose at me like I was shit someone had smeared on those battered front steps.

"You're late."

"There was traffic on the way here."

"And you brought company." He had the same tone as someone saying, *And you tracked dog shit on my white rug.*

"Didn't have much of a choice," Ethan supplied, holding tight to Mariska's hand.

Mariska who was, for once, quiet and still.

Hiller pursed his lips. "Really. Ms. Goode is waiting to meet with you before I show you to the facility."

He stood aside and motioned for us to go ahead into the house. While there were definite traces of *other* while I was outside, walking into the house was being body slammed by it. I gasped, unable to stop myself, as my brain and body attempted to go in opposite directions for a moment, conflicting signals tangling my thoughts and senses. Fear, anger, predator, prey... I didn't know where any of it was coming from, just that it seemed to fill the house in every single corner, the very air inside replaced by a miasma of *run, wait, fight, hide.*

Under it all, was a faint and unsettling tang of bodies. Living, un-washed bodies. That animal smell people could get when they went too long without a shower, when they spent days outside, mingled with something more primal.

Sour, bitter, dark, earthy, and cloying all at once. It coated my tongue, my nose, and I feared it clung to my skin and clothes. Ethan cleared his throat softly, his face crinkling as the smells hit him. Mariska had tugged the neck of her t-shirt up over her nose and mouth and was making tiny yuck noises. Beside me, Hiller didn't notice. Maybe he was used to it. Or maybe he wanted to see my reaction. "So, this place seems cozy," I said, breaking the brittle silence.

Hiller's smile was cool, polite, but threatening. "It's been in the Penny Mine community for over a century. Follow me."

HOWL AT THE MOON

He moved ahead of us to the stairs, a narrow deathtrap lined with a worn runner that may have once been green or possibly even blue but was now mostly brown and gray with threadbare spots showing generations of traversing. At the top of the stairs, he hesitated, then turned left, taking us down a few yards and throwing open a door to a small sitting room or lounge area. A flat screen TV was positioned on the far wall between two windows with blackout curtains. A battered but clean sofa had pride of place in the center of the room. Someone had tried to make the space cheery with bright throw pillows and a giant floor cushion covered in soft-looking fabric with a bright floral pattern, but the general air of age and little care hung heavily over the room. Hiller gestured for us to step inside, and after a moment's hesitation, I went first.

"Your company can wait here," he said, baring his teeth in a parody of a smile. "Ms. Goode is only doing business with you and has no time or capacity to entertain your hangers-on. There's a television, movies, other timewasters."

Mariska jerked her chin defiantly. "I need to pee."

Hiller curled his upper lip and pointed to a door set in the corner of the room. "Through there. Use soap when you're done. No touching things with dirty hands."

"I'm seven, not dumb," she muttered, and hared off towards the door.

"Ethan..."

He nodded at me. "It's okay. I'm with her. You got this."

"This is very heartwarming." Hiller sighed. "But I'm on a schedule and, frankly, those bodies are not keeping well. Doctor Babin?"

"Okay. Okay, I'm coming." One last look at Ethan, who was watching Hiller with narrowed eyes, and I turned to follow our host.

Samara's office was at the end of a long hallway lined with carpet similar to the stair runner. The funk of the unwashed bodies permeated upstairs as well but was overlaid with the smell of old wood, dust, and something sweet but unappetizing. Overripe produce or the very start of vegetal rot maybe. Despite the odors, the house was painfully neat. *Houseproud* my aunt Cleverly would've said. She'd always respected people who kept their homes, no matter how poor, pin-neat and, in her words, *respectable.*

The thought of Cleverly brought a mix of anger and sorrow that mingled with the uneasiness that'd begun when I stepped into the house. I must've made a sound or something that alerted Hiller because he stopped, hand raised to knock on Samara's door, and raised a brow at me. "Problem?"

"It's been a very long week."

His smile was slick. "Well, let's see if we can hasten the end a bit, shall we?"

That didn't sound good at all.

Samara was pretty—I could see where Mariska got her chin and her near-violet blue eyes. She was also mean as a snake. It was in her eyes, I decided, the way she watched me, the way she kept herself so still as Hiller led me to her desk. When she raised her hand for me to shake it, I half-expected to feel a sting of venom from the touch.

"Doctor Babin. Mr. Hiller has told me so much about you."

"How? He doesn't know anything about me."

She and Hiller shared a fake, hearty chuckle. "Well, now, surely you're aware of a thing called the internet," she chided.

"Then am I safe in assuming you're one of my ten followers on Instagram? I was wondering who the other eight were beside my boyfriend and my friend from work."

Samara's eyes crinkled for barely a heartbeat, but the amusement was gone before it truly put down roots. "I believe you know my ex-husband and our child."

"That's definitely not on the internet."

"Depends on where you look."

Score one for Diz. "I'm guessing it wasn't Google."

HOWL AT THE MOON

Samara nodded to Hiller, and he stepped out of the room, closing the door behind him. Samara rose from her desk and moved around it to sit on the edge, affecting a casualness that was definitely not mutual. "Let's drop the pretense, alright? I know about Mal's past and, thanks to some careful research, yours."

"I don't even remember Mal. I couldn't pick him out of a lineup if you paid me."

"But you do know our child. Mariska, I believe her name is? When I last saw her, it wasn't. I named her...Well. Mariska?"

I nodded. No use lying at this point. "Yeah. Mariska."

"I've been looking for her, Doctor Babin. It was wrong of Mal to hide her from me."

I kept my mouth shut. It was *Scooby Doo* villain 101: let them keep talking so you know what you're working with before you volunteer any information.

Who says you can't learn anything from cartoons?

"Keeping a child from their mother seems like something you'd reject, Doctor Babin. Given your own fraught family history." She tilted her head, bark blue eyes keen on my every expression. "You just lost your aunt this year, didn't you? The woman who raised you? And your father... He's out there in the wind somewhere, isn't he?" Samara pushed to her feet and moved past me, stopping at the old wooden bookcase near the door. She picked up a silver-framed photo of herself holding a baby wrapped in a blue and yellow blanket, beside her a man who looked both startled and thrilled. *Mal Benes*, I knew. "Would you want Mariska to go through the same pain and uncertainty as you have, Doctor Babin?"

I deftly hid my wince. Christ, what did Diz leave out there to be scraped? "Do you know my shoe size and which side I dress on, too?"

"The only way that would happen is if she lost her only surviving parent to greed and addiction while being raised by someone who only saw dollar signs when they looked at her. Is that what you're suggesting, Ms. Goode?"

She set the picture down, giving it a lingering look before turning back to me. "I want Mariska to thrive. And I want her to know her roots. What's that saying, roots to grow and wings to fly?"

"Is she a tree or a parakeet, Ms. Goode?"

My phone buzzed in my pocket. Samara didn't overtly react, but there was a small twitch of her fingers, a barely-there-flutter.

Goddamnit, Tyler!

"She's my child. And she is very important. Very special."

"Because she's your child, or because her father is Mal Benes?"

Samara's smile became fixed. "Because she is special. As is her father. As are you." Her laugh was breathless, tired. "I've worked for a very long time to make Penny Mine what it once was. Before I was born, the rift between us and the Shoot Well weres destroyed everything Penny Mine had been, reduced us to this life in a dying town, unable to do more than simply exist. When I met Mal, we were both in Denver for school. He was..." She trailed off, eyes straying back to the picture on the bookcase. "I knew he was different. He was excited for my plans for Penny Mine. And when I revealed my nature to him, he wasn't afraid. He told me about his past and..." she paused again, closing her eyes. "And it was enough for the time being. But when my child was born..."

"She wasn't a were or a shifter, and you were disappointed."

"No," she snapped. "Never. I was disappointed that Mal was excited for her lack of our traits. I was disappointed that, when it came down to it, Mal wasn't willing to stand by me as I remade Penny Mine and brought it back to its former glory. He stood with Shoot Well, with the weres."

"Did he know?"

"That they were weres? Of course. They brought him into the fold. Made him a sort of pet, really. He was coddled as a child and, as he grew older, treated as a valued friend of the community. At first, I thought he was refusing because Shoot Well is far more powerful, wealthier than Penny Mine has been in years. But I realized it was his loyalty. He was more loyal to them than me. No!" She shook her head, correcting herself. "He was more loyal to them than to the reality of me, of my plans. He was plenty loyal to the *idea* of me he had before Mariska was born."

"Ms. Goode, why am I here?"

"Because," she opened her eyes and smiled thinly. "There are dead shifters in a makeshift morgue in town. And they were killed by a were. We need your assistance as a professional to prove they were killed by a were, so we may proceed with seeking reparations from Shoot Well."

My throat and mouth were dry. "What are these reparations?"

"We want our territory back. We want the blood money they are due to pay upon proof of death, and we want their fealty to our clan leadership." She spread her hands and smiled. "Me."

"So not much at all," I breathed. "Shit."

Hiller knocked and opened the door at the same time. "Ms. Goode? We're ready for him at the morgue."

She nodded. "Go. Bring him back here when it's over."

THE DRIVE TO PENNY Mine was shorter than I expected, Hiller taking a shortcut through a narrow valley between the hills that made me feel claustrophobic, the sheer rock walls towering above us as he navigated the curving road one-handed.

"Breathe, Doctor Babin. I haven't lost anyone on this road yet."

"How about other roads?"

"Well. That'd be telling."

"You're not very funny."

"You're not very bright."

"That was unnecessarily hurtful," I scolded. "I'd think you'd be nicer to the guy you convinced to cross state lines and do vaguely illegal autopsies on dead shifters."

"Hmm."

The rest of the drive was pointedly silent. Hiller brought us into Penny Mine via the far side of town, not the touristy western side where I'd entered with the charmingly decrepit old storefronts intended for photo ops and a scattering of modern shops with faux-Wild West signage. The town itself was on its last legs and it showed, but there was an effort being made.

At least on that end of town.

The eastern side was less charming by a wide margin. Rather than the Wild West kitsch the west side was trying on, the eastern side had very obvious signs of a more modern era that didn't quite get off the ground. Several small, blocky apartments that looked mostly empty save for one where a woman leaned out a window, watching us go by, and another with a scattering of children's toys in front of a downstairs unit. A few houses dotted the main road, but it was mostly businesses, long closed with papered over windows and telling signs: *For Lease! Contact Mountain Pine Commercial Realty to Give Your Business Owning Dreams a Home!*

Hiller turned off the main drag towards a downslope where a hulking gray building waited, covered in graffiti and two cars sitting in the weedy lot near a door marked *Office*.

"This was a grocery warehouse once upon a time, when there was talk of annexing by Denver. When it never took off, the company pulled out of the area. Penny Mine is too far to justify having a warehouse here without a strong connection to a bigger city, and too small to have a warehouse on its own. When they left, they had it retrofitted as offices, or tried to." Hiller shot me a small smile. "The company that owned this place did a slap-dash job of building out. But for our pur-

HOWL AT THE MOON

poses, it doesn't matter. We just needed the refrigeration units and the space for the trial."

"The trial," I repeated. "For the people who murdered the shifters."

"Just so." He stopped at a flimsy wooden door and paused, hand on the knob. "This isn't going to be like the facilities you're accustomed to, Doctor Babin. They're basic, to say the least."

I could already smell the faint, sweet smell of decay. The refrigeration was slowing it but not halting it entirely. No refrigeration unit was that good. But this was far more advanced than I usually encountered and would only make things more difficult. "I need to understand what specifically I'm looking for. Not what you hope I'll find."

"Cause of death, types of markings, that sort of thing," he assured me. "We couldn't trust this to the local ME because, well, obvious reasons, I'm sure."

Evidence of an animal attack would be a problem, evidence of an animal attack on multiple people would be a crisis. I nodded.

He opened the door with a small flourish, and I stepped into a wide, beige on beige on beige, office situation. Two desks sat facing one another and they positioned a third near a door on the far wall.

"Yeah, you weren't kidding," I said. "Nothing like the labs I'm used to." *Red alarm, red alarm...*

"I thought we'd have a bit of a chat first, Doctor Babin. I understand you've had some unpleasant visitors the past few days." He gestured to the marks on my neck from where the were had grabbed me during the fight in the hotel. They were healing rapidly—thanks, recessive genes triggered by Lycaon—but still looked gnarly. "And word has reached me that your Sheriff Stone, I'm sorry, *Mister* Stone, was also involved?"

"How did you hear any of that?" I asked, feigning confusion while my instinct to flee struggled to break loose from my iron grip on it.

"Well, those marks," he said, affecting a sheepish chuckle. "They look rather like claw marks."

"What Ethan and I do in the bedroom is private, Mr. Hiller."

That had the desired effect, startling him into a moment of flustered silence. "Well," he finally said, "I hope you understand that, while our initial meeting was rather fraught, what you are doing is very helpful."

I rolled my eyes, ignoring his attempt at buttering me up. "So, what do I sign for this?"

"Excuse me?"

"I need to sign some paperwork or something, don't I? Business on a handshake isn't exactly legal, especially not when it involves cadavers."

Hiller's smile was oily, quicksilver and unsettling. "Of course! Have a seat and I'll be right back with the contract."

I nodded, heading for the desk nearest the far door. The smell told me that was where the bodies were being held. Wherever Hiller was going, it wasn't to get a pre-made contract for me to sign. I had no doubt in my mind he had hoped to keep this off any official records and maybe intimidate me enough that I wouldn't ask for recompense.

Checking my pocket, I winced. My phone was barely alive, so that was fucking great. I couldn't call for help even if I knew who to call. Ethan? So he could run down here with Mariska on his back and save me?

Waltrip? If he ever answered his damn phone?

I wished I'd kept Dunnigan's number on me and hadn't put it in my bag instead of my wallet.

I gave the doorknob to the morgue a try and found it locked, so I checked the desk drawers. The one nearest me held the usual offices supplies and detritus of desk work. The next one, to the right of the main door, apparently belonged to someone who had a fancy for making chewing gum wrapper chains because there were several all looped together in the narrow middle drawer. The last desk (*and it was juuu-uuuuuuuuuuuuust right,* my thoughts sing-songed) held what I hadn't even known I'd been looking for. A slim portfolio labeled with a line of numbers but containing a familiar-looking print out of lab work and dosages of a substance labeled *L8*.

My own lab work called it *L2*, the second generation of Lycaon. The lab work had been similar, tracking not just the basics but also the effects of Lycaon on my markers and the buildup in my system over time.

The top of the sheet had the string of numbers from the front of the folder followed by the initials *MB*.

Hiller opened the door, and I didn't even bother trying to pretend I hadn't been snooping. "Why are you interested in Mal Benes' labs?"

Hiller pressed his lips into a thin smile. "Because it's better to know your enemy, or however that saying goes."

"Mal's your enemy?"

"Anything that threatens clan integrity is our enemy. Whether it is loner weres thinking they have a right to our territory, or mutts bred in a lab thinking they're not an abomination. Now," he held out a sheaf of papers, "these are for you. Standard NDAs, acceptance of payment via a third party, and," he flipped to the last page, "proof of credentials."

Slowly, I signed the forms. "Now what do you want me to do?"

"Follow me, Doctor Babin, but best take a good deep breath now because you won't want to past those doors."

THE MAKESHIFT MORGUE smelled so strongly of rot and animal that I was sure, for the first time since medical school, I was going to throw up at an autopsy. "It's not cold enough. By a wide margin."

Hiller shrugged, shooting me a pointed glare. "We had no intention of keeping them for so long."

I smoothed my hands over the plastic apron he'd handed me, wishing I had my full PPE gear from the office and not just what amounted to a garbage bag open on the seams. The room had been cold storage at one point but not intended for bodies. The remains were laid out on thick plastic sheeting on what looked to be desks.

The bodies weren't covered.

"I won't be able to give you more than a gross exam unless you have access to a path lab and histology as well as microscopy. These remains are in advance states of decay. It'll be difficult to ascertain much of anything," I said in a rush, unwilling to inhale too deeply.

Hiller handed me a basic surgical mask. "Do what you can. I'll wait for you in the outer office."

He left me with six bodies and locked the door behind him.

"Fucking hell."

The bodies were much like what the pictures showed, just further along in their decomp. It was the work of two hours to determine they all had signs of tearing and puncture wounds, but beyond that I couldn't say much else. When I knocked to be let out, Hiller was waiting expectantly on the other side. "Without equipment I can only tell you they died by violence and likely hypovolemic shock."

Hiller nodded impatiently. "And the wounds. Can you tell what caused them?"

"I scraped some samples," I admitted, "but without analysis it's all guess work. Two of the subjects had thick, dark fur caught in their nails, and one of the victims was partially shifted at the time of death suggesting they possibly were the last or among the last attacked, as the others hadn't shifted, potentially indicating the attack was fast and unexpected. And *potentially* is doing a lot of heavy lifting here, Mr. Hiller. Without access to lab equipment or, frankly, prior experience with examining shifters, I can only make educated guesses."

Hiller smiled. "Thank you. Your services are greatly appreciated." He shut the door behind us and ushered me towards the other door, the one we'd first come through. "The weres in Shoot Well have several members with dark fur when they shift."

HOWL AT THE MOON

"A few hairs doesn't mean anything," I protested. "Hell, I could find a dozen dogs between here and Denver with dark fur, I bet. And three times as many people, if not more."

"To us it does," he assured me, pausing as he reached the door. "I do have a question for you, Doctor Babin. What is it *you* hoped to find by snooping around here? Proof we're some evil gang of murderers? Something tying us to your Bluebonnet clinic?"

"I'm not sure," I admitted. "But given the fact Mal Benes has ties to Penny Mine and is currently missing..."

"Mal Benes is just as worthless as you are, Doctor Babin," he murmured, leaning back against the desk. "And your ego needs to accept that."

The tight, hot, *now, now* feeling from the hotel fizzed in my veins. I half expected my fingers to be stretching, curling even as I looked at them. But nothing had changed outwardly. Not yet.

"If we're so worthless to you, why are you so interested in our backgrounds? Why did you seek me out, specifically?" A stray thought popped into the forefront of my mind, and it settled with a heavy certainty even as I asked, "Was it you at my house a few days ago?"

He smiled slowly, easily. "What big ears you have, Grandma. All the better to hear me with."

"Why?" I breathed. "What are you doing with me? Us?"

"Ms. Goode is waiting," he said, pushing away from the desk and ignoring me with a sideways smirk. "She'll be able to fill you in, I'm sure."

The ride back to the compound was, somehow, worse than the ride out to the makeshift morgue.

Samara was waiting on the front steps for us when we returned. As I got out of the car, she held out her hand, motioning to the front door in a welcoming gesture. "Let's go to my office, Doctor Babin. Have a chat before you're done here."

"And if I refuse?"

"Then you refuse," she said with a slight tilt of her chin. "Why would you, though? I would just like to speak with you. After all, you've just done a service for me and before I pay you, I'd like to have a little conversation." Without looking back to make sure I was following, headed up the steps to the front door. The driver opened my door with a sheepish sort of smile and gave me a nod and another of those searching looks before Samara called out. "Hopkins, you're on rounds at three."

"Yes, ma'am," he replied, giving me one more look, this one almost... pleading. Like he was expecting me to know something I hadn't been told yet. Then he trotted up the steps and into the house after Samara, leaving me to follow on my own.

She had waited for me on the stairs, only making sure I was coming before heading up to her office with me trailing behind. We passed the lounge where Hiller had shown Ethan and Mariska and I wanted to stop, just peek in and make sure they were okay, or I thought more realistically, tell them to run like hell while they still could.

Samara cleared her throat and gestured to her open office door. Hopkins stepped out of an adjoining door at that moment and froze mid-step, watching me pass. I'm sure it was sheer desperation on my part, but I felt like his gaze was screaming at *me* to run then, like I wanted to do for Ethan and Mariska. But the moment was swift and sparked out of existence between one breath and the next. He shrugged into the denim jacket he'd been holding and headed for the stairs, leaving us behind.

"Have a seat, Doctor Babin," she said, motioning to the leather chair in front of her desk. "This won't take long."

"It's already taken too much of my time," I said, my skin itching with *run, danger, wrong*.

She smiled a smile so sweet that I could almost, for one moment, believe she wasn't the monster I knew her to be now. But only for a moment. "My clan is small, much smaller now than it used to be. Some

HOWL AT THE MOON

of them lacked the vision, the dedication, to return us to our former standing. They were seduced by the appeal of being untethered by a community such as ours. Or found partners willing to bring them into their own clans. Or, in the most disappointing cases, chose to turn their backs on us entirely and marry humans, partner with them, just merge into their society as if they truly belonged. We find ourselves rather light on the forces required to truly make a good showing against Shoot Well."

"I don't know what you think I can do for you there," I snapped, thankful my voice wasn't shaking. "I can't shift, and even if I could I have no interest in helping you enact some sort of fucking blood vengeance against a clan of weres."

She laughed, reaching out to tweak my chin like she was my doting auntie or something. "No, Doctor Babin. Your value to me lies only in what you're worth in trade. You and Mal, you're unique. I'd say two of a kind, but I think my daughter might prove me wrong there. You left some very important people in a bad spot not too long ago, Doctor Babin, and once they found out my dear ex was here, it didn't take much to work out a deal with them. Once they found out you were coming here, the deal got sweeter. I give you, Mal, and Mariska to the Associates, and I get the bodies needed to make up my numbers when it's time to strike against Shoot Well."

My mouth was so dry it hurt. The ringing in my ears surely must be my blood pressure going nuts, I decided. Otherwise, it was the shrill ring of panic. "You're fucking insane," I said, surprisingly calm. "Whatever these *associates* promised you is bullshit. They're liars."

Samara sighed, her expression momentarily apprehensive as she strode to the door and opened it on Hiller, waiting with a bored expression on his face. "You have no idea what you did when you destroyed the lab, Doctor Babin. Years of research were nearly lost. It's only because of the Associates that the most vital information was saved."

"You're going to hand your own child over for experiments?" I demanded, trying a different tack. "Mal may not have told you what they did to him, but I'm more than happy to tell you all the nitty gritty about the experiments. We're the only two who survived, did you know that? They had zero problem killing children, Samara. Children younger than Mariska is now. And you're happy to just hand her over to these monsters?"

"Mariska is special," she hissed, gripping the side of her desk so hard one of her acrylic nails snapped. "She's a hybrid, born to a mongrel and a shifter. She might hold the key to what..." She trailed off, glancing past me to stare at Hiller. I whipped around to find him scowling at her, sheer loathing pouring from his expression.

"What do you mean?" I asked, slowly looking away from him, back to her, though I was sure turning my back on him was the worst idea. "Samara, what is it about Mariska?"

The sharp pain across the back of my skull came with the floating, throbbing thought *Yep, that was a bad idea, dumb ass* as I slumped toward the floor, not fully unconscious but definitely disoriented.

"Take him to the cell," Samara ordered. "Muzzle him first."

I REGAINED MY WHEREWITHAL somewhat a while later—maybe an hour, maybe only a handful of minutes. The room I'd been taken to was poorly lit, most of the illumination coming from a high, narrow window made of thick plastic like you'd find on cheap RVs or in those national park shower room windows. The place was too warm, the humid heat that came from a lack of circulation and the sun beating down on the space for hours at a time. There was a drain in the floor which was both concerning and... No, it was just concerning. The walls and floor were concrete, but the roof was timber, the wood looking fairly new and treated with some sort of stain to make it look like cedar. *One of the buildings we passed on the way to the morgue,* I realized. There had been a handful of outbuildings that looked like concrete bunkers, the sort I'd seen back home on some larger properties, meant to keep out wildlife or just be sturdy and stand whatever disaster their owners assumed was coming. Faintly, I could make out the sound of someone on the other side of the wall cursing and a muffled shout, wordless with rage, before they fell silent.

I think they might have been crying.

Still aching, I pushed myself to my feet and took a better look around the room. A narrow vent, high overhead, told me they did have some sort of HVAC, but it wasn't on just then. Other than the drain (way too narrow) and the plastic window (also too narrow), the vent might be the only way out, unless I could figure out how to get the door opened. It was a heavy looking wooden door with several locks on it, all of which were controlled from the outside.

Of course.

I paced back to stare up at the vent and entertained a brief fantasy of suddenly being able to shift and leap that high, but the daydream fell apart when I remembered that, if I was in a wolf form, I'd have no opposable thumbs much less a tool to open the vent and get my furry ass through the duct work like some lupine John McClain. "Hell of a time not to be a were-monkey or something," I muttered, sliding down one of the walls to sit on the floor. "Hello?" I shouted. "Hey, next door! Can you hear me?"

The vague thumping and shouting stopped for just a moment, then started up again but louder. Through the vent came the muffled sound of someone shouting *help! Let me out Goddamnit! You can't do this!*

"I think they can, and they did," I muttered. My phone was gone, my head ached, and apparently, I was destined to be the dude in distress, at least this year. I was out of fucks to give at least for the moment. Closing my eyes, I listened to my neighbor shouting at me, as if I were the one responsible for his confinement, and a thought occurred to me.

MEREDITH SPIES

Pushing to my feet, I moved closer to the high vent and shouted, "Are you Mal Benes?"

Silence, then, "Did you say Foul Finish?"

Oh my god. "Why would I say that?"

"I don't know!"

"Mal. Benes!"

"Yes! Get me out of here!"

I fell back to my heels and pressed my forehead against the surprisingly cool wall. "Do you think," I muttered, "I'd be here if I knew how to get out?"

"Hey! You still there?"

"Yeah," I shouted. "How long have you been there?"

"I don't fucking know! Who are you?"

In for a penny... "Landry. Landry Babin."

He fell quiet. Then, much louder than before, shouted, "*Fuck you! Where's my kid?*"

Chapter Ten

Mal shouted for help and shouted abuse at me for... Eh, I'll say an hour. Long enough for the sun to move noticeably. He finally got quiet, but I knew he was still there on the other side of the cement wall. *Where's Ethan? Is he looking for me? What have they told him? God, I hope he gets Mariska out of here first.*

Hunger cramped my stomach, and my eyes felt gritty with dirt and exhaustion. Despite the cool walls, my clothes clung to my body with sweat both dried and fresh.

The stench from the morgue still teased my senses now and then, the faintest whiff of decay mingling with my unwashed body and the dusty room.

I had almost convinced myself to try to sleep, even if it wasn't a good sleep, just to get some rest and ignore my discomfort in the hopes it would refresh my mind and I could think of a way out, when I heard thumping and shouting next door. I couldn't make out the words, but the tone was frantic, angry. Then a clanging sound.

The door shutting, I realized.

Mal shouted again, thumping underscoring the words. I thought he must be hitting the door, which was good in a way since it meant he was still there and not being dragged off to... Well. Whatever Samara wanted to do with us. Hand us over to the Associates, which must be those experimenting in Garrow's name still.

Oh, shit. Justin!

Were these the same people Justin had been heading toward?

Fuck... If Tyler hadn't gotten to him already, was he now with these Associates? The same people who wanted to renew their experiments on me and Mal? On a *child*?

The door to my little room rattled and, a moment later, opened just far enough for the guard to step in and slide it shut behind him. He motioned for me to be silent, and I flipped him off.

Chuckling, he reached into the pocket of his light jacket and handed me a bottle of water, still cold from the fridge. "Here, take this. Look, still sealed," he added when I didn't move. "It's not poisoned."

"That sounds like something someone who figured out how to poison my water would say."

He chuckled. "Yeah, you're right there. But if I poisoned you, then Samara would be pissed. I mean, she's gonna be pissed, anyway, but..." He reached into his other pocket and pulled out my phone and a slip of paper. "Be quiet," he murmured. "Trust me, okay?"

I shook my head, my brows drawn in an expression of *are you fucking kidding me.*

"Look. My name is Terrence Hopkins. I'm a shifter, like Samara. My family's been in this clan since the silver mine days, alright? There's some of us who think she's nutty as a fruitcake and want her gone but..." He trailed off, cutting his eyes toward the door. He motioned for me to be quiet once more and pressed himself against the metal, listening. *Turn on your phone* he mouthed. I shook my head. He rolled his eyes and took several long, quick steps toward me.

"Look," he whispered, "we don't have a lot of time, okay? Those guys who jumped you and your fella? They're mutts. Half shifter, half human. They think Hiller's gonna get them in this clan, got it? They'll do whatever he says. They were supposed to kill you and your friend there, piss off Samara's friends who are coming *tonight*. You hear? *Tonight.* So, if you want to get out of here, you gotta do what I say."

"I gotta?"

HOWL AT THE MOON

"Oh, for fuck's sake." He tapped my phone and said urgently, "I put my cell number in here, and I fucked with the Wi-Fi, so it'll work now, you got me? But keep it on silent. You gotta get word to someone, text or email."

"Why should I believe any of this?" I hissed. "I don't know you from Adam's ox, and you were driving Samara around just fine earlier. Maybe this is her way of trapping me."

"Worse than you already are?"

"For fuck's sake!"

"Read your note," he said with a broad grin. "Go on. I'll wait."

"Jesus..." I flipped open the folded paper to see Waltrip's slanted scrawl.

Trust Hopkins. He was my 'errand' in Denver. I'm working with him. The IC is aware. Hold tight.

"And he couldn't have told us this yesterday?" I muttered. "Fucking hell!"

"Look, we want Samara gone, okay? We don't want war with the weres. We'll be wiped out, forced out, or both. Me and my group, we're gonna nip this in the bud, but it's gonna be ugly and it's gonna be fast. Just... don't do something dumb, alright?" He nodded at the phone again. "Your friend inside, the signal jammer is fucking things up for him, but I'll be shutting it off in about an hour. Let him know you're okay. It'll be dark soon. Tell him to make Mariska go to bed, even if she's not tired." Hopkins glanced at the wall where Mal waited on the other side. "I have someone waiting who can get her out, over to Shoot Well. They know her there."

"I know. Shit, shit, shit." My head throbbed. I started pacing, my blood thrumming with anxiety and anger. "I'm going to give him a password to give her, okay? She's not a trusting kid. She's smart as hell and won't just go with a stranger."

"Tell her we'll use the word... umm..."

"Snicklefritz," I said, smiling faintly at Hopkins' *what the fuck* face. "It's from a cartoon she loves."

He nodded. "Fine, fine. Look, Waltrip helped set this in motion yesterday but he's in the wind right now. I'm sure he's fine but don't wait around here for him thinking he's coming, got it?" I nodded, and he continued, "Mal's too riled up for me to go to him with this but when the time comes, I'm gonna get him out too."

"Hey!"

He paused, one brow arched in question.

"We met Dunnigan, the Shoot Well clan lead, last night. He knows we're here."

Hopkins nodded. "I'll send a runner. My friend Trent, he's like the fucking wind. Skinny as a streak of piss but whooo can he run. Even on two legs!"

"Tell Dunnigan we're alive," I urged. "He said he wouldn't interfere, didn't want to start the fighting himself but..."

Hopkins gave me another nod and slipped from the room, the heavy thump of the lock echoing oddly in the small space.

I looked at my phone to see he had indeed added his number next to the simple letter H, which wasn't as stealthy as he imagined, really. Adding insult to injury, the damn thing had been reset to factory and only had that H number. Thank god I knew Ethan's by heart, but I had no idea how to get in touch with anyone else. Even Waltrip's number was hazy at the moment. Carefully, I typed out a message to Ethan and sent it.

I'm okay. Getting help. On site. Help coming for M. Tell her the code word is Snicklefritz.

Then as an afterthought, I added:

Go to Dun. Call Cullen. Garrow assoc. On the way here.

I waited a few minutes for a reply, but none came. Finally, I sat down, back against the wall again, and waited, my brain supplying me with a never-ending scroll of what could possibly happen next.

HOWL AT THE MOON

The door to the cell rattled, then swung open to reveal a tall, gaunt shifter with either moss or a very sad beard happening on his face. "Get up," he ordered. "Samara wants to see you."

"When I wanted something to happen," I muttered, "I'd hoped I'd have time for a rest or something."

"What you saying to me?" he snapped, grabbing me around the throat before I could react. He bared his teeth and leaned closer, his nicotine tainted breath heavy and foul. "When she's done with you, me an' some of the others are gonna have fun tearing you apart. Gonna be like throwin' a rabbit in a dog fight." He shoved me away, and I stumbled, nearly going back down before catching myself.

"The hospitality here leaves something to be desired," I rasped, hating the tremor in my voice.

He smiled, too wide and too sharp. "Get your ass in gear or I'll drag you. How's that for hospitality?"

I followed the shifter down the corridor, feeling each step rattle my bones as he led me toward Samara's office. It was only a matter of yards, but it seemed like miles, the unwashed body and mildew stench of the carpet and peeling wallpaper only making it worse, triggering a gagging sensation in my throat each time a waft of the odor puffed up from beneath my feet. The shifter knocked twice and pushed open the door, shoving me ahead of him into the office and closing it behind me.

"Samara's otherwise occupied," Hiller announced, sitting on the edge of her desk. "And will be for some time. Arguing her case with the Associates isn't going as well as she hoped." He sighed, giving me a fake-sympathetic frown. "You look disappointed because you thought, perhaps, she was a soft touch beneath the whole"—he flicked his fingers to indicate me, Mal, the whole god damned situation—"trading your lives for her glory thing?"

"She's not a monster," I said, fighting not to sway on my feet. "She's just confused. Scared. I get it. I mean, I don't condone it, and I'm gonna fight like hell to stop her, but I get it."

"Do you?" He pushed away from the desk and closed in on me, stopping just inches from my face. "Because I don't think someone like you can truly understand why Samara thinks this is a good idea."

"Because I'm not desperate?" I sneered. "Trust me, I know desperation. It's very familiar to me."

"Because you're not a shifter. Or even a were. You're a useless bit of trash on the side of the road. You're a genetic failure. Creatures like you have no benefit to our kind."

"Then why do you want us so bad?" I whispered. "Why are you so desperate for us? Why not just leave us alone, let us die of old age? No one will be any wiser and you'll have your precious true bloodline of shifters."

Hiller tapped the tip of my nose with his finger and smiled. "Because you are valuable to someone. Or someones, rather. Your very genetics are thanks to the Associates and Garrow, wherever his sorry ass is rotting away right now. And you belong to them. I'm merely returning their property." He smiled, spreading his hands wide. In a confidential tone, like he was telling me a great secret, he added, "I'm the one who convinced Samara it was a good idea. Left to her own devices, she'd have just whined to Mal until he broke, agreed to come back to her and then dragged him to that facility in Texas."

I closed the distance, pushing against his chest to shove him away as I snarled, "It doesn't matter who did it, we're not going with them. We're not their property. We're—"

"It does matter." He laughed. "Very much! Because they're trying to screw me the fuck over. I'm the one who reached out to them. I'm the one who set this in motion to bring you here. Those dead shifters, they were useless to us! To me! They wanted to leave but Samara begged—begged, like a child! —for them to stay. But I knew their hearts because you see"—he shoved me back, pushing me until I fell on my ass and he towered over me— "I did the same damn thing. The very same thing. I left Shoot Well because Dunnigan is such a sorry

HOWL AT THE MOON

piece of shit. All he wants to do is keep his little corner of the world. Doesn't want to expand. Has zero scope, you know?" Crouching beside me, he grabbed my hand and spread my fingers with a push of his thumb against the pad of my palm. "I was promised things, Doctor Babin. Samara was to be removed from her position. She is ineffective as a leader. She is a selfish, whining brat who has no plan for the future other than seize our old land and show the weres who's boss."

"I don't see how that's any different from yours," I remarked, trying to jerk my hand back, wincing when he tightened his grip. "Let me go."

Tsking, he examined my fingers more closely. "Did you think that would work?" he chuckled. "I saw what happened. I felt it. How did you do it?"

"I... I don't know," I admitted. "Like you said, I'm a genetic defect. I can't control it."

He dropped my hand and grabbed me by my upper arm instead, dragging me to my feet. "You're of no personal value to me—I'd as soon kill you as look at you, frankly. But you are exceptionally valuable to the Associates. You and Mariska both. Did you know she is the only child ever born to an experimental cohort? Well, considering only you and Mal survived, I suppose that was fairly obvious. But Mal... Poor Mal. He didn't get a single beneficial trait, did he?"

"He kept his humanity."

Hiller affected a shocked face. "Well, rude! Are you saying only humans can give a fuck, Doctor Babin?"

"I'm saying he managed, even after everything they put him through, everything Samara put him through, to be a good person." I supposed—I barely knew him, but I did know how to push buttons so might as well. "If he's nothing, even less than me why keep him. Let him go. Let him take his daughter and leave. I'm the one who can partially shift, right? I'm the one who has more of the were traits, aren't I? Hand me over and let them go."

"Your optimism is at once adorable and annoying." He let me go and, at some unspoken signal, the door opened again. "I need both of you, you see. Because they're going to renege on my promise in favor of Samara. She's far easier to control. Far easier to bleed dry. But I have what they want."

The shifter who'd brought me into the office stepped in with Mariska slung over his shoulder. A strip of duct tape covered her mouth and mittens, of all things, were taped around her hands. It wasn't even an effort this time. I turned and threw myself at Hiller, my hands starting to change again. With this came a hot, slick shiver up my spine and through my jaw. Sharp pain exploded in my face as something cracked beneath my ears. Hiller looked, momentarily, stunned, then burst into crowing laughter as he danced back. "This is wonderful," he said. "Set her down. Let her go for a moment."

Mariska saw whatever was happening to me and, instead of the scream I think we all expected, she did a little jump up and down cheer muffled by the tape. I'm not sure what she said, but I'm sure it meant she needed to add money to her swear jar once we got free. Hiller motioned for the shifter to scoop her up again, scowling at us both. "She doesn't fear you," he muttered. "And you didn't turn on her. Well, that makes this next part easier in terms of conserving my trade. Put them in the guest house."

I was still changed, still heaving breath as he paced toward me. His own change simmered beneath the surface as he closed in. "Go on. Attack me. Do it in front of the girl. And let her see what a monster truly looks like. And, in turn, I'll show you what happens when I have to defend myself."

The shifter holding Mariska produced a long, thin blade from a sheath at his side and pressed it against her bare throat. She stopped struggling, but her eyes flashed with hate, and I knew that if she had been able to shift herself, she would have been mauling that shifter before I could blink. Instead, I nodded, sinking to the floor as my body returned to normal, or whatever passed for it. Hiller nodded at the shifter, and he adjusted his grasp on Mariska, using his free hand to drag me to my feet. "Take them the back way," Hiller ordered. "We keep this quiet."

MARISKA AND I WERE taken to a cell in the block where I'd been held earlier. For a moment I had high hopes that it was the same one I'd been in before and I'd be able to get to my phone, to call for help, but it was one door too far. The shifter dropped her on her rear on the floor and shoved me into the back corner before locking us in. She lifted her hands to me in a silent plea, knee-walking toward me for help. I met her halfway, and after some cursing of my own and more than a few failed attempts, got her hands untaped. "This part is going to hurt, kiddo. I'm sorry."

She scrunched up her eyes and nodded, panting through her nose as I pulled the tape from her face as gently as I could manage. "Can I cuss?" she sobbed.

"Go for it."

Mariska let loose a string of words that could peel paint off a battleship before sinking back to sit and cover her sore mouth with her hands. "Dang, kid. I don't think I've heard most of those combinations before, and I used to date a longshoreman."

She lifted her teary face to mine. "What's that mean?"

"Uh, they're a group that's really good at cussing."

"Oh. Maybe I should be one when I grow up."

"Maybe." I scooted closer and, after a moment, she leaned against my side. "Want to tell me what happened?" *Where's Ethan? Is he alive? How did you get back here? I thought you were out!*

She sniffed, shook her head, then nodded. "A guy came to the room they put me in and he said the password you told Ethan to give me."

Go, Hopkins!

"Then what?"

"Then we snuck out and were super quiet. Ethan came, too. He looked like he was hurt cuz his leg was all bloody and he was limping again, but he said he was okay. Mr. Waltrip was waiting at the road for us, and we had to walk a long time to get there. I heard people trying to find us, but Hopkins said to keep moving and we were okay. Hey, did you know there're mines here? I bet they're haunted. I heard that Colorado had a cannibal guy like two hundred years ago or something; do you think he lived here?"

"Uh. No? I think he was in another part of the state. But he's long dead now."

"I figured, but his ghost might be here, and that'd be kind of cool, seeing a ghost."

I could only stare at her for a moment as my brain tried to make sense of that train of thought. *Kids...* "Hon, I need you to tell me what else happened."

"We got to Mr. Waltrip, and Hopkins helped Ethan get into the car with his bad leg. Hopkins went back the way we came and said he had to pretend not to know us, and Ethan said that was okay, so we drove off and it was super bumpy. The road sucks! We got to this big twisty part, and then Mr. Waltrip cussed a lot, and the car went"—she swayed her hands in the air, making crashing noises and doing this circle thing with her head and sticking her tongue out—"and it was scary. I think I fell asleep or something, but my head doesn't hurt. I checked!"

"Good, good," I muttered. "That was very smart of you."

"I'm pretty sharp." She pressed closer, her voice quieter now. "The car was on its side and Ethan was wiggling around a lot, like he was stuck. He said to stay down and be quiet. Mr. Waltrip was really quiet and," she whispered, fingers twisting in her shirt hem, "I thought he was dead or something, you know? But he made this funny noise." She imitated a wet, bubbly cough and I winced. He might have a punctured lung, I realized, or something was draining blood into his throat. "We were quiet, but Ethan was really hurt and couldn't stop making these ow noises whenever he moved. I know he told me to stay still, but it was really hard."

"Where's Ethan now?" I couldn't help but ask. I had to know. "When did you see him last?"

She tipped her face up to meet my gaze and, so softly I could barely hear her, said, "He got out of the seat belt and fell down and cussed some more. The windows were broken an' he helped me get out." She mimicked climbing with her hands, which I could see now bore faint cuts and red marks, whatever healing factor she'd inherited from one or both parents hard at work. "We tried to walk, and he said he needed to get help for Mr. Waltrip. He said someone was coming and told me to run. We were near the ranch—I could see the lights on the goat barn, but it was down this big hill. I tried to run to it but"—she closed her eyes, fat tears trickling down her cheeks—"someone grabbed me. That mean guy who taped me up because I bit him and scratched him. Not like a coyote though," she added with a hint of bitterness. "Just like a kid."

"And Ethan?"

"He changed. It was pretty cool! I've never seen someone do it in person before! And he had a limp, but he ran, and he tried to fight the guys, but they were fast and not hurt like he was..." Opening her eyes, she met mine again and shook her head. "I don't know where he went. He didn't come with us though."

My heart gave a painful, funny lurch and seemed to stop for a moment as I thought of all the reasons why Ethan didn't go with her, wasn't brought back or didn't follow.

None of them were good.

Outside, the sky was darkening, and I knew from experience it would be cold in here soon. "I wish we had some blankets. Or heavier coats."

Mariska glanced up at the thin window near the ceiling and frowned. "I wish I could climb the walls. I wish I was like a gecko shifter or something."

"Do those exist?" I asked idly, an idea starting to bubble up in my thoughts. "Lizard shifters and stuff like that?"

"No." She laughed. "That'd be weird!"

The window was too small for either of us but the vent... I looked at Mariska, then back at the vent high up on the wall.

But not so high she couldn't reach it with a boost... "Mariska, you're very brave."

She shrugged. "I know. I rode a goat once."

Huffing a surprised laugh, I pushed to my feet. "Well, you're very brave, and very fast. And I think I have an idea to get you out of here."

"Just me?" she asked, her voice tiny. "I can't go on my own. I need to help Dad!"

"Well, you'll go first," I said. "Then help me get out."

She stared at me thoughtfully for a long moment. "And you promise you're not trying to get rid of me?"

"I promise. Um, but there might be spiders," I added, motioning to the vent. "Do you think you can handle it?"

Mariska nodded, bouncing on her toes. "Does it go outside?"

I definitely hoped so. "It should. Just... be careful, okay?"

She rolled her eyes. "Kinda late for that."

"Are you sure you're seven and not like a forty-year-old in there?"

Mariska wrinkled her nose at me, making a confused face. "Why do you and Dad ask me that?"

I laughed, unable to stop the sound from bursting out. "It just means you seem more perceptive than we're expecting."

"Dad said it means I'm a grumpy middle-aged person in a kid's body."

"Same thing, really. Okay, let's try this."

HOWL AT THE MOON

I wished we were in the same cell where I'd hid my phone earlier—at least then we'd have some light. Or, you know, a way to call for help somehow... It took some maneuvering and a scary amount of delicate balance, but I got Mariska onto my shoulders and lifted to the vent. "Are there screws?"

"Uh huh. But they're not really tight. Oh! I have an idea!" She wiggled, and I grunted as her foot dug into my chest. "Dang it! Hold on!"

Something metallic clicked, and she shifted her weight, pressing on the back of my neck hard enough to make it difficult to breathe. Suddenly, there was a tiny *plink*, and she gave a quiet little cheer. "I used my barrette like a screwdriver!" she announced. Three more wiggles and *plinks* followed. "I'm so awesome."

"You know, you're not wrong."

She dug her heels into my pecs again and gasped as she pitched backward. "Help!"

"Hold tight, Mariska. Okay, this is going to be scary. Can you pull up on the vent? Like you're getting out of a swimming pool?"

"I swim in the pond. There's no edge."

"How about getting onto the counter then?"

She was quiet as she assessed the space. "Maybe."

I patted her leg reassuringly. "It's okay. If it's too scary, we'll think of another plan."

"No! No! I need to help Dad! I'm not gonna just sit here while he's scared!" She leaned forward, and with a push off my chest and a flailing kick that nearly caught my temple, she was in the vent, her feet sticking out for a moment before she gave a fishtail flop and disappeared inside.

"Mariska?"

"It's dark," she called, her voice wavering. "What do I do?"

"Find the outside, kiddo. Don't go into the other rooms. *Only* outside!"

The sound of thumping and metal buckling was the only thing I heard for several minutes, and whispered swear words as she wiggled her way hopefully to freedom.

Finally, it was quiet. "Mariska?" I called softly.

Nothing.

I sank back down and closed my eyes. Please let her just run fast and far. Get off the property. Get to Shoot Well territory. Hell, run into Hopkins! Something!

The shuffle of feet on gravel startled me out of my panic spiral, dragging me to my feet as the sound of someone fumbling with the lock bounced around the room. After a moment, the door dragged open slowly and Mariska, dirty, sweaty, and red-kneed, grinned up at me. "These people are kinda dumb, huh? The locks are like the big slidey ones on the barn door at the ranch. Just go flip, slide, and out!" She grinned. But still looked tired and likely in desperate need of something to eat and drink.

"They're pretty awful," I said, shaking in a mix of relief and anticipation. It was late dusk, and the sound of life happening around us was muted but clear. A truck coming or going on the long drive to the house, voices calling to one another, and the ever-present sense of *flee, run, live* thrumming under my skin made my muscles twitch, senses on high alert as I looked around us quickly. "Okay, we're gonna have to run. Do you think you can?"

She nodded, but there was a hesitation. "My legs kinda hurt. I ran a lot last night, and I fell down too." She nodded at her scraped knees. "But I can do it!"

My own feet were aching, sore and cut up, bare. But I could deal with it better than a child could. I think. "Tell you what... You want to go for a piggyback ride?"

She shrugged. "Sure. But can we call it a pony ride instead because pigs scare me a little? Did you know they can eat an *entire* human body, bones and all?"

HOWL AT THE MOON

161

"Uh, yeah. How did *you* know that?"

"Discovery Channel. Oh! Did you know there's a body farm in Tennessee? You can donate your body to science there and they let it just rot in the woods and stuff?"

"Yes, I'm well aware. Here, climb on," I said, pulling her up to get on my back. "Don't choke me, okay?"

"Have you ever been to the body farm?"

"Once, in med school," I said.

"Oh my *god* that is awesome! Did it smell bad? What was it like? Were there zombies?"

"What?"

"I mean, there're werewolves so why not zombies?"

"Tell you what... you keep quiet until we get off this territory, and I'll tell you all about the body farm." *Like hell.*

She nodded, her head resting against mine. "Okay. But don't tell me it was no big deal because I'll know you're lying."

I huffed. "Yes, ma'am." Carefully, I crept to the edge of the cell block and peered out. The nearest person was close to the main house, a quarter mile or so away. The doors were facing away from the house, meaning we had cover for a bit, so long as we kept the block between us and anyone on ground level. The second floor, however... I glanced up. Two windows had heavy wooden shutters pulled, but another was uncovered. I couldn't see inside. If someone was peering out at us, I wouldn't know.

Damn it.

Nothing for it then, I thought, and started moving low and carefully away from the block, toward the low rise of hills I remembered from the drive to the makeshift morgue on the farthest edge of the property. I'd be able to find the old road into town if we kept heading this way, I was sure of it. Remembering the ride back with Samara, I knew we'd cut close to the route Hiller had taken, so there must be at least one point where I could get off the compound and onto the road, where it would be easier to get into town and hopefully off their territory before they noticed.

"Wait!" Mariska hissed. "Wait! Where's Dad?"

"We need to come back for him," I said. "Getting you to safety is first."

"No!" She bucked and twisted, flinging herself backward until I had to set her down or risk dropping her on the rocky ground. "Dad's in trouble! We can't, Landry! *Please!*"

"Mariska," I crouched low, silently cursing this delay even while I understood her panic. It was similar to what I was feeling for Ethan, I was sure of it. "We need help, okay? We can't do this on our own. I can't get both Waltrip and your dad out. And if we can get to Mr. Dunnigan, I bet we can get him to send some big, tough weres back to help."

She shook her head, lank hair flying with the vehemence of it. "No! We get him *now!* Mr. Dunnigan said they wouldn't help, remember? And Dad needs me! And... and..." she choked on a sob. "I need him."

I had known before we even got past her opening argument that I'd end up capitulating, but it didn't mean I felt confident about this. "Mariska, if we get caught, it's going to be really bad." I sighed. "I need you to do exactly as I say, without arguing, okay?"

She set her jaw mutinously, folding her arms across her middle as she glared.

"Look, I'll show you pictures of the body farm if you do what I say. And," I paused, closing my eyes on a sigh. "And I'll let you read some of my notes from med school labs."

She sniffed. "Deal."

THE LAST PLACE I'D seen Mal was in the house so that was as good a place to start as any. It wasn't terribly hard to figure out where he was—he was still kicking up a fuss which I was thankful for. It meant he was alive. It meant he still had some strength left. And it meant he'd be more likely to get the hell out of dodge and not argue about it. "Mariska, this is important," I whispered. We'd managed to slip in through the kitchen door, the mildew smell somehow worse in there than anywhere else in the house. "Do you remember my car?"

She nodded.

"I need you to get in it. And hide."

"*How?*"

"If it's locked, then just hide beside it or behind it, okay?" I muttered. "Stay out of sight and I'll be back with your dad soon, alright? If anyone other than me or your dad comes to you, *run*. Don't look back. Run as fast as you can. Follow the drive to the road and then turn left. Keep going. Stick to the shadows if you can and keep moving. We'll find you."

She stared at me, openly doubtful, but gave me a slow, considering nod. "And if you don't?"

"Then Ethan will."

"But my dad..."

"You'll see him again. Just please do what I say, alright? Hide."

She nodded again and slipped away in the thick shadows between the house and the cars. Mine was still where I'd parked it the day before. Or was it two days now? Mariska disappeared into the dark in silence and, after a moment, I heard the soft click of metal and a gentle thump.

I hoped it was my car door.

Chapter Eleven

The house was quiet but not empty. The faint sound of a television somewhere, the smell of recently cooked food mingling with the mildew odor, the press of my senses warning me that *others* were near, that I was on the verge of being prey. I moved quietly as possible, wanting to just run, to keep Mariska safe by not leaving her alone, but I forced my steps to be slow and cautious.

A rack of keys hung by the back door, and I nearly crowed with relief to see my familiar keychain with my car keys and house keys mingled in with the lot. I snagged them, shoving them deep into my pocket to keep from losing them because if I had to hot-wire a car to get out of here, we were all fucked. It wasn't far from the kitchen to the stairs, but it would mean being in the open for several yards, across the lit foyer and then the open staircase until I reached the second floor. At the kitchen door, I hesitated, swallowing the rising bile in my throat. *Remember practice. I worked on this with Ethan. There's more to being were than just shifting. Use my senses...*

It was still hard, despite the practice with Ethan. Hell, despite the fact it had been hardwired into me since childhood, using my senses effectively was still a burden at times, still anxiety-inducing. Because the part of me that was purely human was afraid of what the part of me that wasn't could do, could feel and hear and taste and smell. It—I—feared that part of myself that was just different. Not more, not better. Different. I didn't know if it was because it was simply the unfamiliarity of it that made me afraid, or if it was the human in me fearing the *other*, parts of myself at war. But I knew that, with each partial shift, it was becoming easier to allow. It hurt, but it passed. And I was afraid, but with

HOWL AT THE MOON

the change came a confidence, a certainty that what was happening was *good*, *right*.

But standing at the foot of the rickety stairs, waiting to see if I was about to be attacked? It was easier to lean into the fear than embrace the confidence.

Mariska is waiting. Don't be a dick, Landry! Move! I forced myself up the stairs, overriding that panic voice, and made my way down the dark corridor to the lounge. Inside, Mal was ranting, his voice raw and strained as he shouted for help, to open the goddamn door. A thump rattled it in the jamb, followed by a grunt. "God damn it! I'll kill you myself!" he roared. "Let me out!"

The door had a simple latch on the outside, easy to pull and lacking the necessity of keeping up with keys which made sense from a certain administrative standpoint, but in terms of keeping your prisoners locked away? The odds were definitely better for us than for the clan. I slipped the lock, and before I could turn the knob, Mal flung the door open and tackled me to the ground, his hands on my neck and thumbs pressing just right to do serious damage very quickly. Thankfully, he stopped mid-choke and gave a startled cry, flinging himself to one side at the sight of me on the floor beneath him.

"Great technique," I rasped. "Ten out of ten, would have you choke an enemy for me. Highly recommend."

"Oh my god," he sobbed. "Waltrip needs help and Mariska is gone and—"

"I know where she is. She's waiting. We need to move *now* though."

"Something's happening out there," he muttered, helping me to my feet. "About an hour ago, Samara and Hiller got into a shouting match. I don't know what happened after that, but there's a whole group of people setting up literal camp by the pole barn." He gestured toward the window. Against my better judgment, I strode over to peer out, and sure enough, at the very edge of the available view was a white tent, the sort you see in scary movies about viral outbreaks and zombies.

Just our luck if Mariska jinxed us about the zombies.

An RV sat on the far side of the tent, one of those fancy rockstar sized jobs that had actual room to move in. Mal joined me at the window. "I saw Samara heading out there a while back, but she hasn't come out yet. At least not that I could see."

Waltrip's labored breathing grew loud as he tried to stand. Mal and I rushed to his side, each of us taking an arm. "We need to go," Waltrip muttered. "Something's going wrong. The Associates..." He trailed off, blinking rapidly. "I told Mal..."

Mal growled under his breath, adjusting Waltrip's weight against him. "After we heard Samara and Hiller fighting, Waltrip said something about plans falling apart."

"There weren't any guards on duty downstairs," I muttered. "No one seemed to be in the house."

Mal's eyes were wide as he glanced between the window and the open door. "Holy shit."

I nodded. "Now. We need to go right fucking now."

Getting Waltrip down the stairs was not as hard as I'd worried it would be. Despite his injuries, he managed to walk while supported and only had a moment of wobbliness on the stairs. I couldn't imagine what it took for him to push through his lingering pain and injuries in order to keep from slowing us down.

By the time we reached the ground floor, Mal was visibly antsy. He was murmuring something over and over, too quiet for me to make out, but I was sure it was his daughter's name. Putting on a burst of speed, we made our way through the kitchen and out the back door. Outside, the rumble of voices and yips of coyotes were audible, drifting on a cool evening breeze. "Mariska," Mal whispered. "Where is she? You said she was waiting!" In a slightly louder whisper, he called her name again.

"Shut up," I muttered. "We're not alone out here. Waltrip, are you good?"

HOWL AT THE MOON

He nodded, wobbly. "Jesus, everything is moving. Swear to god, if I die from this head injury I'm gonna kill someone."

Mal glanced askance at us, and I shook my head. "I'd say it was the injury, but he talks like that even when he wasn't in a rollover accident."

"Was Mariska—"

"She's fine, I promise. Come on. My car is there. I told her to hide at the car."

We shuffled as fast as we could, a quiet mutual decision to fuck trying to be quiet and opt for speed. "I can't shift," Waltrip murmured. "If they come to us and you need to run, go. I can't shift to protect you. Too hurt."

"Shut up," I grunted, nearing the car. "I'll get you out of here even if we have to strap you to the roof like a surfboard."

Waltrip snorted and Mal made a startled little squawk of laughter as we reached the back of my car.

With no Mariska.

Mal shot me a wide-eyed, furious glare before shoving Waltrip against me, so I had to take all of his weight. "Mariska? Mariska, it's Dad! Come out, baby. It's okay, I promise!"

"You guys are the loudest assholes I've ever met!"

Waltrip groaned in disbelief (or maybe pain. Or both. Probably both). Tyler, holding a sleeping Mariska, slipped out of the thickest shadows between a jacked up truck and an SUV. "What the *fuck?*" I hissed. "What the fuck, Tyler?"

"Remember I told you I was following Justin?" He shrugged, nodding toward the house. "The Associates were heading here. So... looks like we're getting the band back together."

Mal made grabby hands at Mariska, and Tyler passed her off without hesitation. Mal's soft sob made Mariska snuffle and shift, but she didn't wake up. If anything, she snuggled in deeper, pressing her sweaty, dirty face against Mal's neck as he cradled the back of her head, tears streaming freely down his face. "I'm so sorry," he muttered. "I'm so, so, sorry, baby."

"Hey," I said, "you did nothing wrong, okay? We need to go. Now. We can have our nervous breakdowns later."

"Justin is with the Associates," Tyler murmured, staring past us at the soft glow of the encampment's lights. "I'm going to give you the keys to my truck and—"

"And nothing. You're not going in alone. We're getting Waltrip help, getting Mariska out of here, and then we're going to figure out what to do next," I said sharply. "Come on."

Tyler shook his head, still scowling. "I don't like leaving him here. They picked him up outside of Abilene. He's been with them three days already, and I don't like this."

"Tyler," Waltrip said, voice still rough and a bit thick, "going in alone is a damn fool thing to do. Ethan's here. And the weres in Shoot Well..." He trailed off.

Tyler rolled his eyes. "That's what I thought."

Loud voices and yips sounded, coming closer. Hiller's angry tone was clear among the tangle of sounds, demanding someone *go get her ass in here now.*

Yep. Time to go.

"We can all fit in the car," I started, but Tyler shook his head.

"My truck's down at the road. Pulled off into one of the ditches."

"We'll take you there, you follow us to Shoot Well," I ordered. Tyler quirked a brow but didn't argue.

Chapter Twelve

The Shoot Well Ranch was a solid fifteen-minute drive at ten miles over the speed limit which, honestly, was super not great of me to do since the drive was one long curve. "Whoever made the roads out here has never heard of a straight line!" I complained on yet another sloping, graduated turn.

"It's kind of fun," Mariska protested, still wrapped around Mal like an octopus. "But I might puke again."

Mal set to soothing her, occasionally offering shortcut suggestions. Finally, we reached the imposing gates of Shoot Well Ranch.

The imposing, very *locked* gates.

"Let me out," Mal said, setting Mariska in the seat beside him. "I can get them to open it."

Even as he scrambled out, two large wolves were trotting to the gate from the inside, and the rumble of an ATV getting closer resolved into Dunnigan himself riding one with a shotgun across his back. "It's all go here tonight on the farm," he announced, sounding equal parts exasperated and amused. "Mal. You look like shit."

"Feel like it too," he admitted. "Mariska's here."

"Thank god," Dunnigan said, motioning the wolves back and getting off his ATV to open the gate. It was electrically locked along with a more traditional heavy bar latch and a difficult to maneuver latch, which told me they were not fucking around with security.

He stepped back as the gate swung wide and called, "Follow me up to the main house. I'll show you where to park."

Mal climbed back into the car and Mariska wrapped herself around him once more as we slowly followed Dunnigan on his ATV. Glancing back, I saw a tall, very naked man, shutting the gate behind us.

Dunnigan led us to a wide, paved area near the sprawling ranch house, indicating I should park facing out. Mal cradled Mariska to his chest as Dunnigan jogged over to open the rear door and let him out. Mariska, yawning again, smiled. "Today sucked," she announced. "I was in a car wreck!"

"*What*?" Mal barked as Dunnigan said, "I know."

"She was with Ethan and Waltrip," I told Mal. "Ethan..."

"He's here," Dunnigan said, and the relief was so intense I sank to sit on the ground, heart pounding like it was trying to escape through my mouth. "He's pretty bad off with his leg, but he's here. Let's get y'all inside and see what we can fix up and what we need to summon Doctor Lafayette to handle."

"I'm a doctor," I reminded him. "Why does everyone forget that?"

"Because we're not dead?"

"Mariska!" Mal admonished gently.

"Come on," Dunnigan urged. "Inside. Shit's going off right now, and I'm not loving being out in the open with..." He trailed off, his eyes flicking between me and Mal.

With non-weres, I wondered. Non-shifters? Injured people?

Did it matter? Because I sure as hell didn't want to be out in the open either.

I held my shit together until Dunnigan led us into the ridiculously huge living room (seriously, if any real estate agent wanted to use the term 'great room' to describe the space, it would be entirely unironic). A few shifters lingered, talking in a small cluster around a desk, but what drew my attention, what I could only focus on, was Ethan.

"Oh my god," I exhaled, stumbling over my own feet to get to his side. "Ethan!"

HOWL AT THE MOON

171

He lurched up, trying to get to his feet, but between the way his leg was elevated and the shitty wrapping job someone had done on the wound, he only managed a sideways lean that nearly put him on the floor before I dropped to my knees beside him, grabbing him in a tight embrace as he slung one arm around my back, the other bracing himself in a sitting position. He breathed me in, his lips moving silently against my temple.

I love you too, I thought. I was terrified too. I'm so sorry I dragged you into this.

"You didn't," he murmured, and I realized I'd spoken aloud. "I made you bring me, remember? I said you needed help." His chuckle was mirthless and dry. "See how much I'm helping?"

"Ethan, stop," I ordered a bit more sharply than I'd meant to. "Talk to me about your injuries. Mariska said you were in a roll over. Waltrip—"

"Shit," he exhaled. "Is he—"

Dunnigan and one of his clan were bringing Waltrip in, helping him to one of the huge sofas around the room. "I need to help him," I murmured, and Ethan nodded, letting me go, though we were both obviously reluctant about that. "Waltrip," I called, and he turned his head toward me as I walked over. "I'm gonna poke and prod a bit, okay? Just to see how bad things are?"

"On a scale of no pain to *I think I just saw Jesus*, I'd say about a thirty," he muttered.

"I bet. Let me see your eyes. This is gonna suck." I checked his pupils, then gently palpated the goose egg on his head before checking the gash at his scalp. "I need to listen to you breathing, but I don't have a stethoscope, so don't get too excited here." He chuckled, the sound turning into a groan as I lowered my head to listen to his lungs. Even without assistance, I could hear a wheeze with each breath.

"He needs a hospital," I said, sitting back on my heels. "Not a clinic, not a house call, but a hospital. I think he's got some broken ribs, and that concussion is not good. The wounds are looking a little infected. No pus yet, but it's coming. My big worry, aside from traumatic brain injury and possible lung damage, is blood clotting and sepsis."

Dunnigan nodded, motioning to one of his clan. "Call Lafayette."

"I said a clinic isn't going to cut it."

"Lafayette has a connection in Wyoming. It's not ideal, but it's the best we've got. The hospital's small, but the staff is almost entirely shifter and were, or their spouses. It's the only safe place for us to go if we need more intensive care than Lafayette or home remedies can provide."

"Jesus, what do you people do for vaccines?"

Dunnigan shot me a confused look. "Go to CVS and stand in line like everyone else."

"Your bodies can accept them like a human?"

He shrugged. "I'm fifty years old and haven't had the flu in like a decade so I'm guessing so."

Waltrip groaned. "Don't mind me, just dying."

"You're not going to die," I scolded. "I'm still pissed at you, so you have to live long enough for me to yell at you later."

"Noted." He sighed and started to drift off.

"Carlton, keep an eye on him," Dunnigan ordered before I could ask for someone to monitor his breathing.

Ethan was sitting up by the time I turned to check on him. Mal was slouched at one end of the sofa, Ethan at the other, and Mariska curled up between, drifting in and out of a drowse as she tried to tell them about the vent adventure.

Dunnigan nodded toward the group at the far end of the room and motioned for me to come along. "They're shifters," I said. "I thought you didn't do business with shifters."

One of them broke away, smiling at me tiredly. "Hey, Doc. I was kinda hoping this would go better but..."

"Hopkins," I said, eyebrows creeping up in surprise. "Dunnigan, what's going on here?"

"These guys," Hopkins said, then paused, blushing slightly, "and gals. Sorry Melissa, Becky, Dian. Well, we're not thrilled with how things are going under Samara and we're working to change that, but now..."

Dunnigan sighed heavily. "Things are so far off the rails you can't even see the tracks."

A commotion of snarls and shouting drew our attention to the foyer, where two weres came in with Tyler held between them. He looked annoyed and dirty but unharmed.

"Tyler!" Ethan struggled up, cursing when his leg buckled. "Where the hell are your pants?"

"In his car," he said, nodding at me. "Good to see you too, favorite brother."

"What's going on?" Dunnigan snapped. "He's your brother?"

Ethan nodded. "I can vouch for him. He's my brother and works with Waltrip."

Waltrip groaned. "Freelance."

Tyler shook off his captors and, glancing around, grabbed a throw pillow to cover himself in front of Mariska. "I lost my trackers at the border of your territory. Whatever Samara's planned, it's beyond just trying to get her clan's old lands back. She's in deep with Garrow's crew."

"I think," Mal said softly, "we need to get our shit together right now and start opening up."

"You think?" Dunnigan muttered. "Alright. Someone get him some pants! Ethan, Mal, Landry, Hopkins and your lot... Kitchen. Now."

Our kitchen table gathering lasted until nearly dawn. Mariska had been put to bed in one of the guest rooms, gently sponged clean by Mal and slipped into a clean set of clothes someone had retrieved for her from the cottage she and Mal shared.

"I still think we should just go," Mal muttered. "Leave. Get Mariska as far from here as possible. Samara... she wasn't the woman I thought I married," he admitted. "The Samara I knew, she wouldn't think of turning her kid over to these people to... to..."

I laid my hand atop his and patted gently. He shot me a sideways, confused glance. "I know. Out of all the people in this room, I know what they do to kids. The two of us are the *only* ones who know, at least from our perspective. Whatever those ghouls think they're doing, it's not worth the harm."

"How many were there?" Dunnigan asked. "Before?"

"Before the others in our cohort died?" Mal asked bitterly. "More than I want to think about."

Tyler answered, "Diz says fifty."

My stomach dropped, every thought becoming white noise and screaming. "Fifty. Fifty children?"

"And adults." Tyler sighed. "More than Bluebonnet had on official records. They were using families of the scientists who worked for them, poor clan members desperate for money, desperate to help their kids..."

"Fucking hell," Ethan muttered, rubbing his hands over his face. "And they have Justin now."

"And the plan is to hand me and Mal over."

"And Mariska," Mal added, terse. "Mariska is most important to her for this little trade."

"Mariska and Landry," Hopkins corrected. "Since that neat little trick of his got witnessed, they're damn near frothing at the mouth about him."

I sank lower in my seat, face hot and ears ringing. "They can have me," I said. "If they back off Mal and Mariska. And Justin."

"No!" Ethan's sharp snarl made us all jump a little. "There's no way in fucking hell I'm letting you just throw yourself at them in the hopes they decide to not be monsters in exchange."

"Maybe," Tyler said thoughtfully, "maybe that's not a bad idea."

"Tyler!"

"No, Ethan, listen. We go back in the morning. When the sun is actually up. Mal asks to speak with Hiller. Goes along with shit. He's a distraction while some of us get Justin out, you know? And then"—he shifted his gaze to Dunnigan—"we call in every favor and bit of goodwill we can manage and offer whatever you want in trade for help."

"Wait, you said Hiller. Samara's the one in charge," Mal said. "She's the one who got this ball rolling."

"But Hiller's the one behind it," Tyler said. "Last night, while I was trying to get closer, before I ran into Mariska, I heard Hiller talking to some of the shifters on guard duty. Hiller's the one pushing hard for this trade right now. Samara was thinking of backing out. Apparently, he"—Tyler pointed to me—"said something that got under her skin yesterday."

"I just told her that trading us in wasn't going to save her," I muttered. "Something like that."

"Well, whatever it was got her thinking. She wanted to renegotiate. Just you for the hired help." Tyler shook his head. "Hiller was pissed."

"So, Hiller's taking over now?" Ethan asked. "There's been a coup?"

"Not yet. Or maybe. Who knows at this point."

Hopkins spoke up. "Hiller's been after Samara's position since he got to the compound. Even though he's a were and there's no way the clan would let that happen, he's sure..." He trailed off. "Well. We trust Hiller even less than Samara. Samara's grasping for ghosts, but Hiller?" He shook his head. "He's out for blood."

"Hiller left this clan under a cloud," Dunnigan said heavily. "He was violent. Attacked some humans in Denver, allegedly hunted some tourists for sport before he was stopped by one of the rogues outside Silverlode."

"For sport?" I rasped. "Holy shit."

"Some weres," Ethan said in a measured way, "they let the myths get to them. Live in their heads. End up thinking they're owed fear, that humans or weaker shifters and weres are deserving of whatever carnage they can dish out."

"And Hiller was one of them?" I asked.

Dunnigan looked very tired now. "He was close. Maybe he was all the way there. When he was cut out of the clan, it was after several incidents with higher-ranking members, and threats against the humans who do day labor here. He went running to Penny Mine within days. Samara was openly antagonistic toward us, had been for years by that point."

Hopkins nodded. "She was thrilled that Hiller came to her. He bowed and scraped just enough then, well"—he spread his hands—"skip ahead a few pages and here we are."

Tyler pushed himself to his feet, the too-big clothes hanging off him, making him look almost like the teenager I first knew him as over a decade ago. "This group is determined. They're building a new facility—hell, it's likely done by now since Diz's info is only as fresh as the last upload. And they need four of y'all to make this work. If they don't have you," he paused, meeting my gaze.

"They'll start over."

He nodded. "So, I'm going tomorrow. I'm getting Justin out. And then I'm gonna start taking them apart."

"Wait." Ethan pushed to his feet. "Don't go off half-cocked, Tyler. We should." He sighed. "We should call the IC."

Dunnigan sneered faintly. "What do you think they'd do, Stone? Come in and hold our hands while we talk about our feelings with the shifters?"

HOWL AT THE MOON

"No," Hopkins put in, sounding far less genial as he glared at Dunnigan, "but it's the closest thing we got to some sort of structure in our world. And I mean a wide-reaching one, not just each of us playing king of our own hills. If we call them in, they might be able to provide backing and support while we get shit settled. And making them aware of the associates and what's going on will mean more eyes on them and less chance for them to do what they did to Mal and Doctor Babin!"

Mal groaned. "I'm going to bed. Fuck all this. I just want my daughter to be safe, and all I'm hearing right now is more ways to make her world confusing and violent. I'm out."

No one tried to stop him because we all knew he was right.

Also, he looked like shit and needed the sleep.

Dunnigan broke the silence after a moment. "Call the IC in then, but I'm not offering my people up to get shot at and torn apart to satisfy your vendetta."

"It's not about us," Ethan protested. "Don't play dumb, Dunnigan. You know damn well that if Samara or Hiller has their way, your ranch is going to be an open grave as soon as they can manage it!"

"Stone," Dunnigan said in a low, threatening tone, "your clan is your business. Mine is mine. You're welcome to stay here the night, but come tomorrow, once you leave this property, that's it. Your welcome is over."

Ethan stared at him for a long moment, his expression unreadable, before nodding sharply. "Understood."

We were shown to a small guest room next to Mal and Mariska. Tyler had sloped off outside as soon as the meeting broke up, Hopkins behind him. But all I cared about was sleep, and possibly food, but mostly being with Ethan as we curled into the too-soft bed and, instead of talking or even making love like I wanted, we fell into heavy, dreamless sleep.

Tyler shaking me awake only a few hours later, when the sun was finally up but not high, was an unpleasant thing that made me want to claw his face. "Come on," Tyler murmured. "We need to get going. Hopkins is gonna try to help from the inside, but I don't know if they realized where he was last night or not."

Ethan struggled to sit up and groaned. "Goddamnit!"

"He's not coming with us," I told Tyler. "I don't know what Dunnigan wants us to do with him, but he's not coming."

"Lan," Ethan began but sighed when I swung around to glare at him. "Okay. Let me talk to Dunnigan. Kiss a little ass. I'll buy us some goodwill at least long enough for you to get back."

I nodded. "Keep Mal and Mariska in sight. Just in case."

"I'm coming," Mal said in the doorway. "I have to. Samara... Samara might listen to me."

"Did she before?" Tyler asked archly. "Why would she now?"

"Because," Mal sighed, "she has to. I mean, I want her to have to. This is our daughter's life she's playing with. I need to at least try."

Tyler looked less than thrilled but didn't argue. Ethan was staring at Mal with a searching expression before relaxing a little and offering me a small smile. "He really does remind me of you sometimes."

"It's the Lycaon," I joked. "It makes us charming, handsome, and idealistic."

"And ridiculous," Tyler muttered. "We leave in ten. Be ready."

Mal trailed after him, calling softly for Mariska.

"I don't envy him that goodbye," Ethan murmured.

"We have one of our own."

He shook his head. "It's a *see you later*. Not goodbye. Because I'll never forgive you if you get killed or try to be a big damn hero and give yourself up or some bullshit."

"Well. Can't have that," I said, reaching for him hesitantly. He closed the distance between us swiftly, pulling me against his chest and into a deep kiss that verged between filthy and desperate. His fingers pressed bruises into my back and hip even as his breath shook against my face. I clung to him, fingers sank into his hair, leg flung across his good hip, as we kissed until we burned for air. Finally, we pulled apart, and Ethan's eyes were shiny as he looked down at me. "See you for dinner?" I offered, breathless.

He nodded. "You'd better. Because I have plans."

Reluctantly, I stood and started to dress in the clothes I'd had on the day before, stiff with sweat and dirt. It made my skin crawl and throat feel thick with disgust, but I had no choice. Finally, I offered Ethan a small smile. "I'm thinking Italian for dinner?"

He nodded. "I'll see what I can do." When I opened the door, he called out sharply, "Landry, I love you."

"I love you too."

He sighed. "See you tonight."

WE PARKED IN PENNY Mine, behind an old theater that had last seen life in the eighties judging by the sun-bleached posters in the display cases out front. A tattered *For Sale or Lease: Commercial Use Only* sign dangled from the front marquee. A few shops were open at that hour of the morning, and I had the feeling they were the only functioning shops in town. A feed and grain store, a small grocery store that looked more like a convenience store than a place that sold actual healthy food, and a very tired looking CVS with a sign proclaiming: *Minit Clinic Inside!*

"Christ," Tyler muttered. "Why does Samara want this place, anyway?"

"It's not as bad as all that," Mal said quietly, his face flushed as he looked up and down the street. "It's home for a lot of folks. And they get by as best they can. Samara doesn't care about that, though. She doesn't want Penny Mine the town. She wants the territory. What it represents. The people in this town won't know one way or another who has the land when it comes to weres and shifters, but the clans will. And Samara is bound and determined to come out on top."

"Not if Hiller has his way," Tyler said. "If the Associates decide he's the one they want to hitch their wagon to when it comes to getting what *they* want long-term, Samara doesn't stand a chance."

"Something Hopkins told you?" I asked lightly.

"Yeah. That and a bit of snooping on my own last night. Come on. It's about two miles through the grasslands, and I want to get moving before it gets all snakey."

"It's too cold to get snakey," Mal said. "Trust me, I've lived here most of my life."

We were about a quarter mile into the trek when he added, "Spiders, though..."

"Oh, fuck you," I muttered, and Mal laughed softly. We kept to the edge of the territory, heading for the rocky outcropping where the mine was an attractive nuisance for bitey things, tetanus, and traumatic injuries. Once we reached the mine, Tyler shed his clothes, and I shoved them in the empty backpack we'd taken from my car.

The fact it was a *Sassy Dragon Princess* backpack had no bearing on my masculinity, thank you very much. The fact it was a tiny bag might have though. Tyler kept ahead of us, his senses far keener than ours, and we made our way closer to the compound itself. Signs of life started to pick up as we got within half a mile: the sound of raised voices, of vehicles, and a generator roaring. Tyler nudged us back, tugging at our jeans until we dropped low.

"There's a fucking camp," Mal breathed. "I saw the big tent last night but this..."

"Looks like her mercenaries have arrived," I muttered. "That barn there? That's where they had the bodies of the shifters." People were going back and forth from the barn to the tent, a regular circuit. Some were carrying boxes and pieces of equipment. Others were just hustling along.

HOWL AT THE MOON

"Are they setting up something?" Mal asked quietly. "Like... I don't know. Improving the morgue?"

I shook my head as Tyler huffed in disagreement. "I think... I think maybe they're setting up a lab."

Mal made a low, unpleasant noise and I could only agree. "Maybe they don't want to wait to get us out of here."

"If it's a lab setup, it's not something that's long term. There're a dozen places in town they could easily buy for something like that. Hell, there's land cheap enough out here so they could build a dedicated space." And that thought brought me up cold and short.

Tyler moved in a low crouch, us following until we got closer. He stopped us again and pawed at the ground, pointing his sharp muzzle toward the encampment.

"Here goes nothing?" I asked him. He gave a soft bark of agreement. "Okay then. Let's go."

Tyler moved swiftly, not at full speed so we could keep up, keeping the buildings between us and them as much as possible. We reached the back of the pole barn and he stopped again, sniffing the air. He hesitated, visibly confused, and shook himself.

"What is it boy, Timmy's fallen into the well?" I murmured, earning a sharp (and deserved, I admit it) nip to my hand as Mal snorted. Tyler took a few steps toward the barn, paused, then a few toward the big white tent. He sniffed the air again and shook himself, his gaze zeroing in on the RV that had been parked there last night, then started loping toward it.

"I hope this is something and not Tyler deciding to go Mad Max with a motor home," Mal said as we jogged behind him.

The RV was unlocked and inside someone was talking.

"This would be easier if you had thumbs," I muttered at Tyler, who bared his teeth at me in either a grin or *fuck off*. Both, most likely. Mal eased the door open, and the owner of the voice became clear.

Hiller.

"You're going to tell them you fucked up," he said, tight and low. "You're going to tell them you're a pathetic liar and *beg* forgiveness. I want to see you on your knees, Samara. I want to see you being the piece of shit you really are."

Samara's reply was a high-pitched whine and some muffled words.

"Gagged?" Mal mouthed. I nodded, and we eased back. Tyler's hackles were up as we moved away from the door. "What now?" Mal whispered.

Tyler's ears cocked back, and his lips curled.

"I know," I murmured. "Someone's coming."

Mal looked around frantically for a place to hide, but Tyler didn't give us a chance. He threw his head, indicating the RV, then set out at a fast run, disappearing around the front of the RV. Shouts rang out and he came out running in the other direction, heading for the tent. A handful of shifters followed and two large men in black, tactical get ups with matching tattoos on their biceps.

"Jesus," I muttered. "His arm's bigger than my head."

"Imagine them as wolves," he muttered. "Fuck."

Inside the RV, Hiller's voice rang out. "Say it, Samara!"

I exchanged a look with Mal and opened the door, stepping up onto the metal stair to peer into the RV. "I was right. This is a fucking rockstar set up."

Samara sobbed behind the duct tape over her mouth, cloth sticking out around it where it had been stuffed between her lips to muffle her further. Her arms and legs were all but mummified together with more tape, and she was strapped to a folding chair with lengths of bungee cord and rope. Hiller had one moment where he looked startled, but it quickly melted into annoyed amusement. Easing into the RV, Mal was right behind me, pulling the door shut.

"You can't even escape right," Hiller sneered. "Saves me time, though. I won't have to waste the Associates' gift by tracking you down."

HOWL AT THE MOON

Samara gave a futile lunge against her bindings, a growling, choking sound in her throat. "She can't shift," Hiller smiled, reaching out to tug one of Samara's curls, so like Mariska's. "It would break her bones, you know? Her body has no room to move."

"I don't know what they promised you, Hiller, but you're not going to get it," I said. "They're using you like they were using her."

Hiller rolled his eyes. "Okay, let's go. You give me your good guy speech, and I'll villain monologue, we'll fight. Then what? Your cop boyfriend comes riding in on a white horse to save the day? Or better yet, the Shoot Well clan finally unclenches and offers to help?"

"I know what you did," I said, pretending like I hadn't heard a word he'd just said. "I know about the man you killed in Denver. The tourists you hunted. Who else, Hiller?"

He laughed. "Did Dunnigan tell you that? Did he forget to mention why? The man in Denver tried to buy out the ranch and wasn't going to take no for an answer. The tourists were investors. They wanted to bulldoze Shoot Well and turn it into one of those shiny bedroom communities."

"And you want to be in charge of it," Mal said. "You don't give a fuck that it's clan territory, so long as you're the one everyone answers to. Whether it's a ghost town or a suburb. That's true, isn't it?"

"Samara thought she could trade us in, trade her *daughter* in, to get her clan's glory back. But you're not even that principled, are you? To you, it's all about power. Control." I took a step toward him, my hands out where they could be seen. "Samara didn't think it through, did she? But you did. You'd be getting rid of the *mutts* all while getting some powerful new friends."

Hiller huffed. "You're too stupid to understand any of this."

"I can understand. Samara made a bad decision out of some sense of loyalty to her family. You're doing it out of greed."

"Does that make it better or worse?" Hiller asked, turning to fully face me. Samara sagged behind him, not even bothering to struggle.

"Six of one." I shrugged, affecting a nonchalance I definitely didn't feel. "Either way, me and Mal and even Mariska would end up dead in the end. Used up, turned into spare parts in a lab."

Samara made a choked, sobbing sound. Mal flinched, looking away.

I didn't blame him. The truth was violent and awful and was not going to end well for someone.

"They're not going to help you, Hiller," I said, moving in for the metaphorical kill. "They're using you. You hand us over, they leave you high and dry. You're a traitor to your clan. You're a murderer. You have no leadership here. You're of no use to them once you hand us over."

Hiller swept his hand out, knocking a stack of plastic boxes and soda cans off the counter, everything clattering and loud. Samara jerked back, her chair tipping to one side, wedging her between the open bathroom door and the wall.

"You're a liar," Hiller ground out. "You don't know what you're talking about and trying to, what, scare me? Trying to scare me out of doing this is pathetic!"

Samara made a low, angry noise and wiggled to a sitting position.

Hiller whipped around and kicked out at her, aiming to shove her back down, but she was fast.

And unbound.

Samara rolled to one side and was on her feet before Hiller even finished moving. "You're not taking my clan from me," she spat. Hiller growled and lurched toward her. Samara was shaking but quick, dodging him and moving around to stand between us and him, but I did not for one moment think she wanted to protect us. We were just in her way.

"Samara," Mal began, but I shook my head.

"Move. Get out. Now."

We backed toward the door, stumbling over our feet as Hiller and Samara clashed. Mal fell out first, providing me a bony landing spot. "Fuck! Get off me!"

HOWL AT THE MOON

The sounds inside the RV were distinctly feral now, growling and snapping. A few shouts went up behind us, but no one came over. God only knows what they thought was happening. Soon a sharp yelp and whine went up, and the two of them tumbled out, one lithe, bloodied coyote and a huge wolf with a deep gash across his throat and more on his flanks. Samara did not give him time to get to his feet, twisting as she fell and landing atop him, her teeth sinking into his throat. Hiller thrashed once, twice, then was still.

"Oh my god," Mal breathed.

I nodded. Nausea was thick in my throat, but I couldn't look away as Samara, bloodied and blowing, sank back onto her haunches, then tipped to one side, slowly changing back into human form. Mal shed his jacket and threw it over her as she stirred, the red marks from her bindings clear on her skin even amidst the gore staining her face, chest, and limbs. Pretty much everything.

"My clothes," she rasped. I nodded and very gingerly stepped over Hiller's still body, caught partially shifted and definitely, definitely dead, easing back into the RV. Her clothes were near the bathroom door, tape still stuck all over and fabric torn and bloody in places.

"Um, here." I pulled out Tyler's t-shirt from the bundle in the backpack. Samara made a face but took it, Mal and I both turned our backs as she pulled it on.

It came down to the middle of her thighs, and she gave it a few annoyed tugs as she tried to make it longer to no avail. Samara blew a sigh through her nose in a very canine noise of annoyance before turning her attention back to us. "You didn't come to save me," she said after a moment. "I should kill you both, or tell the others... you're here to stop what I'm doing. Without you and Mariska, I'll lose it all. The territory, the clan... Everything. My entire family is buried here," she added, her voice thin now and distant. "If I lose this to the weres, then I've lost it all."

"Samara," Mal said quietly, "you already have."

She jerked her head up to glare at him, but her face crumpled a moment later. "I can't stop everything, but I can try. Follow me and do as I say."

"I don't think I'm comfortable with that," I murmured.

She smiled at me. "And I don't think you have a choice."

Chapter Thirteen

The low rumble of engines washed over the encampment as we followed Samara through the maze of cars and trucks. We hadn't made it far before the heavy weight of impending chaos broke and all hell followed.

Samara tensed, turning to see who was coming and let out a low, snarling string of curses. "If you want to live, keep moving. Come on!" She ducked between two SUVs and we, perforce, followed. A dozen or more people in those dark tac clothes we'd noted earlier pelted past, some shifting as they ran which was frankly impressive and terrifying. "Shoot Well," she growled. "They came to us!"

"Dunnigan said he wouldn't help," I murmured. "What's happening?"

Mal shook his head. "If Dunnigan's changed his mind, something must've made him."

Samara stood again and motioned for us to follow. The sound of fighting was loud and brutal, howls and snarls mixed with shouting, a gunshot, heavy and wet thuds. More weres ran past, but they didn't even slow when they saw us, their focus on the fighting alone.

"How did you get free?" I asked as we crept toward the giant tent. "Was that all some ruse to trick Hiller? How did you get the tape off?"

She shot me a look and rolled her eyes. "The bathroom door. The edge was sharp enough to break the fibers."

I shook my head. "In another life, I bet I'd have liked to know you."

"In another life, you wouldn't be here," she noted. Stopping outside the tent opening and smoothing her ruined dress. "Follow me. This is the only way to get you out of here."

"So, you've changed your mind, too," Mal noted.

She paused then affected nonchalance with a small shrug. "Not as such, but... I don't want to be what Hiller said. And I could see it. This is the only way now." She pushed the opening wide and strode in. The pair of us followed, wide-eyed and on high alert.

Inside, it was indeed set up like some sort of lab, but not to the extent I'd imagined. Just a few things, mostly instruments rather than anything mechanical, set up on a long table. Several people who looked like they knew what they were doing were huddled around a laptop at one end, frowning thoughtfully and muttering to one another as one of the weres in black came out of a side door, arms laden with equipment.

Oh.

Oh, cripes. It was for the morgue. I recognized those tools anywhere.

They were improving it, expecting more use.

Shit.

Samara didn't let us have time to panic—she called out, "Where are Doctors Klein and Mattison?"

One of the people looked up, frowning at us. "This is off limits, ma'am. Mr. Hiller assured us you were aware of the change in plans and—"

Samara's shift was fluid and swift as she ran toward them, her body arcing and twisting, her clothing falling around her as she hit the table, scattering the electronics and the tools, hitting the researcher who'd been speaking in the chest and taking him to the ground. The others shouted in dismay and shock, one of them shifting to join the fray, but Samara was faster than them.

"Landry!" Tyler emerged from one of the tent flaps, mussed and red-faced, long scratches across his torso. Under his arm, a familiar figure leaned. Justin looked... awful, really. Gaunt, patchy redness on his face and throat. His nails dirty and cracked, hair a tangled, oily mess. His eyes were wild and frantic as the fighting raged behind us, a sud-

HOWL AT THE MOON

den shout and influx of wolves, coyotes, and human forms pouring out through the opening in the tent. "I need to get him out," Tyler shouted over the noise. "They had him in a fucking kennel! A *kennel!*"

Mal shrank back as one of the men in the black gear roared past, bloody and aiming to take down a wolf that had presumably his gore on their muzzle. "We'll get our asses kicked," he muttered to me. I nodded, faintly aware of the new familiar pressure building in my bones, pulling at my muscles.

"Maybe so," I allowed. "Shit, get inside!" More were coming, some on ATVs but more on foot, heading toward where we stood out in the open. Tyler ducked back into the tent and we followed, finding ourselves in a storage space full of boxes and one large, unsettling dog kennel, the door twisted off its hinges. Outside the fighting seemed to grow more chaotic, if at all possible. Roaring, screaming, the sounds of metal and bodies breaking. We had to move, to get the hell out while we could. "Do you have a knife or anything on you?" I asked Tyler.

He looked at his naked body, then back to me. "Guess."

"There has to be something you can use as a weapon. Grab something heavy or sharp or both and go!"

Tyler nodded, shouldering Justin who let out a pathetic gasp of dismay at being lifted, and swiftly made his way toward the tent flap, Justin over his shoulder. One of the Associates saw us standing back and pointed, saying something to the mercenary beside him.

I'm guessing it wasn't, 'Look at those two lovely gentlemen just minding their own business,' because the mercenary bolted for us, not shifting but I knew he would soon—that seemed to be their go-to move. Run then shift at the last moment for maximum surprise.

It'd be way more surprising if they didn't all do it like some messed up stunt team routine.

I felt the pressure build, my muscles locking in my hands and arms as the change started to happen whether I liked it or not. "Go, Mal," I rumbled, my voice thick and rough as my body forced itself to shift at least in part.

"Like hell," he muttered, and reached down to grab one of the metal tent poles, yanking until a segment came free. As weapons went, it would be fairly light and not terribly effective.

I mean, unless you drove it into someone's eye like Mal just did because holy shit would that stop a merc in their tracks.

"Mal!"

"I have a lot of anger built up right now, Landry, and I'm going to use it. They want to take my daughter, they're getting fucking stabbed!"

And I mean... okay, fair. A sharp twist of pain bowed my back, and I went to my knees, Mal's shrill cry of rage and fear rushing past as he threw himself into the fray. Another black clad were ran at me, and this time, I was (mostly) ready. He wasn't expecting the weird abomination I had become in that moment, my hands curved into claws, my teeth elongated, jaw jutting.

This halfway state *hurt*. I hated it, but at the same time, it was going to hopefully save my ass. The man drew up short when I rocked to my feet, an expression of horrified disgust on his features for just a moment before he shook it off and started his own change. I lashed out, raking my claws over his face and making him scream in shocked pain. I didn't linger, running toward where I heard Mal shouting. Around me, were and shifter alike were injured, some dead. Samara had leaped onto a table and let loose a howl that some of her clan answered but others... They were ignoring her in favor of a smaller, but very stocky coyote with sandy blond fur and a loping gait. He barked and yipped, which seemed to be a command because some of the coyotes formed a small pack and shot off after a were that was trying to escape through the opening.

I was glad Ethan wasn't there even while I desperately wished he was beside me. My shifting, partial as it was, made me feel strong, made me feel different from scared Landry Babin who had no idea what the hell was going on so much of the time. But beneath that newfound

HOWL AT THE MOON

boldness, that scared Landry remained. The one who desperately wanted to be anywhere but here, who wanted someone to tell him it was okay, and they wouldn't let anything bad happen to them.

My distraction nearly did me in. Someone pinned me, their teeth snapping at my neck as I pushed against their chest, shouting in shock when their claws dug into the meat of my shoulders to pin me down. A flying dark shape hit them broadside and knocked them away, letting me roll to my feet in time to see Tyler's familiar wolfy grin flash at me before he went back at it with the were who tried to kill me.

"Justin?" I called.

Tyler shot me a look. A reminder he couldn't talk right now for several reasons.

I had to assume he was safe, at least for now. A quick look showed me Mal struggling with a shifter who had apparently decided Samara was right, his bloody tent pole bent all to hell as he shoved it into the shifter's mouth to keep from being bitten. I turned to swipe at one of the unshifted weres who still swarmed the fight, knocking him back when he started toward the coyote who I thought might be Hopkins.

A few of the wolf heads snapped up, and then more. The coyotes paused in the fight as well.

Then I heard it.

Vehicles, heavy and slow, crunching up the drive.

Shit. I didn't think we were going to survive this if there were more of those fucking weres-for-hire.

A large, lone wolf appeared in the doorway, threw back his head, and howled. Outside, several more howls went up. The fighting inside stopped entirely, but the tension shivered in the air like a tangible thing. The wolf stepped aside, and a man in a very expensive-looking suit stepped in, followed by a woman who could've been a Greek statue she was so beautiful. "My name is Harold Gellar. I am the lead security liaison for the International Committee of Were-Shifter Relations. If you don't want to be taken into custody, I suggested you shift now so we can better identify you."

TYLER, MAL, AND I WERE cleared pretty much right away. A handful of the mercenaries escaped, as did all the Associates, melting away like a bad smell.

That didn't cheer me as much as I thought it might—if they disappeared then they had help. I just couldn't tell from who, and my head hurt too much to dwell on it for long. The IC had brought a cadre of agents, three huge SUVs, and a small bus with the bland logo *IC TOURS* on the side. The agents were unsmiling and no-nonsense as they rounded up the remaining mercenaries and started collecting the shifters who had been on Samara's side. Gellar and his companion approached us where we sat against the wall, staring down at us for a long moment before the woman spoke, producing a business card between two fingers and gingerly handing it to me. "Contact us at your earliest convenience."

I nearly burst out laughing, but I managed to swallow it down and accept the card, which I promptly shoved into my pocket to better forget it.

"Your abilities have not gone unnoticed," she added with a slight tilt of her head. "Be aware of that fact as you make your choices."

"Well," Mal muttered. "That's not ominous at all."

"I think you'll find," Tyler said, "this is pretty much a typical Tuesday for Landry."

"Oh, fuck off," I muttered, and for the first time in what felt like days, I closed my eyes and cried.

Chapter Fourteen

"Yeah, this is gonna hurt like a bastard." I sighed, gingerly tugging torn fabric away from a Shoot Well were's belly wound. "It's not too deep though, all things considered. You should get stitches."

The were winced, hands coming up to protect her belly before I could push them back down gently. "Ain't a doctor nearby who we can trust."

"Uh, hi? I didn't go to medical school just for fun."

She rolled her eyes. "Aren't you a pathologist? The kind that cuts up dead folks?"

I shrugged. "Still, I had to do rotations through general and emergency medicine. And this"—I pointed to her stomach—"needs stitching."

She looked down at her wound and sighed. "Well, I guess I can cover the scars with a bad ass tattoo later, huh?"

"Whatever floats your boat." The first aid kit Dunnigan had produced was one of those huge jobs that preppers like to stockpile. When I gave him a *really* look, he shrugged. "I have a ranch to maintain, Doctor Babin. People get hurt."

The were—her name, I finally found out, was Deborah (*if you're gonna see me topless might as well introduce myself*) handled the stitching well, but the antiseptic was another thing entirely.

She could put Mariska's cursing to shame, really.

Most of the injuries were similar—a few stitches here, a brace there. "I can't prescribe anything, but some of these folks are going to need antibiotics, at least a prophylactic course," I noted to Hopkins when he came over to see how I was doing.

He nodded thoughtfully. "I bet Doctor Lafayette will make a house call if we ask him nice."

I couldn't keep the surprise off my face, apparently, because Hopkins laughed and nudged me none too gently. "He's the only shifter friendly doc for like a hundred miles. 'Course I know who he is. And I know he ain't here, and you are so I want to say thank you, Doctor Babin." He nodded toward the injured—from both sides, thank you very much—sitting on the floor or leaning against the wall, waiting for what would come next. "I know this is a bit out of your wheelhouse."

"Oh. Well." My face heated—I never did take compliments or gratitude well.

"Now. don't you act like this was nothing." He looked out over the scattered destruction, the upended equipment and the blood, the injured... The bodies had already been moved into that damn morgue, waiting for their home clans to arrange pick up, or in the case of the unaffiliated, their families. "This was... Well, it was fucking awful. But I figure it's like one of those crucible things from high school chemistry. Burning off the impurities."

"That is actually kind of terrifying to think of," I admitted. "Do you think this had to happen?"

Hopkins sighed. "No, I do not. But it did happen, and now we just have to rebuild and go forward."

A small commotion drew Hopkins away as the doors slid open and three suit clad men, one of whom I recognized, entered. Cullen was purse-lipped and looked disgusted as usual, but the other two men were bland as oatmeal. They might as well have been walking through a grocery store for how interested they looked in the goings-on. "Shit, here we go."

I watched as Hopkins strode over to them, ready to glad-hand and shoot the shit and whatever it was the cowboy types did when meeting people. I thought about getting up, but my body was too tired, too sore and too crashed after all the go-go-go of the past week.

HOWL AT THE MOON

"You do get used to it," Samara said, sitting beside me. She was still bloody, dried blood overlaid with fresh. Her dress was beyond redemption, but she didn't seem to care, tugging on the hem to cover her knees as she got settled.

"This?" I asked, gesturing to the barn, "or the shifting?"

"Shifting. Though most of us learn when we're children. I suppose it's more difficult for you."

"Bones already fused and all," I murmured. Is this real life? What is happening here? I'm just talking with her like no big deal?

She nodded, staring at the smear of blood where one of the dead—or maybe a badly injured survivor—had been dragged nearby. "Are you going to ask?"

"Has your answer changed since earlier?"

"Not really," she admitted. "It was what I thought was right. I still think it is, but maybe... maybe not as right as it was presented to me."

"So, you'd still give up your daughter? Mal and me? Justin?"

She took a long, deep breath and sighed. "If I could see a way to give the Associates what they wanted without the four of you being... potentially lost, then yes. Blood samples, perhaps. Or medical records."

"That's not how they work."

"I'm aware."

Her far-off stare made me think that, just maybe, she was seeing the near miss we just had. Maybe regretting the things she'd set into motion?

Turning back to me, she smiled a little, lifting one shoulder in a shrug. "I wanted what was best for my clan. I wanted to right wrongs."

"But you wanted to do it at our expense."

She fell silent, staring at the blood on the floor. After several minutes, Hopkins led the IC group over and Samara pushed herself to stand. I got to my feet far more slowly, audibly creaking. "Ms. Goode," Cullen said, nodding. "Doctor Babin. You look... awful."

"Thanks."

"Mmm. Considering you usually look terrible, that's something." I snorted as he turned away to address Samara. "This is Mr. Markham and Mr. Dodson. Mr. Markham is the lead agent in charge of the Mountain West division of the IC and Mr. Dodson is the North American security chief for the organization."

Samara held out her hand to greet them out of habit, I think, but drew back when she saw the blood. "Gentlemen. I assume you're here to negotiate again."

"Hardly," Dodson, a tall and gaunt man who could have been anywhere from thirty to fifty murmured. "We're here to offer you help, of a sort."

For a moment, Samara's eyes flared bright with excited hope, but the spark burned out quickly as his meaning hit home. "Ah. Taking me away, then?"

Markham nodded. "We're offering you an opportunity to receive help, and also remove you from this situation while allowing your clan to rebuild."

"My clan—" she began, but Dodson cut her off.

"We're not in the business of meddling with clan affairs, but the chances of your clan allowing you to remain in control after this"—he flicked his fingers to indicate, well, everything—"are slim to none."

"It's true," Hopkins said. "Samara, those of us who wanted to split off, we don't trust you. We can't. And the ones who followed you... Well, they're either dead or they ran off when it became clear they were on the losing side."

"But this is *my clan*," Samara whispered. "My home. My territory."

"This is clan territory," Hopkins corrected. "Clan. Not yours. Ours. And we're going to keep it that way. Our status doesn't come from how much we control. It's how well we do it. How well we work together." Straightening, Hopkins lifted his chin and announced, "I'll be stepping in as the clan lead, unless anyone objects."

Samara snarled softly. "I do, Goddamnit!"

HOWL AT THE MOON

"Anyone else?" Cullen called out. "Anyone object to Terrence Hopkins taking over as clan leader?"

"Hop's kept our asses out of the fire while Samara went wild," someone called out.

"He's not a fucking mass murderer," someone else muttered. More voices chimed in, mostly for Hopkins, some suggesting a few other names. Finally, Hopkins raised his hand and silence fell.

"I'll stand as leader pro tem. After we clean the compound out and ensure we're safe, we'll hold an election."

"Clan leader election," Samara said. "Seriously?"

Dodson smiled thinly. "It's a brave new world, it seems. Now, Ms. Goode, you have a choice. You can come with us. Get help. Or we leave you here, and Hopkins decides what happens to you."

Hopkins tried to look like a hard man, a man who would do something violent or terrible, but he only looked tired. Samara sighed, though, and nodded to Markham. "I'll come. I... I need help. I need help."

Cullen stood aside as Markham and Dodson led Samara away, picking across the puddles of blood and piles of fur and god knows what. "Are you sure you want to do this, Hop?" I asked quietly.

He nodded. "I do. It's why I organized the dissidents. It's why I put myself on the line to try to stop her. This is my clan too. And my parents before me. And their parents. Hell, most of us here are from families that came with the original Goodes to settle our territory. And we were hurt by the clan wars, too. Not just Samara. But those of us who fought back? We know that the clan is more than what we own, how big we are. And that's all we want, to be a clan. A real one. The property, the status, sure it'd be nice but..." He trailed off, looking over his people. "It's more important that we keep one another safe and support one another."

Someone called out for Hopkins, so he hurried away, leaving me and Cullen just standing there awkwardly. Finally, Cullen cleared his throat and gave me a small nod. "You did well, Doctor Babin. More violent than I'd expected but... you did well. And I'm assuming you met Doctor Lafayette?"

"I met Marty," I said. "The nurse."

"Marty. Oh, him. He's... acceptable."

A small commotion at the door resolved into Ethan, Mariska, and Dunnigan clattering in. Mal broke away from the shifter who was gently bandaging the cut over his eye and sprinted to scoop up Mariska. Dunnigan peeled off to find Hopkins, but Ethan made a limping beeline for me. Cullen sighed and stepped back but didn't move away.

"Oh, thank god," Ethan muttered, grabbing me by the shoulders and kissing me. I uttered a muffled squeak of surprise, and he smiled into the kiss. After a moment, my hands were in his hair, and I was melting into him. *He's okay, I'm okay. Everyone I care about is okay. We're going home and getting the fuck out of dodge and... and... and...*

I can't help it. My brain function doesn't do so well when Ethan kisses me.

Finally, he pulled away and pressed his forehead to mine. "When Dunnigan sent his people, I nearly lost my shit," he whispered. "I couldn't stop thinking of you caught in the middle of a clan war, of what could happen. I..." He let out a shaking breath and pulled back enough to look me in the eyes. "I feel like I failed you by not being here."

"Ethan." I pinched his chin lightly between my thumb and forefinger, making him focus instead of close his eyes. "You're still injured. You would've likely been hurt worse. I'd never forgive you if you tried to do something brave and ridiculous like protect me while at like 75 percent capability."

"Gentlemen," Cullen said lightly. "As charming and unnecessarily emotional as this reunion is, I have a schedule to keep. There is a proposition the IC wishes to offer you."

HOWL AT THE MOON

"Me?" I asked. "I already did the freelance shit for y'all and see how it ended up."

"Yes." Cullen smiled faintly. "With a catastrophe averted, a secret experimental group revealed, and the replacement of a half-mad clan leader with one who wants the best for their clan and to work with the neighboring weres to ensure peace and safety for both communities." He sniffed. "How terrible for you."

"Well, you left out the whole getting kidnapped and injured thing. And Mariska and Mal and Ethan and—"

"Yes, well. The proposal is actually for both of you. Rather, it is two proposals. And will require your consideration before we accept an answer either affirmative or negative." He reached into the inside pocket of his bottle green blazer and pulled out two thick envelopes, handing one to Ethan and one to me. "Doctor Babin, as you have become abundantly aware this week, medical providers who weres and shifters can see without worry of their nature being revealed are rather thin on the ground, and our kinds have some... idiosyncrasies when compared to human patients. The IC wishes to encourage your acceptance of our offer but will not pressure you."

I pulled out the papers in the envelope and skimmed the first sheet. "A clinic in Misston? What is this?"

"It would be the only were and shifter friendly clinic for about two hundred miles," he said. "And you would be the provider. Along with any professionals who wish to move to rural East Texas which, honestly, don't hold your breath. The IC is willing to help fund the clinic as well as any fees and expenses required when you change your specialty."

"How did you know," I began, but clamped down on the words. Ethan made a startled sound beside me and I shook my head. "Damn it, I hadn't told him yet," I grumbled.

I could help people like Ethan and Mariska... Maybe even people like me and Mal.

"I need to think about it," I finally said. "It feels like a lot."

"It is. You'd be well compensated." He nodded at my packet. "The last page has the compensation details."

The number listed was ridiculous. Like, doctors could get paid quite well, but this was Dallas plastic surgeon money, not rural East Texas general practitioner money. Cullen was smirking when I looked up, stunned. "Think on it," he urged. "But remember to read the fine print. At least twice. And you," he added, turning to Ethan like some weird shifter Willy Wonka doling out job offers instead of sketchy golden tickets. "The IC is aware of your current situation, and in light of the fact we are in need of a field agent in the southeastern region, we're extending the offer to you."

Ethan pulled out his papers and scanned the first page. "I... don't know about this."

"My advice is the same as before: read the fine print. I'll be your neighbor a bit longer," he added, "so we can discuss this at length at a later date, but not too much later. I'm returning to Chicago in the near future."

Mal and Mariska wandered up just then, Mariska bouncing in Mal's arms as she stared around the room. It was still a mess and a half, but the more able survivors had made great headway on the bloody floors and the bodies were, at least, out of sight. "Hey." Mal sighed. "I'm... I was going to say ready to go home but I don't know where that is right now."

Cullen raised a brow. "Are you not staying in Shoot Well, Mr. Benes?"

"That sounds like a leading question, Creepy Fairy Godfather," I muttered.

Cullen didn't smile, but he did have a tiny little flicker of movement near the corner of his eyes that made me think he wanted to.

Or maybe I was so tired I was seeing things.

Mal set Mariska down before she managed to wiggle herself free and shook his head. "Dunnigan didn't say as much, but I don't feel

HOWL AT THE MOON

like I belong here anymore. And I don't want to raise Mariska here. Hopkins seems great, but there are too many ghosts." He didn't say her name, but I knew Samara would be haunting him for years to come.

"Broken River isn't bad," Ethan suggested gently. "Low cost of living, lots of kids for her to play with. And you know people there."

Mal huffed a small laugh. "And I'll be able to get a place to live with the job I don't have, I suppose?"

"If I may?" Cullen interrupted. "I'm moving soon. I own the home next to Doctor Babin, and I'd be willing to work out a very fair rental agreement with you, Mr. Benes. One that would not require payment until you had a new job and at least two or three paychecks under your belt?"

Mal blinked rapidly, his eyes bright. "Seriously?"

"Seriously." Cullen's gaze traveled to Mariska, who was peering closely at the bandaging a shifter was doing on her own leg just a few feet away. "If you tell anyone I said this, I'll call you a liar, but Mariska reminds me of me, really. When I was small. Making sure she has a place to grow up, at least for a while, in safety..." He trailed off, cleared his throat again, and nodded. "Think on it. I'll be back in Broken River by tomorrow and await your arrival. All of you," he added. Without another word, he turned and strode toward Dunnigan, leaving us all in silent, slightly stunned confusion.

"What the hell is my life?" Mal muttered.

"When you find out, let me know because I have the same question about mine," I replied.

We drifted to help with clean up, Mal making sure to keep Mariska away from the worst of it. I made Ethan sit after a few minutes, his limp worse than he wanted to admit. Tyler joined us, finally breaking away from the weres who had been doing the worst of the clean-up and were now decompressing with cold drinks outside of the barn.

Lucky bastards.

"Hey, guys. Justin's sleeping in the truck," he said quietly, as if Justin could hear us from there. "I was wondering if you could take a look at him before we head out later, Landry?"

"I guess so, yeah. What's up?" I set the bucket of soiled rags aside gladly, shedding the nitrile gloves someone had given me as I turned to talk to Tyler.

"He's just... not great. I know he's been living rough, but this feels like more than that. I don't know how to explain it." He sighed.

"I mean, he's been through a lot of trauma, just in the past few days alone, not to mention the past six months or more."

Tyler nodded, frowning. "I just want to make sure he's going to be okay for the drive back."

"Where are you taking him?"

"Ah. Well. He doesn't really have anywhere to go, so I was thinking my place."

Was Tyler blushing, or was it just the heat in the crowded barn?

"Not a bad idea," I said. "He's going to need someone with him for a while, I bet."

Tyler nodded. "I figured I'd help him get his shit together, you know?"

I chuckled dryly. "Yeah, I get it. Ethan did the same for me. Or he's trying to, anyway. Hope Justin is less of a jerk about it than I am."

"Dude. Ethan loves you. He hates hearing you talk shit about yourself."

"Yeah, well."

Tyler shoved some lank curls out of his eyes and shook his head. "Look, you gotta sort your own shit out, too. It's not something Ethan can magically fix. But he can help you. He's trying to. He *wants* to. And we're all flying blind here, you know? So just... be easy on yourself, Landry. It'll help."

HOWL AT THE MOON

Dunnigan waved me over, and I sighed. "Keep an eye on Justin. I'll check on him in a few. Get him some water or something," I added over my shoulder, trotting over to join Dunnigan and Hopkins.

"I wanted you to know we got Waltrip up to the hospital in Wyoming. Gave 'em your number to call. He was conscious and talking when they left this morning."

I nodded, feeling a spike of relief I hadn't anticipated. "Good. Great. He's... I wasn't sure he was going to be okay," I admitted. And I knew he still might not be. But getting him to medical care was a huge step toward making sure he was as good as could be.

Dunnigan shoved his hands in his pockets awkwardly and looked around. "There's no good way to say this but..."

"We're getting gone soon," I promised. "Likely tonight. Least as far as Denver," I added. "I don't think I can drive much farther than that without falling asleep at the wheel."

He nodded again. "Sorry. But right now, we just need to get things as back to normal as possible."

"And we're definitely not part of that normal."

Dunnigan had the grace to look abashed at my flat statement.

Mal's panicked shouts of, "Mariska? Mariska! Where are you?" interrupted whatever awkward and hurtful thing Dunnigan could've come up with next.

"What's going on?" I called. "Where'd you last see her?"

"With me," the woman with the bandaged leg said. "She was yawning and said she was going to go back to her dad."

Mal shook his head. "I haven't seen her. She couldn't have gone far, could she?"

One of the shifters called out, "She a coyote?"

"I..." Mal shook his head. "I have no idea. Maybe? I don't know if she can..."

"Well," the shifter said, nudging a large plastic tub full of clean rags. "Someone is. and none of us have pups this age."

Mal ran to the box, followed by me and Dunnigan, Ethan coming more slowly. "Oh my god." Mal sighed, dropping to his knees beside the box. Inside, a small coyote pup was curled on her side, nose hidden beneath her paws, snoring softly on the clean cloth.

Dunnigan chuckled softly. "Reminds me of mine when they were that age. Keep an eye on her, Mal. She's gonna be a handful."

Mal scooped her up and Mariska yawned, squirming in his arms, before falling back asleep. "I don't know how to deal with the shifting," he muttered. "I don't guess someone wrote a book or something?"

Hopkins grinned. "I'll give you my email. You can ask me anything once y'all get settled."

Mal glanced up at Dunnigan. "Sir, I want to thank you for allow us to stay on your ranch for so long and—"

"Hey, just because you're moving away doesn't mean we'll never talk. You've got my number. I expect you to use it. And maybe... next year or so, y'all can come up at lambing to see the babies."

"Mariska would like that," he whispered. "Thank you."

WE LEFT MORE QUIETLY than we had come. Justin riding with Tyler, his thousand-yard stare firmly in place, Mal, Mariska, Ethan, and I in my poor car, which was definitely getting the mother of all detailing when we got back home. We stopped in Denver for the night, getting two rooms at a mid-grade hotel with an adjoining room available. Mariska wiggled her way back into her little girl form before we arrived at the hotel. Though she'd kept the light up shoes Reba had chosen for her, she was delighted to be reunited with her wardrobe of brightly colored outfits, including the [insert way over the top outfit here] that she'd slipped into after her change. We drew a few strange looks from guests as we made our way through the lobby, though I suspected it had little to do with Mariska's outfit and far more to do with our scratched up appearances. Or perhaps it was just the strangeness of five grown men traveling with a seven-year-old. I didn't much care. I had grand plans for Ethan that would have to wait till morning, because we were both as able to get aroused as a pair of boneless chickens by the time we closed the door behind us. Instead, we curled into commas of exhaustion, barely able to move once we were down. But despite that, we were too wired to sleep. Words fuzzy and soft, Ethan murmured, "I love you. I was terrified when you were still at the compound. If something had happened to you..."

"But it didn't." My speech was no sharper than his, but I forced my mouth to move, to spill the words I needed to say despite wanting to just flop. "You're stuck with me, Ethan. For better or worse."

And maybe that was the wrong thing to say. We both went even more still, if that was at all possible. Those words had a weight to them neither of us anticipated. An echo of vows that we had never discussed.

And were frankly too tired to consider even remotely. "I love you and I'm glad you're not dead."

He snorted. "I'm glad you're not dead, too."

MAL AND MARISKA LOOKED better when they joined us at the car in the morning, promises of a stop for hash browns and juice doing the lord's work when it came to getting her out the door. Her bag with her tablet and books had been rescued from the ranch before we left, so she was happily ensconced in the back seat with Mal as we got on our way back home. Ethan drowsed beside me, the sun slanting in at midmorning angles as we wound down yet another mountain road, Shoot Well and Penny Mine getting farther with each second.

"Do you think Justin is okay?" Mal asked after a while. Ethan, snoring beside me, startled, sputtered, and dozed back off before I answered.

"No. He's really not. But I hope he can be. At least something like it. I don't think he'll be the same as before."

"We were kids when they did it to us," Mal muttered. "I wonder what we'd have been like if they never had..."

We were quiet again, and the road seemed unending. If I hadn't been dosed, if I hadn't been experimented on, would I have met Ethan? Would I be here right now?

Who would I be?

Ethan woke enough to lay his hand on my thigh and squeeze gently, as if he'd heard my thoughts.

I wouldn't be the same. I'm not glad about what happened but I'm glad about where it got me.

Mostly.

My phone buzzed, startling Ethan awake again, and he grabbed it out of the cup holder to read the message for me. "Reba," he grunted. "She says *What do you think about macramé hammocks?*"

"Tell her the seventies died."

"I'm telling her they sound lovely."

"You bitch."

Ethan chuckled as Mariska sleepily muttered, "Swear jar," from the back seat. We were going home, finally, and things were going to change whether we liked it or not. But it was up to us to make it for the better.

Epilogue - One Month Later

A cold, wet nose pressed against my face, warm and heavy breath huffing directly into my ear. "Swear to god," I muttered. "Ethan, this is new and weird, and I'm not into it."

Mal's startled laugh dragged me out of my nap on the sofa. "Sorry," he said, reaching down to grab a floppy-eared brown and white dog who was doing its level-best to wiggle out of his grasp. "Mariska talked Tyler into showing her his neighbor's puppies, and well..." He lifted the dog like it was Simba and he was Rafiki, but bashful. "Meet King Floppy Ears von Floofington, First of His Name, Last of His Line after the vet appointment on Thursday. King for short. Or Floofers, depending on Mariska's mood."

I nodded slowly, pushing myself up. My laptop slid to the floor with a gentle thump, the screen powering back up with the motion. "Y'all got a dog."

He chuckled, setting King whatchamacallit down on the floor and watching him waddle-run toward the door where Mariska was barging in at top speed, face sweaty and hair a snarl that had once been a braid over one shoulder. "She did, I just sort of went along with it," he admitted. "It's been such a weird time and..." He sighed. "I probably should've said no, but this was the happiest I've seen her since we left Colorado."

"I get it," I said. "I mean, I don't have kids and don't really know any other than Mariska, but I probably would've done the same thing. Oh my god, he peed on my rug!"

Mariska staggered into the living room, holding King Floofers awkwardly as she grinned her gap-toothed smile at us. "I'll clean it! Dad told me I had to be responsible for his messes. Can I use your bleach?

Do you have bleach? Oh! Do you have that stuff you have to use in the office to clean up biohazards? I bet that'd get rid of pee!"

"Pee and the color in my rug," I grumbled, getting to my feet. "No offense but who let y'all in?"

"Ah, the door was open," Mal admitted. "Tyler said we could just come in, he'd be right back. We ran into him in the driveway. He said he was getting stuff to grill for dinner."

The last vestiges of sleep fell away—today was the day Ethan was coming back from his training trip, and Tyler had suggested a little welcome back get-together. I'd tried to suggest just an evening at home with me and Ethan but was outvoted by, well, everyone.

Someone taught Mariska the word 'misanthrope' and that became my nickname for two or three days before she got distracted by a newfound love of CrimeTV, despite Mal's best efforts to get her into *Bluey* and Nat Geo Kids.

Mal hurried to get paper towels and cleaner to get Mariska started on the rug, returning after I'd gotten my laptop back and opened to the page I'd dozed off reading. "You're doing it then?" he asked, nodding at the screen as he joined me on the sofa. "That's a big change."

"A necessary one," I admitted. "It'll be weird working with the living but..."

"But most of them will be freaks like us, huh?" he teased gently, though his gaze was troubled. "Maybe."

"Maybe. Definitely weres and shifters. There's no clinic for over a hundred miles that the local clans feel safe going to, so there's definitely a need." The fact the IC was funding the clinic I'd be working at, less than half an hour from Broken River over in Misston, which itself was more accessible to the surrounding clans thanks to being right off I-45, meant that I was tied to them whether I liked it or not. Regular people would be welcomed—all part of building community goodwill, but also because it was just easier to hide in plain sight—but the money and the focus would be toward the 'hidden' communities.

HOWL AT THE MOON

No pressure, right?

Mariska came thundering back in with King Floofers on her heels. "Done!"

"Wash your hands," Mal ordered. She groaned and stomped back to the kitchen, where the sink came on full blast a moment later, the sound of King's tippy-tapping claws loud on my wood floor.

"How's living next door?" I asked quietly.

"Different from living on the ranch." He sighed. "Smaller. Cozier, though. And weird."

"Cullen has that effect on people and things." I nodded.

Mal chuckled. "No, he's been a good landlord so far, and Mariska really likes him. Don't make that face," he added, poking my arm.

"Sorry, just... someone liking Cullen is seems wrong somehow."

"He's not that bad. He's a lot like you, really."

I set my laptop on the arm of the sofa and got to my feet, pointing dramatically at the door. "Go. Leave. I never want to see you here again."

Mal's laugh was loud and long. "You're such a dork. Both of you have trust issues, prefer to be homebodies, and are very particular about your homes."

"That's it?" I said, sinking back down. "We're both fussy and introverts?"

"Well."

"Well?"

He shrugged. "We'll go with that for now. Did you decide to talk to Reba or not?"

I narrowed my eyes at him and pointed. "Don't think I'm letting this go," I muttered. "And yeah, I'm gonna ask if she wants the job at the new clinic. I mean, it's a bit away, but that gives us time to work out a contract and let her wrap up her newest side hustle."

"Oh god, she's not still selling macramé sex swings, is she?"

"She swears they were hammocks," I reminded him. "At least that's what I'm gonna keep telling myself."

Mal laughed again, pushing himself to his feet as Mariska's cries of, "Not on the floor!" burst from the kitchen. "I'll get this one and we'll get out of your hair till tonight. Want us to bring anything for the barbecue?"

"Puppy pee pads?"

"On it."

ETHAN ARRIVED JUST after four and I had him in the bedroom less than five minutes later, making sure the doors were locked since my house had apparently become Grand Central Station for werewolves, shifters, and their pets these days.

"Hello." Ethan laughed as I kissed him down to the mattress, pushing him back when he tried to sit up. "I've only been gone a week."

"You've been gone a week," I reiterated. "A whole week. First you move in with me then you fuck off on a business trip." Peppering his face and neck with tiny nips and licks, I went on, "You left me here with your brother and Mal and Mariska and a menagerie of animals and—"

"A puppy is hardly a menagerie," he chuckled, slipping his hands down my back to grab my ass and pull me closer, positioning me where he wanted me. We both sighed, a shiver of want rushing through my body as his arousal pressed hard and hot against mine through our layers of clothes.

"Well, there was a mockingbird out back that seems way too comfy," I grumbled, bursting into a startled laugh when he flipped us, so I was on my back and he pinned me down. His sure fingers had my jeans off and underpants down before I could formulate the request to do it. "Oh, I missed this." I sighed, closing my eyes and tipping my head back against the pillows.

"It's been a week," he reminded me. "We've gone longer without when I'm home."

"Yeah, but you're *home* then. And I miss this then, too. It's just tempered by the fact you're not off doing god knows what with Cullen and the IC flying monkeys."

He leaned up, frowning. "I thought you were okay with me going?"

"I was! I am! Come back down here, damn it." I sighed. "I'm just a grouch. I missed you and I'm thrilled you're home and I want to hear all about the training trip but first I want you to make me come so hard I see stars, and I'll do the same for you, alright?"

"You make a convincing argument, Doctor Babin," he murmured before sliding down my body to settle between my legs, taking my leaking cock into his mouth.

And I'm not ashamed to admit that he had me floating in outer space sooner rather than later, my breath heaving in short, sharp bursts while he worked me over, drawing me deep into his throat as his tongue did this *thing* that made me reconsider my agnosticism.

We ignored the knocks on my front door as he crawled up my body to settle his knees on either side of my shoulders, feeding me his cock in shallow thrusts as I grasped his ass, finger slipping into his crack and teasing his hole as he groaned, throaty and loud, above me.

The knocking stopped—thank god for werewolf hearing, I suppose, because at least Tyler could fuck off once he realized what was going on.

Ethan shot his load down my throat with a shuddering sigh, his thighs trembling as I licked him clean, finally letting his softening dick slip from my lips, smiling as he slumped to one side and kissed me, tasting one another on our tongues and lips until we were too sated to do more than lazily lean against one another, lips barely touching as we just breathed.

"I guess I'll need pants soon." He sighed. "Tyler won't stay away forever."

"Want to test that theory? I bet if we keep making sex noises every time he knocks, he'll get the hint."

"Or he'll think we've got a disturbing new kink for fucking while people are waiting for us, and knowing him, he'll tell everyone I know about it just to get back at us for not letting him in when he came by."

"Ugh. You're probably right and I hate that for us."

As if on cue, Tyler's familiar, heavy knock fell on the door again. "Coming, coming," I shouted. A muffled, *Yeah I know* came back to us and I felt my face heat.

Ethan laughed, getting to his feet and padding toward the bathroom. "Come on. I'm hungry after that and I'm really feeling the urge for ribs."

The barbecue was small but, dare I say, fun, even with the presence of a purse-lipped Cullen who held court under the pecan tree out back, a glass of sweet tea and lemonade in one hand and a plate of untouched ribs in the other. "Too messy," he announced when he caught me eyeballing his plate. "However, Mariska assures me it would greatly hurt her feelings if I didn't have food tonight, so here we are. I, technically, have food."

"Touché," I murmured, letting my gaze slide from him to find Ethan and Mal talking about something just across the yard.

"He did well," Cullen said. "He's a natural at this job, being an agent for the IC."

"Is he?"

He cut me a glance, one brow quirking in question. "Shouldn't he be? You sound as if you doubt my assessment."

"It's not that," I said. "I just..."

When I didn't continue, Cullen sighed and carefully set the plate down on the card table between us, borrowed from Tyler to make up the lack of seating arrangements out back. "It's not going to be a perfect fit. No job is, really. But Ethan enjoyed what he did and while it was quite an easy assignment, he took to the culture readily and asked good questions, took initiative on several interviews and demonstrated excellent problem-solving skills during a few tricky moments."

"Are you giving me his progress report?" I asked, a bit amused. "Assuring me my partner's absence is worth it?"

"In a sense," he admitted with another shrug. "Ethan is very much a Boy Scout sort, isn't he?"

"I want to be defensive for him, but you're not wrong."

Cullen's smirk was faint and fast. "He'll be an asset to the organization, but he'll do well to have a support system that keeps him from getting into his own head." Tipping his drink slightly in my direction, he gave me a nod. "Now, if you'll excuse me, I promised Mariska I'd help her with her shifting before I left for the evening, and this conversation has become far too personal for my liking. Have some ribs, Doctor Babin." Then, handing me his plate before I could think to refuse, he sauntered across the yard toward Mariska and Mal.

"What the actual fuck," I muttered, looking after him as he crouched down to speak with Mariska, who shot me a glance before laughing.

"Sure, laugh at the guy who lets your dog pee on his rug."

"Good conversation?" Ethan asked, slipping behind me from the shadows of the pecan tree.

"Eavesdropping?"

"Just needed some air," he murmured, pulling me carefully against his chest as we watched the party in the backyard simmer along. "I think I'm more tired than expected."

"Busy week."

"Mmm."

"Have you heard from Waltrip?" I asked after another few moments of quiet. "Tyler's being tight-lipped about him but I figured if he'd died, we'd know. Right?"

Ethan tipped his head in a *maybe* gesture. "He's doing okay. Turned down the IC's private clinic, said he wanted to recover on his own. Diz and Elio are staying with him for now, making sure he's not pushing too hard."

"It's so weird thinking of Waltrip having a house of his own. I just always imagined him popping into existence wherever we see him."

"You're odd, Landry Babin, and I love you."

"I love you too, Ethan Stone."

We were quiet again, but I could feel the tension in Ethan's arms, in the way he held himself against me. So I waited, letting him figure out how to say it on his own, and in the meantime I rambled. "I got the paperwork sent in for the specialty change in my licensing," I said. "I'm taking a few intensives next month and then in December and doing some rounds at the county hospital to make the state licensing board happy. The, ah, IC has arranged for me to pick up some clinic hours in Houston in January, at a facility that sees weres as well as humans. Mostly so I get an idea of the kind of patients I'd be seeing in terms of illness and injury but I'm going to be winging it for the most part."

"Did you ask Reba?"

I nodded. "We talked. She's in, but she asked what I thought about her getting her medical assistant certification."

Ethan let out a low whistle. "That's a lot more school, isn't it?"

I hummed. "A bit more, but she's already got some basic credits to transfer to the community college. She said she'd looked into it and it'd be about a year or so to finish her associate's then take the exam."

"Sounds like she's all in."

"Gotta admit, it's kind of a relief. It was weird thinking about going in to work and not seeing her. She's more my friend than not, but I don't know if she realizes that," I admitted.

Ethan squeezed me a bit tighter. "Maybe you should tell her."

When I just nodded and didn't pick the conversation back up again, he sighed. "I think I'm gonna like this IC gig," he murmured. "It's just... different. There's so much I thought I knew, you know? About clans and our dynamics. Now I'm starting to find out that we're kind of

HOWL AT THE MOON   215

an oddball little group out here. Real isolated. Old-fashioned in some respects."

"And that's a bad thing?" I mean, I knew what I thought about it, but I wasn't the wolf in this situation.

He paused, then slumped a little. "Maybe so. Nothing wrong with being tight knit, but the way we're resisting change... It ain't good, Lan. And the world is changing. I don't know if people like us will ever be openly part of it, but things are happening that make it damn near impossible for us to stick to the old ways, clannish and hiding out in the woods and shit. Being rural is one thing but shutting ourselves off from the world, from the way it's changing?" He shook his head. "It's going to be hard to get the clan on board."

"But it's worth the try."

"More than."

Tyler and Justin burst into laughter suddenly, startling us both. Justin still looked more pale than usual, more drawn. He had a rough look about him that made me think he felt lost, but he had imprinted on Tyler like a baby duck ever since Tyler found him, and Tyler didn't seem to mind. They'd taken over Ethan's house in Belmarais, and after the briefest fuss from the older clan members, it was fairly unexceptional. Justin turned our way and hesitantly waved near his chest. I nodded, smiling in return, and Ethan raised his hand to wave back.

"People like Justin," he said suddenly, "like you and Mal and even Mariska... you're part of this world we're in, whether you like it or not. And we know that Garrow's group is still out there. And god knows how many of them there are. And—"

"And," I said, laying my hand atop his where it rested on my stomach, "nothing changes overnight, does it? Not really."

"No," he agreed on a sigh. "It doesn't. But I think I need to be part of making it happen."

"And I do, too."

Mariska broke away from Cullen and Mal, running Pell-Mell toward us. "Mr. Landry! Mr. Ethan! Guess what!"

Ethan slipped from behind me and knelt to catch her around the middle, turning his face away as King Floofers tumbled up alongside her with face licking mode engaged. "Chicken butt?" Ethan guessed.

"What? No. Listen!" She thew her head back and closed her eyes, letting loose the tiniest, warbliest howl I'd ever heard in my life. Tyler cheered and joined in, howling in an eerie mix of human and wolf tones. Justin looked as if he wanted to try but ducked his face, smiling, instead.

"That's amazing," Ethan praised. "You'll be scaring off the neighbors in no time!"

She grinned and raced back to Mal, leaving us in the grass watching her dance around her dad and Cullen, baring her teeth and curling her fingers like claws, laughing the whole time.

Even Cullen looked amused, just a little.

"Things are always changing," Ethan said after a moment.

"It's not always going to be good."

"No." He sighed, rising to his feet. "But you're gonna be with me, right?"

I looped my arms around his neck and kissed his chin, whispering, "Good luck getting rid of me now, Ethan."

He smiled, and we sank back into the shadows, watching our little growing world move around us.

HOWL AT THE MOON

Marked Book 3 will be coming in Winter 2023/Spring 2024. Follow me on social media or my newsletter for updates!

Also by Meredith

Y ou can find all my books listed my website with links to buy at your favorite online retailers, or ask your local booksellers to order you a copy if you prefer!

THE BEDEVILED SERIES
The Devil May Care
The Devil You Know
The Devil in the Details
Speak of the Devil (Summer 2023)

MEDIUM AT LARGE SERIES
Bump in the Night
Ghoul Friend
Old Ghosts
In the Spirit
After Life (Spring 2023)
Ghost of a Chance (Autumn 2023)
Ghost Stories—A Short Story Collection (Winter 2023/Spring 2024)
Science of Magic Series
Data Sets
Fuzzy Logic

Discrete
Scientific Method (2023)
Marked
Nearly Human
Howl at the Moon (Spring2023)
Book Three Title TBA (Winter 2023/Spring 2024)
In The Pines
Fetch (Spring 2023)
Witch Bone (Winter 2023)
Conjure (Spring 2024)
Damian Murphy's Pet Sitting and Murder Investigation
Tea and Antipathy (book 1): June 2023
Arsenic and Old Ladies (book 2): TBA
Stand Alones
Between the Lines
Ring My Bell (Contemporary MM Fairy Tale Retelling, January 2023)
Shared Worlds
Leo (A Gaynor Beach Single Dads Romance, November 2022)
Final Days: The Calms (An apocalyptic romance with a HEA, October 2022)
Anthology
Easy as Pie, *a MM holiday romance, will be appearing in the* **There Goes The Turkey** *holiday anthology in November 2023.*

About the Author

MEREDITH IS A QUEER, nonbinary cryptid and likes to write about sexy stuff, weird stuff, and some-times weird stuff doing sexy stuff. Originally from Texas, they live elsewhere now with their family and two cats who think they are gods (the cats, not the humans—the humans know their place). Meredith writes queer-centered romances in various subgenres including paranormal, speculative fiction/alternate universe, contemporary, and historical. They firmly believe in happily ever afters and pineapple on pizza.

For sneak peeks at upcoming works and other goodies, check out Meredith's social media, website, and newsletter!

www.booksbymeredith.com

Printed in the USA
CPSIA information can be obtained
at www.ICGtesting.com
JSHW022008100124
55190JS00001B/52